S

OVER 100
GREAT NOVELS
OF
EROTIC DOMINATION

If you like one you will probably like the rest

NEW TITLES EVERY MONTH

All titles in print are now available from:

www.adultbookshops.com

If you want to be on our confidential mailing list for our Readers' Club
Magazine (with extracts from past and forthcoming titles) write to:

SILVER MOON READER SERVICES

Shadowline Publishing Ltd
Box 101
City Business Centre
Station Rise
York
YO1 6HT
United Kingdom

Telephone: 01904 525729
Fax: 01904 522338

NEW AUTHORS WELCOME

Please send submissions to
Silver Moon Books
Box 101
City Business Centre
Station Rise
York
YO1 6HT

Silver Moon is an imprint of Shadowline Publishing Ltd
the print publishing division of the Convecto Media Group
First published 2008 Silver Moon Books
ISBN 9781-904706-61-8
© 2008 Francine Whittaker

Pleasure Control

(A Whipmaster Novel)

By

Francine Whittaker

Also by Francine Whittaker
The Connoisseur
Punishment Bound
Amber in Chains
The Slave Path
The Slave Path 2
The Slave Path 3
The Whipmaster
Bad Blood (with Sean O'Kane)

FemDom Titles
Mistress Blackheart
Lady Nightshade

THE WHIPMASTER

The Whipmaster told the story of Tyler 'Lanky' Morrison's meteoric rise to inherit vast wealth from his grandfather; Whitby, Lord Morrison-Grenfell. A chance meeting in the grounds of Whitby's manor house introduced the young gypsy, Tyler, to the delights of SM.

As the two men grew to know each other, Whitby supported the young man as he explored his darker desires with women – especially as they applied to Chelsi Laird; now a famous singer but once a local girl who had accused Tyler of rape when they had both been teenagers. As a result, Tyler had spent a night in police custody and narrowly escaped prosecution. While he plotted her downfall and enslavement, he amused himself by ensnaring her sister Charlotte, who already worked for Whitby.

When Whitby died, Tyler inherited his title and fortune, including 'The Ramparts' the stately home where he determined to create the best SM club in the country. Whitby's disinherited son got nothing, but on the day The Ramparts opened its doors to prospective members, he turned up unexpectedly…

'Pleasure Control' opens just a few weeks prior to the club's opening and describes events that took place at The Ramparts before and after Chelsi's abduction.

CHAPTER ONE

Tyler took a deep swig of his pint at The Griffin one evening and prepared to explain the details of his plan to his old friend Tully. At least in the pub they were free from Alfred's continued hostility and contempt for the new Lord. Alfred had been Whitby's butler for many years and could not come to terms with the louche young man who had inherited the dignified title and the beautiful old house. It was not that he disapproved of the debauchery, he was quite happy to help discipline any of the young women who inhabited the place; it was just Tyler he couldn't accept.

For his part, Tyler had been working on a scheme for some time; a scheme to regulate the domestic slaves but in a different regime from the one which would govern the Pleasuregirls themselves, of course.

"However the men handle things at home, the contracts I've had them sign make it clear that their bitches ultimately answer to me. I'm their true Master! It's me in the saddle! It's my right to dole out any punishment I think necessary, without prior notice, and their duty to deliver them on time for their shift and have them collected at the end of it."

What he had failed to mention for fear that he would appear a soft touch to eavesdroppers was that, having lived in poverty himself, it had never been his intention to deprive any household of an income. So instead of paying the women the wage they had once earned he paid a slightly reduced amount straight into their Dominant's bank account instead.

"Although the partnership can be dissolved at any time by either party," he continued as he watched Tully wipe his mouth on the back of his barbed-wire-and-dagger tattooed hand, "if any of the Dominants fail to keep their side of the bargain, I'll stop the money pronto and the partnership'll be wound up."

After buying another round served by a surly barman who threw Tyler's change at him, he explained how he planned to extend the system to any additional domestic slaves that he acquired. "Eventually the system'll include you and the Escorts. Maybe some of the other estate workers, too. It all depends on whether I can get enough girls… we need a fuck load more domestics if we're gonna offer a first class service to the members. Anyway, it's my intention to lease them out to you guys! And I've managed to cut a particularly sweet property deal. You know that new block of flats they're building on the outskirts of the village?"

It was the last straw for one of The Griffin's regulars who chimed in with, "Bloody eyesore if you ask me!"

Tyler did not ask him and continued regardless. "Under the Government's scheme the flats are meant for what they call 'key workers.' You know, like teachers and nurses? Anyway, in this case the key workers who'll end up living in them are you guys, The Ramparts' Escorts!"

The Escorts were recruited mainly from Tyler's old friends from his gypsy days and managed every aspect of the lives of the Pleasuregirls, and took full advantage of the perks on offer.

Laughing, Tully pointed out that pretty soon the village would be nothing more than a domicile for slaves. In a sweeping hand gesture meant to take in the whole of Squire's Langley, he said loudly as he looked around at the hostile faces, "These buggers might not like you, Ty, but one way or another, they'll end up dependin' on you for their living!"

Tyler raised his pint. "And so helping me offer some of the very best SM entertainment - with the highest quality Pleasuregirls - in the whole fucking country!"

***

With just a couple of weeks to the club's official opening things were shaping up slowly, Tyler told himself as he turned down one of the carpeted corridors that led off from the cavernous, extravagantly decorated entrance hall, with its huge Egyptian statues and grand staircase.

Padding along barefoot and naked behind him, her head bowed and hands crossed but not tied behind her back was Charlotte. Meek and obedient, she was a woman in love.

Top of Tyler's list for consideration that morning were questions concerning how he could increase the numbers of girls. He had money aplenty to purchase the high-class stock that he insisted should be at the core, but having lived most of his life in poverty, he also had an eye for a bargain. He was a great believer in the two for one offers at the Supermarkets and could not see why that should not apply to slaves as well, though free would be even better! Besides, not all men lusted after the kind of well-stacked-but-slim-lovelies that he was filling the place with, some preferring girls with a bit more meat on them, like Charlotte who, though not exactly plump was nevertheless generously built in the arse and hip department, he mused, as well as having epicurean tits. In any case, there were already enough gorgeous girls to satisfy his own personal needs… well, almost, he thought greedily… but even with the addition of Chelsi in a few days time, there would be nowhere near enough to keep a vast membership of his club happy! And he really believed that the club would attract a huge membership.

At first the business of setting up the club had seemed simple enough, and he had thought only of redecorating the musty rooms that had not been used in decades. But belatedly he had realised that he had not spent enough effort planning the venture. He pushed open the heavy, creaking door to the huge, time-worn, stone flagged banqueting hall and for a moment just stood looking around the wood panelled room. There were three tables; one across the top end of the room, opposite the mammoth inglenook fireplace with its wooden benches of two feet long fitted on either side of the grate so that one could sit comfortably in the warm, the other two adjacent tables running almost the entire length of the room, one with a doorway behind which led to the kitchen, and the other near the door by which he had entered.

He told himself he had simply been swept along with the excitement of it. After all, one minute he had been skint, living on the very edges of the law as part of a clan, he thought as he walked toward the table nearest to him, and the next he was tossed in at the deep end as Lord of the fucking Manor!

He had seen the potential of the great, ochre-walled, elaborately-fronted and antique-stuffed Manor House years earlier when, as a penniless member of the travelling community, he had prowled the grounds on the look-out for game for the cooking pot, and pretty housemaids to tie up and ravish. Then about five years later, finding himself unbelievably but safely installed in the be-chimneyed, crenellated and turreted "house" with its 90 plus rooms and bizarre, totally incompatible ancient Egyptian frieze and statues at the front entrance, it had not taken him long to decide to turn The Ramparts into a club where men of a similar persuasion to himself, men who embraced the joys of the very harshest SM, could torment beautiful young women to their hearts' content.

He came to a halt in front of the table where a large package was waiting to be opened. Charlotte stopped too. She stood a little way behind him, slightly to his left, and he caught a whiff of her banana-scented blonde hair.

Without looking at her, he said, "I made a tidy sum by selling some of Whitby's bitches. And I've already replaced them with more suitable ones."

He often talked to her, sometimes about his previous lifestyle and sometimes even confiding his plans, not because he valued her opinion. Indeed he had never asked for it. Being an obedient slave, she would not dare to volunteer it without being ordered to do so. Nor was it because, as in her ignorance, Charlotte believed that he thought of her as a valued and trusted confidante. Cocooned in her own cosy thoughts, poor Charlotte had no way of knowing that it was simply because he was behaving as he always had; there were few things a gypsy enjoyed more than "telling a tale." But with a slave who was not allowed to speak without express permission or to answer a specific question, any conversation was inevitably one sided.

He glanced over his shoulder toward her and wondered if she had the slightest idea how sizzling a piece of womanhood she really was. She was also so wonderfully docile that it was all he could do to keep from flaying every scrap of flesh from her bones for the sheer hell of it. And although she was far from being the innocent her open, pretty face suggested since she had worked for years as a maid for the old lord and had many times witnessed his cruel debauchery, Tyler delighted in despoiling her and leaving her forever tainted. She blushed so prettily that he took great comfort from drenching her in scorn and leaving her quivering, pink and broken. Her soft, matt skin was so creamy and perfect that he could easily spend his days ribboning it with scarlet and infusing it with pain. Sometimes he even allowed her to orgasm!

Currently she was gagged with a yellow duster which tasted of dust, beeswax and lavender, which he had snatched from one of the sexily uniformed maids on the way to the banqueting hall. She stood with her customary obedience and awaited his pleasure, accepting without question that any pleasure she sought for herself would be strictly controlled, and probably denied. With her long, glossy blonde hair and soft mouth, curvaceous Charlotte had always been one of the prettiest, most eager to please of all the housemaids. It had been her compliance as much as her whippable arse and generous, wobbly tits that had prompted him to make a sex slave of her in the first place.

He recalled how he had first come across her in the woods, and how it was due to her that he had first met Whitby, the corpulent Lord Morrison-Grenfell, with the long, white ponytail and bushy beard. He smiled as he recalled how, under the old man's guidance, he had flogged Charlotte's rump... the first he had ever flogged! Then, a few days after what he thought of as his Damascus moment, he had had his brief encounter with her younger sister the inexperienced Chelsi. What a disaster that had been! he thought. For although he had fully intended to ravish the youngster and practice his new-found skill with the whip into the bargain, it had been Chelsi who had led him on. As he had said at the time, "she threw herself at me like a streetwalker having a dry spell."

Breathing softly, Charlotte stood in the required manner with her legs apart to allow unrestricted access to her cunt. He seldom tied her hands, only at night when she was returned to her new cell, or on those rare occasions when he took her to his bed. For such was her deep-rooted need to obey that she would never move them unless commanded, not even to rub herself after a beating.

His eyes zeroed in on her completely hairless vagina. "You missed one!" he lied. Trawling through his jeans pocket he extracted a pair of tweezers he carried for the purpose and, leaning in toward her and aiming for a non-existent hair just an inch or so above the apex of her slit, he used them to grasp the tiniest amount of tender skin. He plucked it sharply and laughed at her muffled intake of breath and watering eyes before returning the tweezers to his pocket.

He did not tell her everything, of course. For one thing, she was still completely in the dark concerning the imminent abduction of her superstar sister. Within days he would be able to enjoy the degradation of both delightful sisters side by side, he thought as he turned away from her and, surrounded by mounted stags' heads and the incongruous landscapes of Egypt hanging on the oak panelled walls, he opened the long, bulky package before him. She had no idea that he was in a position whereby he would soon… finally… exact terrible revenge on Chelsi. For unknown to the lovely blonde slave, discussions had been underway with Chelsi's manager for some time, and plans concerning her kidnap were within days of being finalised.

With a characteristic, thin-lipped smile he began to extract the contents of the package and lay them out on the banqueting table. As he did so, he began to mentally catalogue the delightful, submissive creatures who were already subject to his cruelty and would soon become whip fodder to paying club members. Apart from Charlotte there were Saxon and Crikette… all at once he remembered the girl currently awaiting punishment in the underground, Egyptian chamber.

Recalling the incident when he had gone down to the girl's cell just before dawn to give her a jism breakfast, he confided to Charlotte, "I haven't decided yet how many lashes her carelessness deserves. It might've been an accident, but I can't start making allowances for bloody accidents! Anyway, she couldn't… or wouldn't… relax her throat!" As he had rammed his cock as far down as she could take it, the girl had snagged his pulled-back foreskin between the tiny gap between her two front teeth.

"It's bad enough she's done it to her own Master but," he reasoned, "supposing she did the same thing to one of the club member's instead? Something like that could ruin

The Ramparts' reputation." Even allowing for the fact that she was a youngster and new to submission, no self-respecting dominant would go near a club where the sluts were incapable of giving head! However, she was an amusing addition and given time she would learn. "I ought to name her soon."

Giving names to sex slaves had always been a bone of contention between himself and Whitby's friends, the Stapletons. They insisted that a slave was in essence a slut and as such, not deserving of a name. Tyler, on the other hand, though agreeing to a principle he would never admit to Lilith Stapleton, always pointed out the practicality of naming them.

"When you've got only five or six it's easy to refer to them as 'the redhead,' 'the thin one,' or 'the one with the enormous knockers!'" he would argue. But when you were moving toward increasing their numbers and building up a suitable stock, names were essential. Unless they had numbers. Except he had never been overly fond of numbers. No, he had started with names and so he would continue. Sadly, he doubted whether he would have time to deal with the girl in the Egyptian Chamber that day after all because there were just too many other matters that needed his attention. "I'll call her Rawnie," he said suddenly. "It's a gypsy name. It means 'Lady.'" He overlooked the fact that at only nineteen, she was most definitely still a girl.

"I'll get Alfred to deal with it," he said suddenly, "give the old bugger something useful to do!" He took out his mobile and put a call through to Tully to relay his wishes.

***

Charlotte was glad that for once Alfred, Tyler's crusty old manservant, was nowhere to be seen. His usual position was just inside the door of whichever room Tyler happened to be in, with his white-gloved hands crossed behind his back and an officious bearing that was born of years of serving the aristocracy. It was in Alfred's blood to serve.

And Charlotte was pretty sure that since he had taken over the role of manservant some fifty years ago, he had never lifted a finger to save any of Whitby's girls from their cruel Master. On the contrary, to her certain knowledge he had offered his assistance. Such had been his loyalty to the family... those he had considered his betters... that he had never seen any reason why even housemaids should not be subject to their employers' whims, even fucked by them. He had also seen no reason why the Lord should not give her the odd thrashing from time to time and had, on more than one occasion, held her down.

So it followed that, as much as Alfred hated the new Lord - and everyone knew he did, probably even Tyler himself since he made no bones about it - he tolerated the maltreatment that took place under his nose; it had probably never crossed his mind to protect even one of the delightful creatures from their Master's sadism. He merely watched from the corner of his eye as he awaited Tyler's pleasure.

She knew that Alfred considered Tyler a usurper, having . once told her that if the two men were to stand side by side, if it were not for his own valet's attire, anyone entering the room would mistake himself for the Lord of the Manor and recognise the other man for what he was - a con artist who had ingratiated himself with Lord Whitby and so swindled the true heir out of his inheritance!

She remembered the occasion when Tyler had first entertained his unsavoury friend, Tully, just a few weeks after he had taken possession of the Manor House. It had been in one of the most highly decorative of the first floor rooms. With its gold and lapis lazuli décor and furnishings, throughout Alfred's long service it had always been called the Day Room. But when the club opened, it was going to be called the Members' Smoking Lounge, something else that she knew had upset the servant.

On that occasion she had found herself suspended by her ankles from a special fixing close to one of a pair of glittering chandeliers, decorated with lapis lazuli pendants, which threw all manner of curious effects across her inverted form. Due to the high ceiling and the special mechanism, a girl could be raised or lowered as desired. And she recalled not only how her head had swum but also Alfred's horror when Tully had arrived.

Tully was a stocky character who wore a ring through his left nostril and two through each ear. Both his hands were tattooed - the left bearing a design of a dagger swathed in barbed wire, and the fingers of his right hand bearing the letters F-U-C-K. His jawline was always heavily shadowed, as if he had forgotten to shave. But worst of all was the odd odour which reminded Charlotte of cat's piss! He was a familiar character in the village and along with Tyler, was one of the chief reasons the villagers harboured such feelings of ill will toward the travelling families.

Even from her inverted position she had picked up Alfred's prickly demeanour when, as soon as Tully had actually spotted her, he had shown what Alfred always called "lack of breeding."

"Stone the fucking crows! What the fuck's that all about?" He had spent a good few seconds examining how her arms had dangled with her fingers fluttering aimlessly in the void a couple of feet or so above the thick, golden carpet and how her loose hair had kissed it. "Nice carpet," he had said in a tone that had suggested he was about to roll it up and put it in the back of a van, it being of more interest than the naked slavegirl.

"My grandfather said it represented the deserts of Egypt," Tyler had told him, pointing out the pictures of Egypt on the wall as well as the weird and wonderful artefacts, including the life-size but thankfully fake mummy.

Tyler had related how it had once inspired a "mummy wrapping" party that had seen all Whitby's girls swathed in colourful bondage tape.

"So, the man was a fucking idiot, then!" Tully had laughed before turning his attention back to Charlotte.

"Look at her tits! She's had one helluva whipping to get them in that state! Your handiwork, Ty?"

She had heard the pride in her Master's voice as he had told him it was.

"She's fucking gorgeous, Ty!"

Charlotte had positively glowed at the compliment. But at the same time she had trembled nervously as she had wondered what kind of treatment she could expect from her Master's friend. She need not have worried; Tully had soon lost interest in her again and had wandered over to the antique sideboard where drinks decanters and glasses were set out alongside the champagne on ice.

"This real crystal, Ty?" he had asked in his boorish, harsh tone.

He had clumsily clinked a brandy decanter against a similar one filled with the finest malt, and at once Alfred had joined the offensively-scented Tully at the sideboard. With his white-gloved hands he had taken the delicate, early 18th century decanter from the gypsy's grasp and she knew he had put all his effort into making the gesture seem polite as he had asked, "Drink, Sir?"

She recalled that Tully had knocked back two whiskeys and a brandy before asking, "Got any beer, Ty?"

Ignoring Alfred's presence as well as the naked girl, Tully had surveyed the room rather like a burglar casing the joint.

"Blimey, mate!" he had commented at last as he had taken in the décor and the bizarre Egyptian collection, "I keep asking meself, is this for real? You're not gonna suddenly find some long-lost 'rightful heir' crawling out of the wood panels, are yer? I mean, this really is all yours?"

"Course it is, mate!" Tyler had told him. "The old man disinherited his son…"

"Your father," Tully had pointed out as he had suddenly plunged his fingers inside Charlotte's pussy hard enough to make her gasp.

"Yeah, just think of it Tul, my Father! All those years we never even knew I'd got one!"

Charlotte had felt her blood run cold at the mention of Digby and had known at once that Alfred's old hurt was reopened. He had always been rather fond of Whitby's only son and just the mention of him had stirred something deep inside. But she had also known that his years of dedicated service would not allow him to show his anger as Tyler had pulled a face and continued with a tight-lipped smile.

"Ha! I wouldn't know the bastard if I saw him!"

Tully had plucked his finger free from Charlotte's squelchy cunt and used it to stir his whisky. "Strictly speaking, Ty," he had laughed as he had reached behind her and pressed his finger against her pink-puckered hole before boring it deep into her rectum, "you're the bastard!"

Coming out of her reverie, she knew Alfred still did not believe that Tyler would "get away with it." He had even told people that "he hasn't a hope in hell of passing himself off as a member of the aristocracy!" But anyone could see that Tyler was not actually trying to! But she was aware that, even now, after almost a year serving the new Lord of the Manor, it really stuck in Alfred's craw that he had to serve a man that he considered a blot on the face of humanity. The ignominy of a common vagabond inheriting the house where he had served the aristocracy for most of his life was almost more than the elderly manservant could stand. He had said more than once that he owed him no respect or loyalty, he merely carried out his duties.

Just as he would once he had finally been located, though

not for Tyler's benefit but because nothing would give the lecherous old man more pleasure than disciplining the new girl with the new name… Rawnie.

And it struck Charlotte for the first time that Tyler had given new names to all the girls… except herself.

CHAPTER TWO

The final weeks were a frantic round of people to see and jobs to do.

"Someone has to be behind the workers all the time," Tyler sighed as he continued examining the new implements, and that left less time for the actual business of disciplining the bitches, a job that he increasingly delegated either to Alfred, as he did then, or to the Escorts, a newly-formed, close-knit band of men.

As Tyler's most trusted and closest friend, Tully had been one of the first men to take up his offer of employment. Tyler had met up with him in The Griffin when Tully had arrived in the area with their clan a couple of months earlier. Over a couple of pints Tyler had explained something of his needs.

"I want guys I can trust to guard the sluts. And keep an eye out for them with the punters. You know what I mean, Tul, make sure they don't get damaged. Just because I tell the brainless tarts they're worthless slave meat don't mean they actually are, Tul. It'll cost a fucking fortune to replace them!"

As Tyler removed a bundle of new riding crops from the package, flexed them one by one and laid them out before him, he recalled Tully's reaction with amusement.

"These guys, Ty… is that it, just guard the prossies? Or do they get a piece of the action?" Tully had enquired in a laid-back kind of way that was at odds with the lust that had flared in his dark eyes.

"Pleasuregirls, Tul, I'm calling them Pleasuregirls," Tyler had corrected him, then gone on to explain more about the girls themselves. "They're not prossies, not in the sense you mean. They won't get paid for sex! They're a whole fuck more than a normal bunch of whores in a whorehouse!

For one thing, they're all stunners. For another, they're all submissives... basically that means they'll wait quietly until they're given an order, then they'll do whatever they're told when they're told. And without complaining! If some guy... you, me or any other bloke, tells one of them to dress in a plastic mac and diddle herself while standing on her head she'll do it. And submit to a whipping if it's not entertaining! If one of the members wants to tie a girl up and suspend her from the chandeliers, that's fine, too... as long as he doesn't break the chandeliers!"

He had paused while Tully laughed. Now, as he examined the keeper of one of the crops, he recalled how he had finally hooked his friend.

"So the guards - they'll be called Escorts - well, they'll be responsible for fetching and delivering the girls when needed, preparing them for the punters and locking them up again at night. And a whole lot more besides! There'll be perks, Tul, real diamond edged fucking perks," he had added with a grin.

Tully had accepted the job there and then. Before the evening was out he had recommended their mutual acquaintance Elvis, a Presley look-alike who took his resemblance seriously. And once Elvis had all the details, he became the second recruit.

All the men taken on so far seemed more than satisfied with their new employment and the responsibilities that went with it, agreeing the work was interesting, varied and the perks far outweighed even the generous salary.

The question of staff had posed problems in one form or another from the very beginning. Tyler considered all men as superior to women and was happy to pay them a wage - all except the gamekeeper! He was a dour man from the village. Like the rest of the villagers, he hated Tyler and all his "thieving didicoy friends." Many were the times that he had turned his shotgun in Tyler's direction and driven

20

him from The Ramparts estate. That being the case, it was entirely inappropriate for Tyler to pay the man a wage! Tyler never doubted that if it had been the gamekeeper rather than Whitby who had come along when Tyler was ravishing Charlotte in the woods, his unbelievable good fortune would have passed him by completely.

However, the female staff were a different matter entirely; and the first thing he had done was give all the female domestic staff a stark choice - either submit to slavery or get out. Those who stayed were subject to discipline, not as harsh as the Pleasuregirls but then they were hardly in the same league as the sex slaves! No longer paid a wage, they were split into two groups… maids and other slaves who would come into contact with the members, and backroom slaves who worked in kitchen, laundry etc… while the first group were never allowed to leave the premises and had their accommodation supplied, the second group were subject to a special scheme.

Everyone who chose to leave was made to sign a contract which prohibited legal action or disclosure of the events taking shape as The Ramparts prepared to open its doors to the more sadistic members of the SM community. Although at the moment there was one kitchen in use and one formal dining room, within weeks, like some multi-starred, world class hotel there would be three very different dining areas to cater for members' differing culinary pleasures… which meant finding additional slaves from somewhere! He could hardly advertise. Even the magazines that ran ads along the lines of Experienced Master seeks slave for discipline and mutual sexual gratification would be way off the mark, for what he was offering had nothing to do with the sexual gratification of bloody kitchen slaves!

He had solved one potential problem - the company who were supplying the marquees for the Grand Opening were also supplying waitresses.

He took up a dog whip from among the new consignment of disciplinary implements which were now all spread out along the table and turned his mind back to the Pleasuregirls. There was Fionola, he thought as he used both hands to assess the instrument's weight and caressed it with more affection than he had ever shown a female... except his ma, of course! He considered Fionola's neat little bottom that he always thought of as a drum-of-an-arse because of the sound the lash made when it struck her tight rump. He smiled as he imagined reproducing the sound with the new whip. She had not been cheap but the Jamaican slave trader from whom he bought her had not lied about the quality of the bitch!

Thankfully, a couple of weeks ago he had had the sense to put in an order with the Jamaican for a few more top notch sluts. It would be expensive because the man with the impossibly white suit dealt only in the best merchandise. But it would be worth it in the end, he told himself. He wanted The Ramparts to be one of the best clubs of its kind, with only the very best girls on offer to the punters. It was not merely quantity he was looking for but also quality and diversity - he had told the Jamaican to keep his eyes open for one or two Chinese girls, and perhaps a couple of black ones as well - and he still hoped he would be lucky enough to pick up a couple of other suitable girls on the cheap somewhere!

And there was Honeysuckle and Brandy, of course. And within days Chelsi would be joining them! She certainly was not going to be cheap and her manager kept upping his price. Turning slowly, Tyler tucked the whip under his arm and removed the polish-infused duster from Charlotte's mouth. With more force than called for, he used his other hand to prise open her mouth and then shoved the dog whip between her teeth.

"Don't drop it," he cautioned unnecessarily, knowing

she would not release it until commanded to do so, "or there'll be more trouble than you can cope with!" He repeated the words he had told her often, assuring her that he would always think of her as the backbone of his organisation. "The central core, the hub that all the spokes spread out from." He noted the spark of pride in her pale eyes and immediately felt the same temptation to crush it that he always did! "But there's going to be no more mister nice guy, Charlotte," he said nastily as he watched her turn peony pink from her chin to her hairline. The half-witted whore was trembling, he noticed. Time to turn it up! "It's time you realised I don't - never have had - your best interests at heart! I care fuck all for your well-being. To me you're just a worthless set of holes to fuck and a convenient body to flog. It's like I've told you before, I'm going to make you scream longer and louder than all the other whores put together! From now on, it's shock and awe for you, my girl!"

Satisfied with her distressed expression, he reached between her legs and inserted a couple of fingers. She was wet again! The most placid and tractable of all his slaves was always ready for a fuck and discipline. No matter how much he humiliated, whipped or in some other way tormented her, she just soaked it up and primed herself for more. He swirled his fingers around inside her for a few moments, feeling her strong, healthy vaginal muscles clamp tightly around them. He would never admit it... to anyone... but he actually had a kind of respect for her. The other girls, too, he conceded as he tore his fingers from her pussy, wiped them on her thigh and turned back to the table.

Switching his attention back to the whips, he considered his intention to use some of the Pleasuregirls as ponygirls. That brought to mind the tall girl, Sparkle. He had great plans for her! She was easily capable of pulling a trap, plus passenger, around the grounds. He had spotted her at a ponygirl event some months earlier and approached her owner there and then, and taken possession of her just a week later. She had come to him ready trained and, being so striking in appearance, he saw her as his primary ponygirl.

However, he also had great plans for Chelsi, seeing her in a similar role. But when he had told his recently appointed ponygirl trainer, the wild-eyed gypsy girl Adria, about his plans for the pint-sized pop star, although unconcerned about the planned abduction, declaring… "people go missing all the time… " she had disagreed with his assessment of the girl. Instead and without even waiting to see her in the flesh, Adria had condemned the stunning, half-an-inch-or-so over five feet tall girl as "too physically weak, emotionally unstable and self-centred" to be anything more than a novelty! Although he had often had rides in pony carts pulled by girls of different sizes and had paid the odd visit to the modern gladiatorial rings where ponygirls raced each other, pulling chariots and fighting off their opponents, he accepted that Adria knew her stuff. . After all, she had actual working experience of ponygirls. Yet he still harboured thoughts of Chelsi's success between the shafts… he would just have to thrash it into her!

Although he wanted to build up a special team of ponygirls, in time he wanted all the Pleasuregirls to be capable of doing a stint.

"I've ordered some special pony traps, Charlotte," he told her as he examined a pack of hoods. "Don't go thinking you'll escape the shafts entirely. Even if you don't take the punters for rides around the grounds, you'll have to take me." Then, for no particular reason he swung around and slapped first one of her whip-scored orbs, then the other, before repeating the operation and watching the gloriously malleable mammaries crash into each other. When he addressed her next, his uneducated tone became rougher as his lust increased. "You call them tits?" She would not dare take the whip from her mouth to answer. Besides, it was not a question. "They're just fucking overgrown chunks of meat with no tasteful quality at all!" he felt his balls tighten at the mere sight of her luscious globes. "They need at least three dozen welts across each before they show any merit at all!" he lied as her nipples stiffened under his gaze. "Just stand there, be quiet and don't get in the fucking way!" He suppressed a laugh... ... she was so obedient and willing to please that she would stand there all day if he did not tell her otherwise! It was one of the qualities he loved about her, that and how enjoyable it was to humiliate her. "Now just shut the fuck up and let me get on with my work!"

The demure Charlotte merely burbled prettily around the whip clamped between her teeth while he returned his regard to the hoods and shifted his thoughts back to ponygirls. He would love to train them himself, of course, but the running of the household in the absence of a housekeeper... he had had to get rid of the previous one because, quite frankly, he could not bear to look at her prune-like face one moment longer... was taking up far too much of his time already. He knew Adria was the right person to train them up to a suitable pony standard.

Tyler selected a cane from the new batch and swished it a couple of times to get the feel of it. Swivelling round once more, he slashed it half a dozen times across Charlotte's thigh.

She screwed up her eyes as fire blazed across her flesh. Yet she did not make a sound nor did she drop the whip. Even more surprising since her hands were free and only crossed behind her, she did not try to save herself or even rub her abused skin as the signatory tramlines of a cane appeared.

"Turn around!"

She turned around.

"Bend over."

She bent over.

Tyler slashed at her backside, his lustful gaze riveted to the luscious swell of her reddening buttocks. He always experienced a sense of real wellbeing as he watched the skin flatten beneath the impact and then, at the same time, there was a whitening that showed up even on her very palest of pale arse skin, something he had first become aware of while flogging that same, glorious rump years earlier. And those delightful effects were always followed by a glorious rippling of her flesh before the actual lines appeared... and all within a nano-second of impact!

Time and time again he watched in fascination as the tramlines developed. After twenty lashes, he reached behind him and tossed the cane on the table while unfastening his jeans with the other hand. His cock reared up in front of him magnificent and proud as he pulled back his foreskin. Grabbing hold of her hips he sank his phallus deep into her warm, wet cunt, relishing the strength of muscles that a few moments earlier had clamped around his fingers. Thrusting his hips he drove deeper into her, choosing to interpret her whip-hampered sighs and whimpers as signs of pain, for he was in no doubt that a cock of such magnitude was cunt-rending agony to even the most experienced of lust-channels.

His hands gripped tighter. He wished he had more time to screw the bitch properly but there was work to be done! He emptied his seed into her, spurt after glorious spurt. He withdrew, wiped his glistening rod on her tramlined bottom, watched a glob of creamy sperm fall from her quim to the floor, then turned back to the table and when his prick had deflated at last he tucked himself away.

Charlotte, however, did not move since she had not been

given permission. Instead, with her hands linked in the small of her back, she bent over with her pale shapely legs apart, unable to do anything but endure the humiliation of his spunk leaking from her pussy and puddling on the floor. With the whip still in her mouth, she dared not make a sound. But if he had bothered to look at her, to lift her head and perhaps even kiss her lips, he would have seen that she was smiling. But he would not look, of course. Why should he care?

Working his way along the table, Tyler examined the new stock carefully. Taking up one of the new pairs of nipple clamps he summoned her with a terse,

"Here, girl."

Immediately she dropped to all fours and, with the whip still held between her soft lips she hurried with swaying bottom and wobbly, generous breasts to stand before her Master. Bending from the waist, he hooked a finger through one of the metal rings of her collar and dragged her upright on to her knees. He did not have to tell her to put her hands behind her back again but merely waited until she had done so.

"I hope you realise how honoured you are to be the first slut to try out these new toys," he told her as he put them down again, and instead selected a pair with rows of tiny teeth embedded in the jaws. Like the other design, they also had a chain joining the two clamps and a rather fiddly screw on each to tighten them.

Charlotte's eyes bulged in horror as he opened the wicked-looking jaws for her to see. Her mouth slackened and he spotted that she was in danger of dropping the whip.

"Drop it and I'll let Tully and Elvis have you for a week!" He watched her lips quiver in distress at the thought of being handed over to the loutish Tully and Elvis, the man who looked as if he were always on his way to a lookalike convention. It had to be admitted that he did look remarkably like his hero, especially as all his clothes were made especially and copied from some of the King's best known outfits, despite the unsuitability of being every day wear! He even wore his jet black hair in the same style and had perfected both the King's curled upper lip and his accent.

Terrified by the prospect of being left alone with the two men, Charlotte tightened her own lips to hold the whip fast. And that was the very moment he chose to snap the first clamp over her coral-tinted, engorged nipple. She emitted a high-pitched, "Mmmphhh!" and her eyes filled with tears in a most amusing way, he thought as the teeth bit sharply into her tantalisingly turgid nipple. He repeated the process with her other nipple. Again the same stifled cry of pain and again, the glistening of tears. Except this time they actually broke free and trickled slowly down her cheeks as her biddable body and obedient nature were rewarded by maltreatment.

While he concentrated on her distorted features, idly he picked up a second pair of clamps. Absentmindedly he opened the toothed jaws and closed them over his own finger. As the teeth pricked, and then punctured, his skin, it was all he could do to keep from yelling out himself. Nonchalantly he removed it, placed it back on the table, then tightened hers again.

"Lower your eyes!"

Weeping, she swung her pain-glazed gaze to the floor.

"Look at you! The backbone of my organisation blubbering like a common streetwalker experiencing pain for the first time. We both know that's a fucking lie so you'd best pull your socks up and start acting like the upgraded bitch you are! I thought you could hack it, but if it turns out I'm mistaken then I'll sell you on to some other gullible mug!" he threatened, grabbing a shining hank of her honey-blonde hair, raising it above her head and then dropping it as if in disgust. "I hear they go a bundle for big-titted blondes in Africa," he said as a recollection of something the Jamaican had told him came unbidden to his mind.

He turned his back on her and continued with his assessment of the new equipment. So engrossed was he that he actually jumped when the door opened.

Charlotte, still on her knees with her eyes submissively lowered and her tortured nipples taking on a darkening tinge, remained impassive.

"Yer got a minute, Ty?" Tully's boorish voice echoed around the vast room as he called from the doorway.

" 'Course, mate." Tyler turned and gave his short, stocky friend his full attention. "What's up?"

Tully stepped into the room, talking as he swaggered toward him. "Had a call from some guy called Snick. Wants to know if there are any jobs going. I got his number to ring him back."

Tyler laughed. "You'd make a good secretary, Tul!"

Tully rammed the knuckle of his forefinger up his nostril and pushed his nose-ring to the side. "Ta, but I ain't got the legs for it."

"Yeah, right. I guess I'll just have to hire one, then." In truth he already had a perfectly good, efficient secretary who had worked for The Ramparts house and estate for several years. But, like Tully, she had not got the legs for it! "Why'd you speak to him, Tul? Sue not in today?"

That was the trouble with allowing certain members of the workforce to retain their freedom… they were still entitled to days off! Of course, that did not apply to the domestics who had found themselves taken into slavery almost as soon as Tyler took up residence.

Unlike Charlotte, who had been forced to give up her own room in favour of a cell, and the maids, whose rooms had been given to some of the Escorts while they were provided with alternative accommodation in a long, low outbuilding, in common with the estate's doctor, Sue had been provided with a three-roomed flat on the estate. Naturally, she would have to give it up when he finally replaced her.

"She's a bit tied up at the moment," Tully grinned. "I've got her stripped on that cross yer had put in the corner."

"Right," Tyler said, as if it were the most natural thing in the world for the hired hand to tie the boss's secretary naked to a St. Andrew's cross in the main office. "Ring this Snick guy back. Can't see him yet because I'm going on a trip tomorrow afternoon. So tell him if he's still interested, he can come for an interview in a week or two… make it three to be on the safe side. When you've finished with Sue, give her a dozen lashes from me for wasting time."

Tully gave a mock salute. "Okay, boss," and slammed the door shut.

Tyler returned to the job in hand and made a mental note of the interview. He still needed a few more men to work as Escorts, and another couple to work as handymen; the place would need maintaining when the interior designers and their teams of workmen had completed their jobs. But once he had "done the math" he muttered in a parody of an American accent, he had realised that he would need a considerable number. The employment nightmare had been partially solved by taking on a number of gypsies, who were willing to try a more sedentary lifestyle in return for a regular wage, much to the displeasure his Estate Manager. But as Tyler had pointed out, running the estate was a different matter entirely and must be kept separate from minding Pleasuregirls and running a club. Besides, he found it rewarding to hire people who, like himself, had long been considered unemployable. Then he had thrown his net wider to include other men who found themselves in a similar position by advertising for "security staff." That had led to an opening of the floodgates that had virtually solved the second part. In fact, there were only a few vacancies left. He had even taken on a couple of locals since the estate manager, who had quietly and efficiently served Whitby for years, had informed Tyler that as Lord of the Manor he actually owned a fair proportion of Squire's Langley itself as well as the surrounding farmland, and therefore had certain responsibilities toward the inhabitants, whether they liked him or not!

He looked up as the door opened again.

"Er, Ty…" This time Tully kept his hand on the door and did not actually enter the room.

"Yes, Tul?"

"Er… Forgot there was another call… about the Grand Opening. They're okay about marquees but they said 'Sorry. No can do.' with waitresses."

Tyler's features were like thunder. "What? 'No can do?' You telling me they're not available after all? They've been booked for over three months! Call them back! Tell them…"

"No good tellin' 'em, mate. They don't want to know, say they can't send waitresses here. It seems someone told them what sort of event…"

"Who the fuck would do that? God almighty! What are we going to do now?"

"Don't worry, mate. You'll sort it." With that, Tully made a hasty retreat.

CHAPTER THREE

With her head lowered and hands behind her back, the whip still in her mouth and her purpling nipples crippled by pain, Charlotte remained on her knees as she followed at a respectful, judicious distance; she had learned a long time ago that as unbelievably fulfilling and strangely pleasurable as pain usually was for girls like herself, any discipline administered while her Master raged was rarely pleasurable and best avoided.

Spinning angrily, he dragged her to her feet, snatched up a cane, and slashed it savagely across the upper swell of her breasts. Then he tightened the clamps again and watched her eyes water as the teeth sank deeper, while poor Charlotte feared the two sets would come together somewhere inside her agonised nuggets.

"As if I haven't got enough to do!" he fumed as he laid down the vicious strikes. "There's no time to finish checking the stock now! I've got to look in on the landscape gardeners, then see what's happening with the rest of the rooms." Despite Whitby's lavish entertaining, living alone meant he had not used as many bedrooms and reception rooms as they had in the manor's heyday, when it had given employment to a vast army of servants. Therefore there were a greater number of musty old rooms to be opened up and made ready than Tyler had at first thought.

"And I've still got to check the bloody cells!" He was not counting as his angry words set the rhythm for his fiendish lashes. Although all the ancient, underground cells were not yet habitable, at least he had had the sense to move Pleasuregirls into the ones that were! "They'll just have to sleep on sacks, like you do, bitch, until the beds arrive! Don't think for one minute I'm going to let any of them continue living in that tower. I'm going to be moving them outta there pretty soon," Tyler informed her, "my slaves don't need silk sheets and all them fucking cushions!"

The tower - originally built as a folly by an ancestor - was quite luxurious. Whitby had had it specially adapted and made habitable for his girls. The same tower was visible from an upstairs window in Charlotte's family's house down by the canal. In her capacity as maid, she had frequently visited the tower on some errand or other. Naturally, the girls had not been free to come and go as they pleased, and the door had always been kept locked. So it had been necessary for her to be accompanied by the old housekeeper, a woman Tyler had paid off with a considerable sum, who had a key attached to the bunch which dangled from her waist.

However, the housekeeper had never ventured inside and so it had been up to Charlotte to deliver the clean linen and remove the soiled ones. The rooms were over several floors and festooned with gauzy curtains of deep pink, red, orange or yellow. There was a divan in each, to which the girls had been chained by the ankle. In addition, there was one room on the first floor where they could relax, read and listen to music. In that room there were no shackles and, with its gauzy purple hangings, couches that doubled as beds and a plethora of purple cushions, they could make-believe they were in some handsome sheikh's harem.

"And I don't see why they should have a fucking Jacuzzi!"

She recalled with only a smidgen of envy that on the ground floor there was a communal bathroom, with a Jacuzzi! In that respect, Whitby's sex slaves had been much better off than Charlotte, whose shared, chilly bathroom had a small, chipped enamel tub that had not been replaced in decades. Of course, the girls had paid a heavy price for their luxuries, a price she now paid for no luxuries at all!

The tower was where his new girls had eventually wound up, though Charlotte had remained in her own pretty, sunny and yellow-painted room in one of the vast attic areas until moved into her cell, and so had never enjoyed the delights of the tower. And that very week, Saxon, Brandy and Fionola had been moved into cells as well.

"I've got other plans for that tower!"

His heart was hammering and his heavy brows, which almost met over the bridge of his nose, were drawn together to make an angry unbroken line. He paused to get a grip on his anger and took in the tramlines which flared across Charlotte's flesh. But his fury refused to abate and he began again, the rhythm of his words once more dictating the measure of the strikes.

"There's this fucking mess with the waitresses for the marquees to sort out! I can't use Pleasuregirls because they'll be needed for the attractions. Right fucking shambles it's going to be!" he ranted as he rained the strikes upon her raw and swollen breastmeat, tipped with purple-clamped-and-punctured nipples.

Yet even his anger did not prevent him from producing. a rather striking gridwork. For such was his appreciation of red-ribboned female flesh that he never laid the stripes down any old how but rather arranged them decoratively, giving as much consideration to how the welts caught the eye as to how much pain they generated. That was something Whitby had taught him. His assertion being that the only justification one needed to hurt a sex slave was, "because you can, my boy!" Tyler's own attachment to the edict was "hurt not injure."

During those early days with his grandfather, it had felt to Tyler as if he had been awoken from an ignorant stupor; it had not taken him long to earn his grandfather's unofficial title of The Whipmaster as well as the official titles - Lord had turned out to be one of many, including Earl of something-or-other - and these days he was recognised as being The Whipmaster more than any of the others!

"If someone's blabbed..." he continued as he paused once more and admired his handiwork, "probably the gamekeeper - about the club's purpose and the activities I've got planned for the opening, I can't really expect any other conventional firm to save the day, not even if I place an ad in the local paper!" Calming down as his heart rate returned to normal and his anger gave way to a consideration of the practicalities, he reconsidered a moment... the paper not only served Squire's Langley but its neighbouring Langleys as well, from Abbot's and King's Langley (the name Langley believed to be derived from the old word Langelei, meaning long clearing in the thick wood) right the way across to Langley Feldon and Langley Ash. He supposed he might be lucky, but heaven only knew what kind of applicants he would get. "Over at 'Ash they think muff diving's something you play on your Gameboy or Wii!"

No, another solution altogether was needed.

He gave her another eight or nine slashes to convince himself that the cane had been worth the money, then set it down again as he took in the sight of his most obedient slave. He gave a slow smile. With his tension dispersed and his mood lightened as he concentrated on the pure pleasure of Charlotte's suffering, suddenly an idea came to him.

Without a word of comfort to the wretched, pain-soaked Charlotte whose tram-lined breasts were ablaze inside and out and whose purple nipples were throbbing, he turned and left the room. Scrambling to her feet, with her heart bursting with joy and her cunt lustily aching to be filled, Charlotte followed behind as he headed for the office.

***

After leaving the banqueting hall, Tyler arranged a meeting with a Mr Peregrine Green of the Hempstead End Young Offenders Correctional Facility. And so that evening, with Charlotte standing beside his chair, Tyler waited in the Red Drawing Room for the man who he hoped would help solve at least some of his problems.

Without the pretence at a finesse he did not possess or even deigning to look at her, the gypsy-turned-lord leaned across and parted Charlotte's glistening labia. Twisting his wrist uncomfortably and deciding she would pay for that later since it was the slave and not the Master who should suffer, he inserted two fingers into her warm, sweetly-juicing channel.

She picked up on his undeclared discomfort and without being told to, the lovely Pleasuregirl shuffled closer and adjusted her wide-legged stance for his easy access.

He did not thank her. Nor did he comment on the state of her quim as he thrust his fingers in and out. He accepted a proffered goblet from his manservant and took a warming slug of brandy. Then, as Alfred returned to his station by the door, with penetrating force he jabbed his fingers brutally and elicited Charlotte's soft mewls of discomfort.

The fireplace before which Tyler sprawled in a chair with his legs outstretched, ankles crossed and his fingers embedded deep in Charlotte's cunt, was one of the few original, cavernous affairs. The surround, with its handy, roughly-hewn and overhanging wooden mantelshelf, was five feet high and seven feet wide. It had a black, iron grate in which a fire had been lit despite the warming weather, and a stone hearth of about two inches high. Although not on the same scale or of the same design as the one in the banqueting hall, Tyler was adamant it must have been conceived with something far more entertaining than a mere fire in mind!

On that particular evening, beautifully demonstrating one

of the purposes for which the fireplace could have been designed, one of the Pleasuregirls was displayed, attractively and muscle-wrenchingly awaiting his guest. Her name was Saxon and her shoulder length, blood-ruby coloured hair flew about her as she tossed her head as if that would somehow ease the cramps. Her beautifully toned, alabaster thighs, Tyler noticed, had marked up exceptionally well after she had dangled from her wrists in the library all afternoon as a practice piece for the escorts. Naked, and spread-eagled with her curved back facing into the room, her wrists and ankles were held in place by heavy chains. Similar ones attached to her black leather wrist restraints were joined to large iron rings, fitted decades or perhaps even a couple of centuries earlier, which hung at intervals along the underside of the shelf. That evening Tyler was utilising those at either end, with the girl positioned centrally. Her legs were spread with her bare toes abutting the hearth, and the chains secured to her ankle restraints were fitted to metal bolts fixed into the corners of the stone itself. Although Tyler had left no slack in the chains, that did not stop her sometimes energetic but always vain struggles to escape. It was most entertaining, he mused, and found her writhing a considerable turn-on.

Although the fire which burned within the old grate was by no means raging, it nevertheless caused grave discomfort for poor Saxon, placed directly in front of it. It crackled and sparked, and Tyler got up to check on her fire-warmed front, and was pleased to note that her skin was covered in a sheen of perspiration. Her bottom lip quivered most becomingly, and she was whimpering in fright as her eyes misted over with tears. Her entire front was aglow and when he clasped her dangling breasts, he was gratified by the considerable heat. Having mauled her for a good few moments until his hands grew uncomfortably warm, he returned to his chair knowing all was well and that there was no possibility of her becoming damaged. At ease once more he slipped his finger back into Charlotte's lust-channel.

As she continued to tug pathetically, he glanced around at the magnificence of the Red Drawing Room as his fingers jabbed and swirled in Charlotte's vagina.

The Ramparts was a wonderful old house which had benefited from his forebears' discriminating tastes and his grandfather's eccentricity until it had become a mélange of treasures and extravagances. Tyler hoped that all the work and the money that he was spending would be worth it in the end. With his own alterations and additions, along with what he thought of as "interior weeding" regarding Whitby's collection of Egyptian artefacts, the place seemed to be shaping up as the pleasure palace he had long envisioned. Everything was geared to the self-indulgent pleasures of men, including suitable décor of the bedrooms and suites available. Only mens' desires and fantasies were the stuff of The Ramparts, he told himself, and the whores' pleasures must be strictly controlled.

Also on offer to the members would be the more conventional pastimes found in any good Gentlemen's club. Luckily, Whitby had long ago established a well-equipped room with facilities for billiards, cards and other similar recreational activities. In addition there was a Members' Bar, a Smoking Room and, when it was completely renovated, a dungeon.

Every now and then, little sparks flew from the grate and Saxon squealed prettily as they alighted harmlessly on her flesh, extinguishing themselves on impact. And Tyler knew that everything was okay in his world - his concerns were as short lived and harmless as the sparks.

The remodelling of the house was almost completed, and the same magic had been applied to the magnificent, sweeping grounds. With the ancient woodland being a natural boundary, the multi-acre grounds had always been a haven of neatly trimmed lawns and parklands stretching for miles, looked after by a dedicated staff of three. But Tyler had promised them that when the landscape gardeners were finished, he would find them additional gardeners from somewhere. The woods were now extended with a woodland garden, complete with rustic-looking seats at intervals, along with whipping posts and trestles set up along the bark chipping walkways.

Although it had been sadly neglected there was also a private branch of the Grand Union, the canal that ran through Squire's Langley, that he had had spruced up since he had bought his own narrowboat. The trip he taking the next day, intended to be part business and part pleasure, was planned to start here at The Ramparts and go on to Napton-on-the-Rise in Warwickshire. It was a round trip that would last a few days. Of course, it would only take a couple of hours or so by road but it was hardly as relaxing as on the boat and besides, Tyler enjoyed the physical work of opening and closing the locks. The canal itself was a popular waterway with day trippers and holiday makers, and the private stretch would not only find popularity with the members but would also be convenient for bringing in new girls.

In addition to the canal there was a well-stocked river running through the estate... Tyler and his Ma, sometimes Tully, too, had often dined on fish caught a mile or two from where it actually joined the canal... and so angling was just another delight that could possibly be on the menu. What could be more relaxing for a man, he asked himself, than fishing with a wet and willing slut at your side? He would have to have special rings inserted in the banks to attach them to... and he would have to get the Escorts to lock them in place, just in case someone got it into his head to spirit the whores away!

And, thanks to major landscaping that was, on the whole approved and overseen by the estate manager, along with the woodland garden there were other themed gardens that would soon be ready. Whitby's original tennis court had been extended and the pony-carting track around the estate was also nearing completion. The downside to all the improvements was that it would take a platoon of men to keep the grounds that way!

He flicked a look at the 18th Century mantel clock. Another fifteen minutes and his meeting should be underway. He had never met Peregrine Green and had no idea whether the man' had any concept of punctuality.

CHAPTER FOUR

Charlotte felt warm eroticism spread through her belly and knew that, as long as her Master continued to direct his lust, savagery and scorn toward her, then there was -and never would be - any problem, and everything would remain as it should be in her world. For Charlotte was exactly where she wanted to be.

Ever since Tyler had come into her life some five years earlier, she had longed to be more to him than just a housemaid who was only good enough for occasional discipline or quick screw when there was no one else available. Given her experiences and inside knowledge of the late, salacious lord and his house, it was perhaps a stupid desire. For who in their right mind would long for such an existence, where harsh floggings, bitter humiliations and sexual abuse were almost daily occurrences? Yet Charlotte had looked on longingly, especially when Tyler had become a frequent visitor. She had watched him closely and whenever an opportunity had presented itself, the busty young maid had offered herself for service. And he had promised her then that one day he would change her life forever - she would never have to work as a maid again!

Charlotte knew it was inevitable things would change when the club was up and running in three… or was it four weeks? she wondered. Yet even with the presence of several new girls, even the one by the fireplace, she knew her own position was safe because, after all, there was a special link between herself and her Master They had weathered a lot together.

In spite of Tyler's gaze currently being fixed on the other girl, she was confident that she, Charlotte, meant more to him than anyone else, something he proved again and again by keeping her almost constantly with him, except when he went to bed, or off on his new and highly prized narrowboat. Other than that, whenever he abused one of the other girls, he demanded that she be there too. And he almost always had her accompany him on his walks in the grounds, sometimes on all fours as if she were a faithful dog.

That evening as she stood naked beside him, she was blissfully happy, the presence of Saxon having no bearing on her high spirits. Why should it? After all, she told herself, in their slave/Master relationship he had all the rights, and it was not hers to complain! As his fingers inside her cunt fuelled her hot swirling arousal, making her vagina squelch noisily, she recalled the day when he had first taken up residence.

He had made her strip off the French maid's costume that Whitby had liked her to wear and had her kneel before him. Then he had taken out his divine, thick rod of manhood and thrust it deep into her mouth. She had had to call on all her experience to relax and cope with his immense girth and while she had struggled he had told her that she was to be kept naked and available for him at all times. He had gripped and mauled her tits while he had told her that all her clothes had been given to charity.

That was the moment when she had first realised that to be truly happy she must accept it all as true, he demanded utter submission and she wanted to give it. So she had accepted, accepted it all, and wondered if he understood how happy she was to bow to his dominance and supremacy, she had put all her efforts into giving him the blow job of his life but even so she had nearly choked on his cock but he had held her face to his crotch and had been so pleased with the effect his news had had that he had immediately come. Charlotte had heard his sigh of pleasure just as the thick spurts had splashed into her mouth and almost choked her all over again, but she had held on, determined to serve him. But there was so much of it! It had seeped from the corners of her mouth, run down her chin and onto her breasts, making it clear he was sated and he had finished with her, he had released her nipples, scooped up the long tresses of her hair and used them to wipe himself clean

His jabbing, spiteful fingers brought her out of her reverie and she welcomed the sharp, redeeming pain once more and while he sat in silence with two fingers of one hand roughly probing her insides and his other hand curled around his goblet, she dared to turn her head and look at the man she was delighted to call Master.

Somewhere in his mid thirties, his hair was unfashionably long and always reminded her of the colour of dried bracken. When the sun shone, or at night when he was seated under the brilliance of the glittering chandeliers, it seemed to be shot through with gold. A better diet had at last put a little meat on his bones and, while his build was naturally lean his old nickname "Lanky" was no longer apt.

That evening he was wearing a pair of scruffy old jeans despite owning wardrobes full of new pairs with designer labels, and one of his old, comfortable western-style shirts. Charlotte thought that no one would ever guess he was a multi-millionaire!

His long legs were crossed at the ankles, his boots scuffed and in need of polish. Rather like the man himself, she mused smilingly as a great depth of emotion swelled up; just because she was in love with the man did not mean she was blind to his faults! Polish, both figuratively and actually, had always been seriously lacking in Tyler's life, and was still noticeably absent since he refused to totally conform, she thought as whorls of blessed pleasure set her insides alight. Such was her devotion that she would gladly lick his boots clean.

43

Her breath caught in her throat as, whether by design or accident she could not tell, his sharp fingernail caught at the delicate membranes of her insides.

"Quiet!" he scolded as, sprawled in the chair, he raised his brandy to his lips. "One more peep out of you this evening, Charlotte, and I'll give you something to really moan about!"

He knocked back the last of his brandy and plonked his goblet on the satinwood, drum top occasional table beside him. "The fucking din in this room is enough to make a man's guts turn sour," he complained though the silence was measured by the ticking and quarter-hourly chimes of the mantel clock, and broken only by Saxon's low-toned groans of distress and Charlotte's sole yelp. "You spoil this meeting for me with your whining, bitch, and I'll really make you suffer."

It was no idle threat, though had anyone been passing they would have thought twenty-five year old Charlotte had already suffered greatly; not only did her breasts carry the shocking marks of her Master's earlier anger but her nipples were speckled with pinpoints of red where the clamps had punctured them. In addition, after a lunch that had put him in a better mood, Tyler had practised his craft with the result that virtually every other inch of her gorgeous body was cruelly marked with a skilfully applied gridwork of freshly inscribed welts that had taken an intolerably long time to deliver. As he waited for his guest, Tyler was pleased to note that their colour almost matched the leather of the wide chair in which he was seated, which itself was perfectly matched to the décor of the opulent Red Drawing Room.

Hoping her master would not mistake Saxon's groans for her own complaints, Charlotte knew she could always simply walk away because, unlike Saxon, she was not restrained in any way. Except she knew that, in the unlikely

44

event that she wanted to escape, she would not get far because her Master was almost six feet tall and much stronger than herself; he would overcome her in a matter of moments. And the punishment would be dire.

Besides, she hated to upset people and had never, in all the years she had been at the house, disobeyed an order or refused a request. It was not in the lovely blonde's nature.

She slewed her pale gaze toward the door where Alfred stood statue-like awaiting instructions.

Tyler summoned him with a terse, "More brandy!"

As he refilled Tyler's goblet, it struck Charlotte that Alfred probably cared more for the crystal glasses and decanters which her Master handled so carelessly than he did the flesh and blood habitually maltreated under his gaze.

She was quite used to Alfred's ways since she had come to work at The Ramparts as a seventeen year old straight from school. The sweet-natured girl had known Alfred since she had arrived as a fresh-faced teenager. On taking up her position as housemaid, it had been impressed upon her that she must show him the all the respect due to a man of his position within the household and offer him every assistance, with the result that by now she knew the lecherous servant's cock almost as well as she knew her Master's! It was just one of the house's secrets, and she had learned many of the old manor's secrets! Of course, the underground cells were part of village folklore as was the dungeon for it was believed that the oldest part of the house was built on the spot of a medieval castle and that its ruins still existed if only one knew where to look... and Charlotte did. And most people seemed to have heard about the centuries' old network of tunnels supposedly running beneath the estate. Some people said they led to one of the nearby villages. But Charlotte knew, though her Master probably did not, more than one location from which the

45

tunnels could be accessed, just as she knew where they eventually came out!

Smiling, Tyler plucked his fingers free of Charlotte's cunt with a plopping noise. Examining them, he noted how they glistened with her sweet sap, then offered them up to her.

Without being told to, she bent toward them and, with her long, wavy hair falling around his hand she took his fingers into her mouth and sucked them clean.

"That's enough," he barked in a way that bruised her heart.

She straightened and, with her legs still apart and her hands still behind her back, she stood with her head submissively bowed.

Ignoring Saxon's increasingly irritating whines, he looked at the clock again as it struck the half hour. Setting up the SM club was more time consuming than Tyler had imagined, and the workmen were beginning to get under his feet. As he lifted his goblet to his lips, he admitted that he could not have done any of it without the help of his estate manager who preferred to be just left alone to get on with his job, and it was largely thanks to him, his easy manner and his contacts that the structural conversions and landscape gardening that should have taken years to accomplish were completed in months.

As to the actual running of the club and taking care of finances... that was another problem altogether, one that could not be solved by hiring a load of gypsies! He gave a wry smile... there was probably not one of his friends who would not rob him blind if they were in control of the funds! The man he had ear-marked for the job was Stapleton, a semi-retired banker and trusted friend of Whitby's. After all, Tyler was the first to admit that he himself was not the ideal man to take charge of such enormous wealth - he needed someone to see that he did not squander it all and end up exactly where he started! Stapleton was surely the perfect choice. Another man with useful contacts, his help in the day to day running of the club would be invaluable. Tyler put it on his mental things to do list… he really would have to talk to the man soon. It was only the thought of Stapleton's appalling wife, Lilith, that made him procrastinate because if he were to employ Stapleton, he would have to offer Lilith something just to keep the bitch off his own back! Perhaps he would give Stapleton a call when Mr Green had gone, and have him come over in the morning. That way he could put a proposition to the man before he left on his trip.

Speaking of propositions, where the hell was Peregrine Green?

***

Mr Green arrived… twenty minutes late… and was shown into the Red Drawing Room where Tyler was pleased at last to entertain him.

He was offered whiskey… rather than Tyler's favourite brandy… which he had Alfred serve in rarely-used tumblers bearing the family crest. He also offered cigars.

And Saxon.

Perry was only too pleased to take advantage of Tyler's generosity and enjoyed everything on offer. Tyler gave him a few moments to pick an implement and enjoy the girl. At the same time he ran through his mind one last time the reasons that had prompted him to summon the man in the first place. When the teams of conservationists and decorators moved out, there would be nowhere near enough suitable looking domestic slaves to keep the number of rooms up to the new standard, which made recruitment of the right sort of girl crucial. And so, as Perry practised his swing with a particularly whippy cane across Saxon's creamy-white behind while she did her best to stifle her cries, Tyler broached the subject he had in mind.

47

"How old are the girls at your facility? Eighteen, nineteen, yeah? Right! Then I'd like to help... some of them at least... by offering them work experience." He swirled his drink with one hand while once again rummaging around Charlotte's amazingly juicy cunt and waited for Perry's reaction.

With tendrils of lust coiling and uncoiling in her depths as she longed for the penetration of something other than her Master's fingers, nevertheless Charlotte remained docile and mute. She felt the leering gaze of Tyler's guest crawling over her bruised and scarlet-wreathed flesh as the man took a breather. And what was visible of Charlotte's pale skin beneath the welts and bruises responded by turning an attractive deep pink.

"What exactly do you have in mind?" Perry swigged his own drink.

"Provided they're suitable as far as looks are concerned, I could offer them experience as maids." Tyler laughed. "Of course, they'd have to be capable of actually doing the job..." Girls who were not afraid of hard work and the occasional flogging by club members, he thought. "At least to the satisfaction of my man." He gestured toward Alfred, still standing in his accustomed position by the door.

Perry flung the old man a look.

On his way from Hempstead End, Perry had stopped off at The Griffin, where he had discovered exactly how unpopular the late Lord's choice of heir was. And yet inside the house itself Perry discovered, there seemed to be little opposition.

Had he but known it, there were even domestic slaves who actually admired Tyler and his angular good looks. There was a raw sensuality which seemed to surround him, the same sensuality which had made Charlotte and the other Pleasuregirls willingly sign the horrendous contracts that Tyler presented them with. Drawn up especially for the sex slaves, it condemned them to a life of carnal brutality.

Tyler did not know or care whether the girls gave any thought to the legality of the documents or gave any credence to his assertion that they were legally binding. The important point as far as he was concerned was that the stupid bitches thought they were! For years he had taken girls' maidenhood, now he took their dignity and free will to boot. In return, though none would ever suspect it, they had his admiration and respect.

Along with the joys of lust, he was also well used to feelings of ill-will directed against him. Ignoring animosity... even Alfred's... was second nature. He summoned the servant to replenish their glasses. Pleased to note that at least he had Perry's interest, when Alfred returned to his station, Tyler continued.

"And then, if they turn out to be all that I … we'd… hope, why send them back to complete their sentences?" Clutching Charlotte's vulva he pulled her down to his level, stuffed a cigar in her mouth and had her draw on it while he lit it. "Surely it would make more sense to let them work out their sentences here? As domestic staff. What's the phrase? 'On licence in the community?' Could you arrange that?" He thought that with the right inducement, the man could arrange anything.

He released a red faced Charlotte, she straightened without comment, her pale eyes watering stingingly as she stifled her coughs.

Perry Green did not confirm, deny or hesitate. "Thereby solving all your staffing difficulties at a stroke." Perry returned his attention to Saxon and dealt another quick, half dozen and totally inept strikes to her red-striped bottom. "If I've understood your set-up correctly, your lordship, you don't employ female staff at all - they're all slaves!"

"Surely your girls wouldn't expect to be paid while working out their sentences? Anyway, like all my slaves, they'd be free to leave once they'd done their time." He did not add how long that period was… he had not worked it out himself yet. "But afterwards, if they fancied getting their housing, food and other costs covered they could stay on and lead good, useful lives as domestic slaves. Perhaps those with the right qualities could eventually become Pleasuregirls."

He watched Perry's lack of aptitude as he resumed his thrashing of the unfortunate Saxon, who threw back her head in a most attractive manner - the response to a particularly ham-fisted strike which grazed her skin with the tip of the cane. The sudden movement of her head sent her fine, attractively-dyed ruby hair flying and exposed her lovely white throat, sensually encircled by a black, Ramparts collar.

"A tidy outcome for all concerned," Tyler concluded in his best business-like manner.

"What would I get out of it?" Perry's comment was accompanied by a particularly harsh but artless strike which must have hurt poor Saxon like hell and almost had Tyler feeling sorry for her… almost, but not quite. He decided to have her taken to the Escorts' newly equipped social hall later for those who were off duty to do the job properly. But in the meantime, he allowed Perry free rein.

"A year's free membership?" Tyler offered. He knew Stapleton would probably balk at his generosity if he got wind of it, which was why Tyler was considering him for the job in the first place, just as he complained about Tyler's continued lack of refinement. But this was his show, Tyler reminded himself. He was now one of the super-rich and could buy almost anything, a fact not lost on his guest.

"Two years would be more acceptable. And I shall need reassurance that…" Perry Green slashed inexpertly with great enthusiasm, making the delightful Saxon howl in pain as she writhed in her bonds. When her cries subsided enough for him to be heard he continued. "I shall need your guarantee that 'my girls' won't come to any harm while 'on licence.' And your further guarantee that not a word of this will get out and that this meeting never took place."

Tyler stood up. "What meeting?" With a tight smile he offered his hand in friendship and to seal that particular deal. "I'll expect to see you at the Grand Opening."

Although weeks of planning had gone into the fête-like event, thanks to that morning's bombshell there was still one problem to be addressed... he needed some fairly decent-looking girls to work as waitresses in the main marquee. His grip on Perry's hand tightened.

"For two years' worth I'll expect something more, call it a favour."

Tyler re-took his seat. He slipped his fingers between Charlotte's peachy buttocks and insinuated his forefinger up her rectum.

Perry Green turned his attention back to the unfortunate, perspiration-beaded Pleasuregirl.

Tyler waited until Perry was engrossed in slashing her poor flesh once more, then told him casually, as he began sliding his finger in and out sending Charlotte on to her toes. "Apart from the domestics we've already discussed, I find I'm short of waitresses for the Grand Opening itself."

With a smirk Perry offered, "My girls?"

Tyler treated him to one of his thin-lipped smiles. "I need good faces, tasty knockers and legs that go right up to their fucking necks! Once the day's over you can take them back with you. There'd have to be some kind of guarantee they'd all keep shtoom about what they see. Got it?"

"Got it!"

A short while later and suffering from uncustomary aching in his arm, Perry indicated that it was almost time for him to return to the correctional facility. Their meeting concluded, Tyler withdrew his finger. He was about to have Alfred show his guest out when he noted the disappointed look on the man's face and being of a naturally generous nature, Tyler left Perry to enjoy the further delights of milky-skinned, ruby-haired Saxon in peace, before he was shown out.

As Tyler left the room, without being told to, Charlotte dropped to all fours and joined her master on his late night walk in the grounds.

Under a clear, star-bright night, as he walked, Tyler occasionally lobbed a stick for her to retrieve. If all went according to plan, he would have a surprise for her when he returned from his trip.

CHAPTER FIVE

The following morning, while he waited for Stapleton and for no particular reason Tyler made his way down to the kitchen for an unscheduled inspection. Charlotte walked at a respectful distance behind him, her hands crossed as usual behind her back and her head bowed.

He was confident that everything was set regarding Chelsi's kidnap and, provided there were no last minute hitches, when he returned from his trip he would be bringing her back on his boat with him. He only hoped that Charlotte had not got wind of the plan.

He pushed open the doors to the kitchen.

Large, steamy and welcoming with its aromas of baking bread, home-made chutney and roasting beef, the very walls were impregnated with the ghostly smells of banquets past. While it was a throwback to previous generations and in need of modernisation, it was still a frantic, working kitchen, and Tyler was reluctant to destroy the atmosphere that had built up over time by ripping everything out and replacing it with new. He often came down here, in truth the allure being not so much the slaves themselves but an atmosphere that was so full of warmth that it always put him in mind of his Ma's caravan. On a more practical level, he had had an additional, state of the art kitchen built at the back of the house to cater for members, which would leave this one free to provide the more basic needs of the Escorts and other estate workers... Pleasuregirls too, of course.

For some moments he just held the doors open and watched the half dozen or so slaves, drinking in their chatter and the general hubbub as they went about their business. They seemed entirely happy in their work, he mused, and their home lives!

For they were not slaves in the same sense the Pleasuregirls and maids were. Instead he had devised a canny system which allowed for the kitchen staff and other "backroom" domestics to go on living their "normal" lives in their own homes. Naturally, there were conditions and he had had the relevant contracts drawn up, though it was not only the slaves themselves who were required to sign on the dotted line! Their spouses and partners found themselves required to take on certain responsibilities, including that of a Dominant lifestyle, and Tyler set up what he called "a partnership" between them in each case. Under the rules of that partnership, they agreed to answer to the title Sir, or Madame in case of the lesbian partner among them, and maintain a certain degree of discipline in their private lives. To help with this, Tyler had generously supplied one set of handcuffs, one brown leather collar, to be worn at all times, and one cane in each case. It was a real joy to see the domestic slaves sporting praiseworthy tramlines. Some of the men had taken to their new position with more enthusiasm than others, and had added a whip or two to their collection, which made Tyler's inspections all the more interesting.

"Outstanding!" Tyler had told one kitchen slave when she came to work sporting quite exceptional welts across the upper swell of her breasts which, of course, her uniform was designed to show off to perfection.

On finally becoming aware of him watching from the doorway with his faithful, busty blonde companion standing at his side, the kitchen slaves fell silent, stopped what they were doing and gave a respectful little bob. Someone coughed, and an almost musical chant went up as they greeted him.

"Good morning, Milord."

"Master!" he corrected.

"Good morning, Master," they said in unison.

" 'Morning, slaves." He almost smiled with amusement at the terror in their eyes and the nervous way they shuffled their feet as they took up the position required of all domestic slaves, with their hands on their heads. He could almost taste their anxiety as quietly they awaited further instructions.

The head cook was a rather bossy, middle-aged woman with short dark hair. She was delighted to have been granted the title "Madam" and had been thrilled when she had been issued with a small whip she carried tucked into the waistband of her white apron; she was a woman who revelled in her new responsibilities over the others.

Even to Tyler's keen eye for the beautiful, fuckable, floggable or merely tasty, the kitchen slaves all looked pretty much the same in uniforms whose only utilitarian components were the cap and white apron which tied with a bow at the back; There were not any worthy of a second look! he thought despondently, and only two youngsters, the rest were approaching his age and spiralling upward.

The black uniform had cap sleeves and a flared, knee length skirt, under which no underwear was permitted. There was a zipper at the back of the bodice, the front of which was nothing more than a flap, made of black mesh, with tiny black studs either side. Bras were not permitted, leaving breasts clearly visible through the mesh. They could be exposed on demand by unfastening the studs, pulling back the flap and tucking it in behind the apron. He was gratified to note that, without exception, they all dutifully wore their brown collars, even Madam!

He reminded himself that even though none of the women were to his taste, most of them were desirable to someone since they all left The Ramparts at the end of their shifts to return to their own Dominants. Well, he may as well give one of them something to report when she got home, he decided.

Without considering Charlotte he let the doors go and entered the kitchen. Wincing as the doors hit her as she tried to follow, Charlotte brought one hand round, pushed open one of the doors, and dropped onto all fours as she entered also. He pointed a long, tapering finger at the woman he mistakenly surmised was around thirty... it was hard to tell with all her hair brushed back off her face and pinned beneath her cap. Brown eyed, tanned and wearing understated make-up, she at least had a reasonable amount of tit-flesh!

"You! Come here!"

It was not until Madam prodded her in the back that she stepped forward into the little clearing the other servants had made and stood on the spot he indicated. Her heart lurched excitedly and for a moment she misguidedly believed he had recognised her as Stephanie, a former barmaid in The Griffin. She smiled, telling herself it must have been five years or more since she had last served him. Then almost at once her smile faded and her heart plummeted as she realised his memories of the occasion were not as vivid as her own. For her, that night had been a momentous occasion, while for him it had obviously been a night like any other; to him she had been just another girl he had ravished behind the bins in a car park.

Except it had not really been rape at all, she admitted now as she looked up into glittering cold, blue eyes which that night had looked at her with the potency of stakes driven through her heart, for she had opened her legs willingly at his command. But then, she recalled rancorously, he and that friend of his, the one they called Tully, had gone sniffing around that fucking Chelsi Laird!

"Turn around."

His voice was every bit as cold as she remembered it. Stephanie flung a contemptuous look at Charlotte... another fucking Laird... she had never had much time for them and could not see why the whole bloody village had thought them and their aunt so fucking special! Just because some relative of theirs... the great Belinda Laird... had been some kind of celebrity in the old days...

Realising he was waiting, she gave a nervous smile. Better not argue, she thought, not if everything they said about him was true... he was their "Master" for Christsssssakes! Besides, Madam had been looking for a chance to get her whip out all morning!

With an exaggerated heave of her shoulders and a rolling of her eyes, Stephanie sighed like a petulant teenager as she pivoted slowly on the spot. She felt her face burning and horrified, knew she was blushing as Tyler unfastened her zip and took in the sight of the fading stripes across her slender back. And for some reason she could not fathom, Stephanie found herself hoping it was with pleasure that he examined them.

Since Stephanie French had left The Griffin she had had a variety of jobs in the nearby town of Hempstead End, before coming to work here shortly before the old lord had died. And now, under Tyler's scrutiny, she recalled how she had reeled from the discovery that the eccentric old aristocrat who looked like Santa Claus and had occasionally wandered into the village and nosed around was actually a kinky bastard who got off on thrashing the daylights out of the beautiful young girls he kept in a tower. But greater still had been her shock when she learned that her ravisher, Lanky the bloody gypsy, was a frequent visitor!

Now here they were again, Steph thought with an excitement that had no right to be pounding away inside her. Except this time they had an audience. And a feeling that had been absent last time almost choked her now as shame set her skin burning.

"Face me!"

Stephanie turned once more and was disappointed to see

his heavy eyebrows drawn together in that demonic frown that she remembered so well.

"Show me your tits!"

With trembling fingers and nausea in her stomach Steph did as she was bid, yanking the studs open as she tried to suppress her… God help her… her eagerness. She wanted to show him! And that was not all she wanted… she wanted his cock inside her again more than anything she had ever wanted in her life before. But worse, she wanted a real dominant, someone like the fucking lord of the manor himself, she admitted as the shame burgeoned in her throat. Her Dominant was alright, she supposed, but his heart was not in it and he only disciplined her for the money.

All at once she found herself wondering if his lordship knew that her Dominant was Kirk Stoner, the village gravedigger… fuck! What if he had found out that it was Kirk who had set light to one of the gypsies' caravans years ago?

Too eagerly she yanked down the mesh and stuffed it into the waistband of her apron. Then straightening her back she stuck out her soft and yielding breasts, proudly . displaying their golden-tanned nakedness.

Reassuringly she reminded herself how Kirk was always telling her that her knobbly, dark brown areolae were nothing to be ashamed of even if they were particularly wide, and how fine her nipples were. Even as she thought it, they seemed to swell and harden, till they were standing out like the corks in the necks of Madam's olive oil bottles. Screwing up her eyes as if that would aid her concentration, she willed Tyler to take them in his hands as he had done in the car park that night, and squeeze them as roughly as he had done then.

But he did not.

"Tell your Dominant you could do with a tit-whipping. They'll look all the better for it," he told her as prosaically as if he were merely telling her to add sugar to the rice pudding.

Steph heard the sharp intakes of breath from her fellow slaves. And a shiver ran through her. A tit whipping? Oh God! No! The very idea repelled her and yet thrilled her at the same time. A tit whipping… yes… Oh no! No! She would never stand it! She could not tell Kirk… he might really do it if he thought there was any chance of extra money! And what if she did not like it? Worse, what if she did?

"Turn around again. Come on, quickly!"

Opening her eyes, she turned around once more for a second time stood with her welted back toward him. In the way Kirk had taught her and without being told to she shuffled her feet apart.

"Lift your skirt. Bend over."

Never had the poor girl felt so humiliated! With her face burning as everyone watched, she had no choice but to do as he commanded. Yet there was a strange sense of elation too, and a feeling of inevitability about it as she did as she was bid and, bending over, she hoicked up her skirt then flapped it upward over her golden, naked bottom. She had always believed he would fuck her again, and now here he was, about to do just that in front of everybody! In front of bloody Charlotte! She clutched her skirt tightly as she felt his strong fingers run over the half dozen welts Kirk had laid down only the evening before.

Stephanie would have been pleased if she had seen the thin smile that twisted his lips as she sucked in her breath at his electrifying touch. Then there was more pressure as his fingers traced the welts, and she could not help but give a little groan of discomfort.

"Six only." He prised her bottom cheeks apart and for one dreadful moment she feared he may enter that forbidden hole. But he did not.

"Tell your Dominant this is an arse that should never carry less than twelve!" he growled.

When he traced the welts a third time it was with his sharp nails. As they scored the lines she could not help but let out a high-pitched squeal. Too late she realised it had gone very quiet in the kitchen and that everyone was looking at her. Her skin burned a deeper shade of red.

To her annoyance it was not Steph herself he addressed next but the blonde

Laird bimbo.

"Fetch me a rolling pin, bitch."

She heard Charlotte moving behind her. Then she came alongside and finally past her. Stephanie could hardly believe it - the silly cow was actually crawling across the kitchen to fetch it! Stephanie watched as Madam proffered one of the well-worn ones and to the round of shocked gasps, Charlotte accepted it with her mouth and returned with it between jaws which, Steph thought, looked really stupid and stretched to their limit. Surely it must be painful? she thought as Charlotte came toward her, then uncharitably told herself that where there was no sense there was no feeling. And the Lairds had never had any sense as far as she could tell!

As Charlotte padded past again, still on all fours, Stephanie craned her neck to see Charlotte present it to her Master as if she really were a she-dog. It was all Steph could do to keep from laughing aloud as Charlotte gave a bleat of discomfort when he tore it from her lips.

"What a stupid tart!" Stephanie snorted as she turned her head to look ahead once more.

Her heart almost stopped when she saw Tyler's trainers in front of her. Before she had time to lift her head, he had snatched the cap from her head. As her warm brown hair fell free and took several years off her, he did not express his delight at the discovery of a sexy girl about Charlotte's age but carelessly tossed the cap aside and began meshing his fingers in her roots. She yelped as he pulled her head up sharply.

"Open your mouth. Wider!"

When her jaws were stretched as far as possible he thrust the rolling pin between them with a sharp "don't drop it!"

"Mmmmphh!" she protested, the unaccustomed ache in her jaws as she tried to retain the heavy object between them overwhelming the humiliation as everyone laughed.

He disentangled his fingers from her hair and allowed her head to fall. Then with a slow smile he sauntered around behind her again. While she held the dress up over her tanned buttocks, he took his whip from the waistband of his jeans.

Had she seen the terrible implement, she would have quaked in terror. She would not have known that it was his favourite, a tan coloured cat o' nine tails given him by his grandfather soon after they met. Its thirteen inch long handle was covered in the finest kangaroo hide, and at the end there was a handy loop which now he slipped over his wrist.

He shook out the nine tails to their full length. It was a magnificent whip that in his gifted hands... the hands of the Whipmaster himself... was capable of delivering either one hefty whack to a selected spot that could knock a girl right off her feet and leave her breathless, or conversely its sixteen inch long, kangaroo hide tails could spread out to deliver a thousand simultaneous stings as if from some super-bee, that would leave a girl stung into a state of oblivion. In either case and if he wished, it could split fragile female skin, leaving a fine peppering of tiny blood spots.

"Forward, six paces."

Steph shuffled the few steps which brought her to enough space to enable him to ply the whip.

Swish!

61

Crack!

There was a clatter as she dropped the rolling pin, followed by a shriek of pain and the sound of the pin rolling away across the floor. There was a collective gasp from the other slaves, followed by silence as they held their breaths. No one dared to retrieve the rolling pin which settled with a light thud against the table leg.

Tyler struck again, fanning the lashes.

"Aaaarghh!"

He took aim once more.

The girl shrieked and howled her way through a dozen of the harshest lashes she had ever received, each one multiplied by nine as the tails spread out across her tender flesh. Hot tears scalded her face. She dared not move.

Without comment, Tyler returned his whip to its usual place in the waistband of his jeans.

Snivelling, Stephanie leapt up at once and rubbed her sore, throbbing bottom. Mascara muddied her face as tears finally escaped. She trembled as she heard the growl of his voice at last.

"Show your Dominant those. Tell him to bring you to me and I'll show him how it should be done! And seeing as how I didn't tell you to get up… " he looked around for Madam and ordered, "when I've gone, give her ten across her palms for disobedience." When the cook had agreed, he turned back to Stephanie and told her, "since you are up, you might as well strip and let me see what you're like stark naked. Quickly, girl, I haven't got all day."

Deciding it was best to do as he said for fear that he may double the quota, as sexily as she knew how Steph stripped off her uniform, folded it and handed it to one of the other women. She was not sure about her collar and wisely chose to leave it in place. Lastly she removed her shoes and placed them on top of the pile, which the kitchen slave set down out of reach on a chair.

"All fours!"

But that was one command too many for the girl whose rash indignation made her instantly forget her previous concern.

"You're not serious?" she snapped testily, watching as one of the women in front of her shook her head warningly, which Steph chose to ignore. He already had one girl playing doggie and there was no way she, Stephanie, was going to join in that game!

If she had turned her head, Tyler's thunderous features would have been warning enough to never disobey. As it was, his retribution was swift and the stinging pain across her already throbbing buttock caught her by surprise and almost knocked her off her feet as his hand delivered a brutal whack.

"Don't question me, girl!"

And if she could have seen the sudden anger give way to sheer delight as he watched the red patch flare up across the still-developing welts, she would perhaps have realised that she was indeed flirting with danger and that the kitchen environment offered little protection. Instead she merely wondered why he did not just fuck her and be done with it. Wasn't it enough that he had whipped her? That he had humiliated her in front of everyone? Once more she rubbed her backside and, with her heart pounding, awaited his pleasure.

"Charlotte fetch!"

So, was that it, then? she wondered as Charlotte crawled over to where the rolling pin had come to rest. Was it over?

Contemptuously she looked on as it took several moments for the blonde to open her jaws wide enough to pick up the pin without using her hands. Then, holding it firmly in her mouth and under gazes that ranged from scorn to astonishment Charlotte crawled back to her Master and presented it once more.

"You!" He brought the rolling pin up sharply between Stephanie's legs and knocked the wind from her.

"Aaargh!" Clutching her vulva she doubled up in pain.

"Next time I give a command you obey at once or face serious punishment. All fours, now!"

With a sniff of dissent, Stephanie finally dropped to hands and knees. Behind her, Charlotte was backing toward her, lining herself up. Then all at once Stephanie was aware of his fingers prising her labia apart. Oh well, fingers were better than nothing! she consoled herself, wishing it was his prick instead. Except it was not nothing… it was the inflexible wooden rolling pin that he pushed inside her.

Steph screeched with pain. "That hurts!"

"It's supposed to," he said calmly as he inserted the other end in Charlotte's readily juicing channel. "Embrace the pain and fuck each other."

"But Milord… Master," Stephanie corrected herself, "it's too thick."

"I don't give a shit. Closer."

Charlotte adjusted her position, placing her ankles on either side of Stephanie's. With a reaction that was more automatic than considered, Stephanie also shuffled, so that their legs became entangled, their buttocks almost touching. That had the effect of pushing the unyielding, wooden rolling pin ever deeper.

"Aghh! Please… no… "

"Rock backwards and forwards," he instructed her coldly. "I want to see you fuck my bitch! Refuse and things'll get so bloody bad for you that you won't believe pain like I can deliver's even possible!"

Stephanie could not believe the pain now! And to make things worse, that fucking blonde haired cow was actually doing it, she realised as the rolling pin moved inside her. This was too much, she could not possibly do it, she told herself as she began to rock slowly, then a little faster as

Charlotte picked up a rhythm. It hurt like hell. And it was so embarrassing as the other slaves drew closer for a better look. But more than that, Stephanie thought as she matched Charlotte movement for movement, thrusting backwards then accepting a poke in her own cunt, she wanted to die! Every once in a while, the swell of Charlotte's bottom brushed against her own. It was oddly thrilling, too, Stephanie thought as she tried to block out all thought. She closed her eyes and bit into her lip, not only to keep from crying out but also to assist in increasing her efforts. God, who would have thought it was such hard work?

And all the while she seethed through the wretchedness of humiliation, the man she thought of as "that fucking didakoi lord" kept up an uncouth tirade that curdled her sensitivities and minced her nerves.

"That's it, you fucking filthy slags. You dirty bitches! That's it. Look at you, fucking like a couple of dykes." His tone became hoarser. "Get a load of that double-barrelled poking! Yeah, you couple of shag-bags. Screw each other cunt-sore. Bring each other off. What a pair of filthy sluts! You're the most depraved lesbos I've ever seen!"

Suddenly and unaccountably, he began pelting them with overripe tomatoes. As the skins split and became detached their welted, labouring bodies were spattered with a slurry of flesh and seeds.

Stephanie stopped to wipe it away.

"Did I tell you to stop? Keep going! You can lick it off afterwards. Ram it harder, bitches! That's it. Dirty whores. Make her come, Charlotte. That's right. Set her twat quivering. She's nearly there. Make her scream, Charlotte. And you…"

Stephanie felt the toe of his boot on her thigh.

"Fuck her brains out. Make that Pleasure-bitch come or I'll thrash you to pulp then sling you to the Escorts. That's right, harder, harder! Faster!"

All at once she was gripped by a savage lust, unable to fight it as rational thought disintegrated. Nothing mattered but the rasping of his voice and the need to obey as all around the kitchen, the slaves were no longer watching mutely but panting softly as they worked frantically at their own cunts with fingers, pestles and even the handles of cooking utensils as their excitement grew. Just like Steph herself, nothing existed for them but the thing inside them.

Drinking in the amusingly horny sounds of women jerking off around him, Tyler's eyes nevertheless remained fixed on the brown-haired kitchen slave, and his compliant Charlotte bitch, only occasionally glimpsing the inch or two of wood separating them.

"You can do better than that!" Tyler rebuked as panting, Steph and Charlotte, their bodies glistening with the concerted effort, continued to rock back and forth, each battering the other's cunt painfully sweetly.

"Work at it, sluts."

Stephanie's insides went into spasm. She cried out as every muscle and every fibre of her being cramped. This can not be happening! she told herself as realisation dawned that unbelievably she was experiencing the most profound orgasm of her life.

"You may come, Charlotte... now!"

Even more unbelievable was the fact that the stupid blonde tart was climaxing too. How the hell had she come on demand? Stephanie wondered as powerful aftershocks overrun her body.

"Good girl!" Tyler patted Stephanie on the head. "By my reckoning that makes you a slut."

Stupidly, as if he had given her a magnificent gift rather than forced her to humiliate herself in front of her colleagues, she smiled broadly and glowed with pride. Without moving a muscle she listened to his footsteps as he walked round to stand in front of Charlotte. Unseen by

Steph, he hooked a finger through Charlotte's collar and eased her forward a couple of paces so that her end of the rolling pin thudded against the floor, glistening with her juices, while the other end remained inside the defeated kitchen slave.

Before Stephanie made a move, Tyler barked, "Don't get up yet, skivvy slut." Tyler yanked the rolling pin from her pussy and examined it. It too was glistening and the corners of his thin lips twitched in appreciation. Holding it by the end, he tossed it across the kitchen into a sink of hot water. While the rest of the slaves either brought themselves off or continued trying, he addressed the pair in dignity-shattering tones.

"Look at the pair of you, covered in tomato puree like you've been in the stocks all day! Clean each other up, or you *will* be in the stocks."

Before either girl moved, one of the slaves offered Steph a damp dishcloth. But Tyler was having none of it.

"No!" He snatched it from the startled woman and slapped it wetly against her head. "That's what they've got mouths for."

Turning around, Charlotte padded toward Steph. When she was alongside, like an overly affectionate puppy she began licking at the soiled and sweaty flesh. For her part, Steph shuddered as the tongue made contact. Except it was not a shudder of disgust but a rather more acceptable emotion which she preferred not to name. She adjusted her own position, craned her head and stuck out her tongue as far as she was able to try and get at the tomato splattered over the blonde.

Within moments and still on all fours they were face to face, and although neither girl knew quite how it happened, they found their tongues entwined as they kissed deeply. As their tomato-flavoured, salty tongues wound around each other's, they could not help but close their eyes and surrender to the hedonistic eroticism of the moment. Breathing heavily down their noses they became more frantic, unable to get enough of each other. And then, in what seemed to the two girls a natural progression, they each lifted a hand and reached for the other's breast.

The multi-lashed strike caught them both so sharply they jerked apart. With eyes widened in shock, they stared at each other as a second, skilfully-directed strike of the fanning lashes caught them both across their shoulders.

"Enough! You fucking bitches!" He lashed first one, then the other across her back, controlling the cat so that the lashes fell as hefty thuds. "The pleasure's supposed to be mine, not yours. Sometimes I might throw you a scrap of pleasure but don't think you can take it whenever you please. Don't ever forget that I'm in control! You'll both be punished, of course. You, Charlotte - you disappoint me! Your punishment'll be left to the Escorts to decide while I'm away. But you!" He reached down and seized Stephanie by her collar, "you'll find out what punishment really is!" Angrily he turned to the cook. "After you've dealt with her," he said as a reminder of the discipline already prescribed, "chain her to the ring outside, in the yard. I'll have one of the Escorts come by and collect her."

"B… but… please…" Steph began as she turned her pleading eyes upward to his.

But it was wasted on him as he furled his whip once more. The anger in his steps as he strode across to the door left no one in any doubt that Stephanie French was in for a very tough time indeed. As for Charlotte…

"Heel!"

Without a word or backward glance, Charlotte padded across the floor to follow where he led.

"That's one hell-of-a fucked-up, arse-licking bimbo!" Stephanie hissed, her hatred returning as if it had never gone away.

CHAPTER SIX

Somewhere in Berkshire

Digby's long fingers curled around the stem of his almost empty champagne flute. Holding it at an 80 degree angle in his free hand as he lounged in his black leather chair, with his other hand he stroked the sleek coat of a gold-and-sapphire-collared, two year old cheetah that sat beside him. Imperiously he ignored the woman in nun's attire who stood some four feet away, facing him with her habit pulled up to her knees, as he waited for Lilith's voice through the speakerphone. It was not long in coming.

"Digby, Dahhhling! You know how much I look forward to your calls. And of course I'll do anything to help. But surely you don't really expect me to go and enquire after the whore's health? I'm sorry, but I really don't understand why it should interest you after all these years." Nevertheless, Lilith went on to give him as concise an account as was possible given that she knew very little of the woman he was anxious to trace… or not as the case may be.

And as he listened to her, his thoughts were not of Lilith, or his 'nun' but the beautiful young gypsy girl he had once known and how luscious her cunt had been. Never before or since had he found a cunt like it, so warm and accommodating that he had almost given the bitch his heart. But the fact remained that she was a didakoi who had birthed a didakoi and, as far as he knew, had gone on to birth a whole tribe of them before her cunt dried up completely.

"If you were here you could go and find out yourself!" Lilith's wounded tone cleverly implied two things at once… … curiosity about where he was calling from and annoyance that he had never shown as much interest in her whereabouts as he currently showed in the trollop's.

Speaking from his secret location, Digby Morrison-Grenfell saw no reason to tell Lilith that he knew exactly where she was speaking from! He had made it his business to know where she was living and on a fact-finding mission had spent a weekend in the area, driving past the place several times. She had done well for herself, he thought, though not as well as she had hoped, of course!

"I merely wondered if she and my father were ever reconciled," he said, remembering how the old fool had turned white with rage at the mere sight of the beautiful, young and blatantly pregnant gypsy girl before directing the full force of his fury on Digby himself. "And whether the sprog she dropped has moved his whore-of-a-mother into my house as well!"

For a few moments their conversation turned to reminiscence of their own brief affair. And if he could have seen her then at the other end of the line, Digby would have been pleasantly surprised to note that her hair was as dark and sleek as when they were youngsters together, and disappointed that her make-up was still applied rather too heavily for his taste. Although they had not laid eyes on each other for many years he would have recognised her in an instant, and noted that marriage to the banker had done nothing to dampen her ambitions over the years.

Digby would have been right in guessing that she had never loved her husband and had only married him because he was a distant relative of Whitby's. To all intents and purposes it must have seemed a good match since Lilith herself was a cousin from a different branch of the family and so had a tenuous claim herself, and so together Lilith and Bellamy Stapleton would have doubled their chances. How it must rankle, Digby thought as he sipped champagne with a thin-lipped smile, that a common vagabond had usurped them all!

That being the case, he could only hazard a guess at how thrilled Lilith had been when he, Digby, had made the first of several calls to re-establish their acquaintance some twelve months previously. It was odd but now they had got the delicate issue of his regrettable fling with the gypsy out of the way, he felt a sudden, boyish excitement at the thought of seeing Lilith again. It would be a reunion that, while not exactly made in Heaven since she had never understood his vocation, would nevertheless be timely, advantageous and, he hoped, sexually rewarding… providing he risked everything by taking her into his confidence. While he was certain of her assistance, he did not know how cognisant she actually was with the facts surrounding his departure from the Church and how she would view his conduct if he were to come clean. They had never seen eye to eye regarding his requirements! To further complicate matters, he knew her husband only by reputation since their only meetings were as children, and so was not sure if he could actually count on Stapleton's support or co-operation. Only one thing was sure at this early stage… Digby could not afford to raise the suspicions of his enemies and so, for the time being, he must urge Lilith to keep their planned rendezvous secret.

***

In her turn, relaxing in the gated, five-bedroomed Hertfordshire property, just fifteen miles away from the grand house she coveted, Digby's smooth and gracious tones were like a balm to Lilith's stony heart. She remembered him as being everything her husband was not… tall without even a hint of a superfluous weight, and arrogantly handsome with a long face and square jaw. But principally he was the rightful heir to The Ramparts!

And if Lilith could have observed him she as she reclined

71

on her Parisian, Damask chaise longue, she would have been overjoyed to see the cassock and dog collar had been replaced by a bottle green velvet smoking jacket with pale green and gold silk cuffs and lapels.

She would also have noted that although his slicked back hair was now steely-grey, he had worn the ravages of the years well. She had known for some time about his altercation with the church authorities and the police…… the "misdirection of church funds"… and "inappropriate behaviour with parishioners"… for quite by chance she had come across a buried article in The Times which had outlined his fall from grace.

***

As their conversation progressed, Lilith's upper-crust tones were as crisp and rounded as his own, Digby thought, though hers leeched considerably more acid down the line than his as she told him, "he's hired every rogue for miles around, even some of the vulgar working-class boors from the village. He's surrounded himself with his gypsy cohorts - even if one wanted to one couldn't get close to him! The place is simply crawling with them. And all kinds of other scum including some burly, military rejects."

Digby almost smiled at the familiar display of resentment. Despite their tempestuous affair and later when he dashed her dreams of becoming Lady of the Manor by moving away to take up his post of rector in Wolverhampton, her spite had rarely been directed toward himself, though she frequently vented her spleen at the plebeians - the inferior beings, poor martyred Lilith was obliged to deal with in her everyday life. In that respect, she had not changed and still considered that people who did not live up to her high expectations were unworthy of her presence. In this instance, it was Tyler Morrison… probably Digby's son… who she had quite understandably branded as a pariah.

But for Digby himself, even pariah was too good a name for him! He only hoped that when the time came, he could pass himself off to the long-haired scoundrel as just another "hanger-on" and keep a civil tongue in his head. If his investigations proved correct, he would soon have his chance.

"What's this I hear about an opening day?" he asked, motioning the "nun" to lift her habit higher so that he could see her sensible, waist-high and wide-legged, white cotton panties.

With Lilith's husband safely out of the way, *en route* to The Ramparts to further ingratiate himself with the new lord, Lilith herself relished the chance to fill Digby in.

"It's going to be a grand affair, Dahhhling," she oozed as she held the white mouthpiece to her ear. With her free, ring-bedecked hand she hooked her finger beneath the collar of the naked young girl who knelt in front of her, with her own hands bound tightly behind her back. Pulling the girl closer, up and round onto the chaise with her, roughly the elder woman manoeuvred her into position between her own shapely legs. She was quite used to carrying on a conversation while engaged in some other activity with a slut and so did not pause as she pulled her chiffon robe aside. "Alfred said he's behaving like some vulgar little emperor."

Stretching her legs like a cat awakening from a deep and contented sleep, Lilith flung them wide, hooking one foot over the back of the chaise and placing the other on the floor. "As well as a 'Triumphal Walkway,' and a throne, no less," she gave a snort of laughter before continuing, "there'll be marquees, flowers, uniformed serving girls, a banquet, several dozen cases of champagne, the works! Not only that, but I understand he plans to display his slavegirls…" she paused to inject just the right amount of righteous horror into her voice.

73

If she could have seen her former beau as he sat in his luxurious apartment overlooking the Thames, Lilith would have been delighted to see the effect her words had as the colour drained from his face, but would probably not have noticed that the defrocked Reverend's fingers tightened on the stem of his glass.

Lilith continued. "…and their purpose quite openly!"

The glass stem snapped between Digby's fingers and fell to the floor. "He's going to turn the ancestral pile into a glorified whorehouse!" He cut his finger on the jagged edge of the flute and threw it and contents to join the stem on the carpet. The cheetah jumped up and dashed from the room. Digby crooked his finger at the 'nun' and motioned that she clean up the mess.

Knowing better than to drop her habit, his wife held it bunched in her hands above her thighs as she scurried across the room. Immediately she dropped to her knees and, transferring one fistful of coarse, black material to the other hand, watched by the cheetah she picked up the flute with its short, jagged spike that used to be a stem. Then retrieving the other half of the broken stem itself she carefully placed it inside. Finding no tiny shards, without letting go of the habit she rose to her feet and gratefully left the room to dispose of the glass.

As unaware of Digby's 'nun' wife as he was of her naked, tight-titted slut, Lilith did not point out that whoring had been a facet of The Ramparts throughout its long history. Instead she told him, "The guest list is impressive, too." Releasing the girl's collar Lilith placed her hand on the back of the girl's head and shoved it downward toward the seat of her black-frizzed womanhood. "They won't all attend, of course!" she said with utter confidence as the girl burrowed through her mistress' curly pubes. As her soft lips closed over Lilith's cunt and her tongue sought entrance, Lilith reeled off a few names that she knew would

74

pique Digby's interest further. Finally, as the girl's tongue squirmed around inside her, she added without even a hint of breathlessness, "He's even invited Lord and Lady Fellbridge."

"Eustacia and Florian? It's unthinkable! One can't believe they would have any interest in such degenerate activities!"

Lilith smiled as she stretched out on her *chaise longue* and smiled at the recent recollection of Lady Fellbridge stripped bare and arranged over the trestle in Lilith's own playroom, her fat arse wobbling as Lilith and Bellamy Stapleton took turns with the riding crop while Florian sat wanking. It had been a regular thing, once a month for several years. "I understand they've dabbled," Lilith lied.

The vehemence that saturated Digby's next words made her heart leap as she realised things would come right after all.

"We can't let that shit of a gypsy steal what's mine. We have to do something, Lilith."

***

To everybody's astonishment, when Tyler finally left on his narrowboat late that afternoon, he was accompanied by the ex-banker, Stapleton. Being as different as kippers and cream, the two had never been friends and the thought of them cooped up on a boat together was inconceivable.

Charlotte, having spent the afternoon following the two men around the grounds and playing fetch for her Master was later taken down to the dungeon where she was disciplined by Tully. She was devastated to discover that Tyler had chosen to take Fionola with them on his narrowboat.

Tully said something rather odd while he was disciplining her over a trestle. He began by mocking her about her sister Chelsi, asking her what it would be like to see her again after so many years. Naturally, he did not allow her to answer and anyway, she had lost touch with her sibling and they had never made any plans to meet up! Besides, Tyler would never allow it!

Then master Tully went on about how he was impatient to discover whether Chelsi's backside was as impressive as her own. At first she put it down to the normal humiliation one learned to accept from a master. But when he started talking about a doctor being sent to examine Chelsi, it struck her that maybe he was actually telling the truth, since Tyler had subjected all the Pleasuregirls to a detailed and humiliating examination by a doctor, or rather a man who claimed to be a doctor. Though Charlotte had always had her doubts about the young man who wore designer clothing. She had often seen him… Dr Blandford… around the place and Tyler had explained that he lived in one of the flats on the far edge of the estate, all that was left of the old oasthouse. Tyler had employed him specifically to keep an eye on the Pleasuregirls' general health, to attend to any issues which might occur from continual misuse and discipline… which the doctor was perfectly at liberty to inflict himself should he feel inclined to do so… and to aid their recovery, then return them as speedily as possible to a fit condition for use. In addition, Dr Blandford was there to take care of their "female problems."

But now she came to think of it, she had not set eyes on the unorthodox doctor for several days.

***

Everyone had assumed that while Tyler was absent, The Ramparts would be left in the care of master Tully as on other occasions.

"Not that he's got any acumen for running anything more complicated than a piss-up in The Griffin," Stephanie told the other kitchen slaves.

And so it seemed when he, along with his friend and

fellow escort - the weirdo Elvis-look-alike - disappeared shortly afterward.

There were mutterings of, "Never could trust a didiakoi!" all around the place as slaves and staff alike feared the place would fall to rack and ruin in a matter of days, if it were not burgled and stripped bare by the workmen or the remaining gypsies.

And during their absence the Pleasuregirls found themselves, including Charlotte, all locked up together in the tower. Instead of taking their meals together in the spartan, refectory-style dining hall, they were delivered by the cook and Stephanie, who also collected the dirty dishes. The only time they left the tower was when one or other of the Escorts made a selection from among them to abuse in the absence of anyone presiding over the men themselves.

It was not until Tully and Elvis returned a couple of days later that Charlotte and the others were returned to their cells. Mealtimes and ablutions also reverted to normal. Only the level of abuse did not lessen since the two men were keen to exact their own share.

When master Stapleton returned, without Tyler but with Fionola, things calmed down considerably. It was not long before the new circumstances were made clear to everyone - from now on, master Stapleton would always be in command whenever Tyler was absent. He and not Tully was Tyler's right hand man. The next day, two men delivered five stunning girls.

Following Tyler's instructions, Stapleton immediately appointed his wife, Lilith, as the second of The Ramparts' dominatrices, responsible for breaking in new slaves to a decent standard.

Tyler's instructions had been clear.

"You're to be known as Mistress Lilith," Stapleton told her. "Initially, Tyler wants you to take charge of the new girls. The others, the ones he calls 'seasoned sluts,' and any designated as ponies, will be drilled by Mistress Adria. But he made it clear that, on his return, what he called 'the lucky ones' will receive training by Tyler himself." Ignoring Lilith's derisive snort, he continued. "When the club finally opens and a routine is established, assuming that training and discipline are ongoing, any slaves not in use will be presented to you in the morning for several hours, and Adria will have them in the afternoons." Stapleton was somewhat surprised that his wife did not object to the arrangement, for he was certain she would rather have sole control of them.

"Don't let the didakoi pretender give the creatures names," she implored her husband in her cut glass accent. "After all, they are slaves, nothing more. And slaves are not worthy of names! Why he insists on calling them Pleasuregirls I shall never know, when the truth of the matter is they are just filthy, perverted slaves!"

"But I do see his point," Stapleton told her. "There has to be a distinction... the whole household are slaves! And while we may think the kitchen slaves and domestics are there to be used for whatever purpose, I hardly think they are of a high enough standard for the club members!"

Content to have a foot in the door at least, Lilith took charge at once of the, as yet, unnamed five new girls. But to her chagrin, only a day or so into their training, she was accosted by Adria, the wild-eyed gypsy girl who Tyler had previously appointed, she promptly removed two of the girls from Lilith's charge and took them to the stables to begin ponygirl training.

Finally, word filtered through to the Pleasuregirls that their beloved Master was on his way home.

Stapleton, once again following Tyler's directions, arranged for the whole household to welcome him home. Charlotte found herself taken to the private stretch of the canal where she was cruelly displayed, suspended by her wrists, on the side of the bridge to witness the return of the boat as it passed beneath her, towed by a ponygirl in flamboyant regalia. Left alone to take in the sight, it had shaken her to the core to see that the girl was her own sister, Chelsi.

***

With only days to go before the Grand Opening, things were buzzing at the

great house as the final preparations were made. With all the cells declared "rodent free and fit for habitation" the rest of the girls were moved in.

Even under threat of punishment the Pleasuregirls could not contain themselves but chatted vociferously whenever they were together. Of all the rules they had to obey, silence was the most often broken; when they should have been resting they called to each other from their cells below ground. They whispered excitedly over their meals in the dining hall, where they were presided over by an escort and served by kitchen slaves. It was the only time when the rules were relaxed and Pleasuregirls were given an opportunity to converse, since house rules precluded slaves talking except to answer a question or given specific permission. Even their mealtime chatter was at the discretion of the man who watched over them.

With the arrival of Chelsi, the first thing Tyler decreed was that as far as possible, except for the times he specifically ordered otherwise or, when the club was open for business and a member wanted the experience of enjoying them together, the sisters were to be kept apart. On no account were they allowed to share a cell!

Aware of his orders, Charlotte had been surprised when, within hours of Chelsi's arrival, they were taken down to the underground Egyptian Chamber where, after whipping them both, Tyler had allowed them a few moments alone. But it had not taken Charlotte long to realise that what she had initially considered an act of kindness on her Master's part… an opportunity for them to console each other and for Charlotte to reassure her sister after the ordeal of being confined with their Master on his narrowboat… was something else entirely. For the cruelty Chelsi had already suffered at Tyler's hands prior to her arrival was as nothing compared to the cruelty of leaving Charlotte no option but to listen to Chelsi spelling it out in such lurid detail!

Chelsi's simpering was still fresh in her mind when, two evenings later, Charlotte found herself once again in her sister's presence, this time with their Master in the Red Drawing Room, renamed the Members' Lounge.

The whole thing was shocking, of course, Charlotte told herself as she stood beside her master, her gaze wandering toward her raven-haired sister, currently bowed low on knees and elbows and serving as their Master's footstool as he slouched in the oak-framed 19th century chair that had become one of his favourites.

Angry with herself for secretly enjoying Chelsi's shame, she wondered who in their right mind would wish such a fate on their worst enemy, let alone their own flesh and blood?

But Chelsi's arrival at The Ramparts had been a thunderbolt out of the blue for poor Charlotte. In her mind's eye she replayed the scene of her sister, dressed up in ponygirl regalia, towing their Master's narrowboat along the canal as if she were some real pony while she, Charlotte, had been cruelly suspended from the bridge under which they passed. Although Charlotte had had time to recover from the shock and get used to the idea, it had not been the happy reunion that Charlotte had expected. Rather than let her put it all behind her, her mind once again replayed the moments when they had been left alone.

Above all, she remembered the way the dark-haired pop-goddess had fluttered her eyelids and dramatically swayed to and fro as she had related the events, as if the stupid bitch might pass out from the memories alone.

"And then, Sis," Chelsi had told her, "when I was completely alone with him, as helpless and vulnerable as any girl could ever be, he flogged me until I was close to unconsciousness. I was totally at his mercy. Heaven only knows what he'd have done with me if I hadn't clung on to awareness, to my… identity. And then he told me that he'd been looking forward to that day for years, and that he'd make me pay for hurting him! And Sis…" Chelsi had smiled weakly, tossing her hair in that way of hers that sent her black curls cascading over her shoulder and men reaching for their cocks, "he said he'd find a way of punishing you through me!" She had raised her cuffed hands imploringly. "Oh Sis, I need to… we need to get out of here! Or, if it's me he wants… … " she had let out a dramatic sob and once again, fluttered her eyelashes, "I'll help you to escape and I'll… I'll stay here! There's no need for you to suffer on my account!"

He was a cruel Master indeed! Charlotte thought as she stood stock still beside him while he relaxed with a brandy and cigar. What punishment could be worse for a devoted slave like herself than to be entombed, no matter how short the period, with someone who was actively seeking to replace her? And at that moment it seemed to Charlotte as if that was indeed her Master's plan, for Chelsi was the one person in the world who he seemed to have any feelings for! Admittedly, they were not feelings of love or affection, but they were feelings, and she was awfully afraid that she had been wrong and he had none at all for her! What kind of warped, evil mind would wish to punish someone like herself when she was totally innocent of disobedience or offence? In fact, if it had not been for Charlotte's tractability

81

when they first met, life would have turned out very differently for Tyler Morrison! What had she done to deserve such punishment? What crime had she committed that warranted she be replaced by a common whore, for Chelsi Laird had been a whore long before she arrived at The Ramparts, if the reports in the newspapers were true! How could their Master favour Chelsi over herself?

Yet despite everything, Charlotte's heart swelled with love for him… she had loved him for months, years… …which only twisted the spear deeper in her heart. Perhaps, she reasoned as the clock struck the first hour, if she were to be even more obedient, more submissive, then perhaps he would not replace her after all. For no one had ever debased herself for Tyler as much as she had!

And so her tangled emotions grew ever more confused. But under-wiring them all and even now uplifting her spirit… quite bizarrely given her adoration of him… was her very real understanding that, no matter how subjugated she allowed herself to become, she would never mean more to him than she did at this moment… she was merely a lump of pale slave-flesh into which he could dig his fingernails or on which he could inscribe the rawest of red lines. It was as if her mind air-brushed out rational thought as she found momentary comfort.

**

Having eaten the kind of evening meal that once he could only have dreamed of, Tyler sat with his feet up and looked around at his "improvements," one of which was the addition of a fairly large construction with a tilting platform. As in all the new public rooms, there were several frames which stood in readiness to provide hours of enjoyment… for the members but not necessarily the girls, he thought as he rubbed a long finger along his angular jawline.

Reflectively he blew out a cloud of grey smoke.

Resting on all fours beneath his feet, Chelsi emitted a strangled sound that would have been a cough had the gag not stifled it, and her mascara-laden eyes watered stingingly.

"Stop your fucking noise! It's my house and I'll fucking smoke anywhere I like!" he growled.

Standing on his right hand side, Charlotte was within easy reach, her feet about fifteen inches apart and her hands crossed behind her. He cast a sideways look toward her and noted that her grey eyes, pale as a winter's day, were looking down at her own lash -patterned breasts. He was well satisfied with her continuing docility. To be honest, he had expected trouble when her sister arrived on the scene. But so far there had been nothing untoward, and for that he was not sure if he was relieved or disappointed.

But Siren, as he had already renamed Chelsi, now that was a different matter entirely, he told himself. He had not yet started to explore her limits! Taking a slug of brandy, it amused him that she probably thought that just because Tully and Elvis had delivered her to him in a crate and she had been taken aboard his narrowboat, that she was already experienced in the worst kinds of indignities and pain. The brainless whore probably thought that during the few days they had spent alone together on the Lashings of Pride she had paid heavily for her teenage mistakes. Well, she was in for one hell of a shock! he thought as he nudged her with the toe of his boot and knocked her off balance so that she toppled over.

"Get up! As before! Move again and I'll give you a thrashing to remember." He slopped brandy as, still holding the goblet, he gave Charlotte's vulva a backhanded wallop to get her attention and told her casually, "Your slutty sister's got a new moniker." As Chelsi settled herself to his requirements again, he leaned forward, trying to keep the goblet steady… the liquor was too precious to waste… and using the other hand still holding the cigar with its half inch of ash, he ran his fingers over Chelsi's olive-skinned bottom. As he kneaded her flesh roughly, the ash fell onto the antique Persian rug on which both girls and the chair were positioned. "Shit! Mustn't set light to the family heirlooms!" he laughed as he rubbed his foot in it and left a dirty mark. Sitting upright he took another drag on the cigar, blowing the smoke out slowly, as if it were something too valuable to let go. Then, as if he were the compere at some concert hall, he announced loudly, "Ladies and Gentlemen, I give you the one… the only…" he flung out his arms dramatically, once again slopping brandy over the side of his goblet, "Siren!" He laughed as the girl beneath his feet squeezed out a pathetic groan.

***

The air was thick with expectancy. Charlotte drew in an aggrieved breath, for she was the only Pleasuregirl who still bore her real name. Even Fionola wasn't her real name! All the girls had been given a new one on their arrival and even those who, like herself, were already resident had their names changed, even those who remained of Whitby's sex slaves. So why, she wondered sadly, had she been overlooked? With a sharp pang of hurt she recalled that even Sparkle had had a perfectly good slave name, given her years earlier by her former master. It was as if she, Charlotte, had been betrayed and she felt tears pricking saltily at the corners of her eyes.

Suddenly, he demanded, "Are you paying attention, Charlotte?"

"Yes, Master," she replied meekly.

"Fucking good job too! You can forget all about stinking rich Chelsi - she doesn't exist anymore. In her place is the dazzlingly beautiful but totally worthless whore called Siren. Hear that name, Charlotte?"

"Yes, Master."

"What's her name?"

"Siren, Master," Charlotte repeated in a soft, steady voice.

Leaning forward again, he pressed his finger against the crinkled star that was Siren's bottom hole. She could do nothing but endure it for several seconds he stimulated it, coaxing it into relaxation, and then used her unsealed anus as a receptacle for his half-smoked cigar. Drowning in shame willing her muscles not to expel it, Siren prayed for delivery, for someone to rescue her, even as she hoped they would not. For her part, Charlotte tried to block out her younger sibling altogether and illogically concentrated on Tyler's rough tones and uncultured accent. She was often present when Stapleton badgered him about it, telling him that if he wanted to be fully accepted into the world of the aristocracy which was his birthright, then he should try to adopt a more genteel manner of speaking. She knew that Master Stapleton had taken it upon himself to "improve" Tyler in such matters, as well as coach him in matters of etiquette. something that Whitby himself had devoted hours to without a great deal of success.

"As Lord Morrison-Grenfell, you'll be expected to attend certain functions," Stapleton had pointed out once. And when Tyler had told him that he was thinking of dropping the Grenfell, Stapleton had advised against it, telling him. "Double-barrels always look good on letter headings." Whether he chose to accept it or not, Stapleton always insisted, Tyler should not think of himself as a gypsy at all, reminding him that he came from a long and noble lineage that stretched back over the centuries.

As her thoughts ran on, her gaze remained fixed on the cigar in its star-shaped holder. And she remembered how the coarsest of Whitby's words had always been uttered in his refined voice!

She was brought out of her reverie by Tyler's voice.

"While the rest of the world speculates on the

disappearance of…" he waved his half-empty goblet in the general direction of the floor, "the sex-crazed pop diva, here in this colossal shrine-to-pleasure, we know she's been morphed into a whore!" Leaning back in his chair again, he continued. "Have you seen the papers, my slutty pair of cock gobblers?"

Chelsi could not answer since her mouth was stuffed with a foul-tasting rubber ball gag. And Charlotte, recognising that it was a rhetorical question, remained silent, her gaze still riveted to the cigar jutting from her sister's behind. She could not help the frivolous curve of her lips as she considered how, in a blink of an eye, Chelsi had gone from being a millionaire singing sensation to a footstool-cum-ashtray. With an upsurge of guilt she chided herself for making light of the scandal. But it was a scandal the tabloids would pay a bundle to get hold of, she mused. Images like these were the dream of the paparazzi! Instead of the normal "Celeb checks into rehab" kind of pictures, anyone with a half-decent telephoto lens could get pictures of the stunning, pampered Chelsi Laird with her expensively maintained, olive-toned flesh horrendously . beaten, with scarlet welts that were as raw as those that decorated Charlotte's own, much paler flesh, and a cigar sticking out of her arse-hole! Of course, even if she could somehow contact the newspapers, or get hold of a camera herself, Charlotte realised she would not do so, not so much for the sake of her sister but, quite damningly she realised, because that would surely bring about the ruination of her beloved Master, and that was something she could never be party to!

"No, of course you haven't!" Tyler answered his own question on a laugh. "It's all over the front pages that the fucking superstar's gone missing from her posh Mayfair flat, just like her mother 'disappeared when the stunning sex symbol was a star-struck child,'" he quoted. "Sorry,

Charlotte," he added mockingly, "but they don't mention that Belinda Laird was your mother as well... ... they don't mention you at all! Perhaps I should invite the paparazzi to my Grand Opening so they can see for the themselves the star-struck bitch who looks uncannily like the missing 'superstar' and who I'll be offering for public humiliation and sexual abuse?"

He paused to laugh, and Charlotte's gaze roamed along her sister's red-welted back upon which Tyler's booted feet were crossed at the ankles, then up toward her head and her trademark long, dark, tiny corkscrew curls. Totally natural, it could easily be mistaken for an extravagant permed creation by some "hairdresser to the stars". She wondered then what it must be like to be rich and famous one minute, adored by thousands... perhaps millions ... and then be an abused sex slave the next. Poor, poor Chelsi! It must seem as if the world had fallen apart around her, Charlotte thought with a sympathetic tear in her eye and a catch in her throat.

Then, as if inexorably drawn by some magnet, her pale eyes swung their focus from her sister to their Master as he swigged the last of his brandy from the engraved goblet and placed it on the drum top table on his other side.

As he stared ahead toward the parklands visible through the window. She became aware that he hardly seemed to notice either Siren... as Charlotte must call her now... or Charlotte herself.

Despite what outsiders, or Alfred thought, Charlotte knew it had not been easy for him to adapt to the demands of his new life. It seemed to her that he was a man trapped between two worlds, one being that of the underprivileged wanderer living the simple life of the travellers, the company he still referred to as "his people." It was a life that had given him the freedom to roam and go about his business when and almost wherever he chose. And she had known him long enough to know that it was not something he had given up lightly. He even had his old caravan tucked away somewhere on the estate! She had heard him say more than once that to have his freedom denied him was to take away the air he breathed… strange then, she mused, that he could take away a girl's freedom so lightly! She swung her attention back to her Siren and frowned. She did not want to think of her sister!

She whirled her thoughts back to Tyler, whose new world of wealth and privilege had given him a different kind of freedom… the freedom to live out his wildest fantasies in a decadent world… a world in which he never went hungry and did not have to poach simply to put a meal on the plate. He no longer had that raw-boned look that had given him his old nickname, although he had lost none of his sharp, angular features. But in spite of having every conceivable luxury available to him as well as the opportunities to mix with the upper classes and the kind of people he used to be denied access to, Charlotte knew he would always remain an outsider among them. For despite Stapleton's best efforts, Tyler still viewed strangers with hostility. It could not be easy for him to shake off his upbringing, Charlotte thought sadly.

Suddenly she drew in a startled breath, and it was as if for a moment the mists had cleared and she was glimpsing the real world for the very first time. Whatever had she been thinking of? How could she possibly feel any kind of sympathy for a man she knew to be savagely cruel, who had calmly had her own sister kidnapped and added to his growing stock of maltreated sex slaves? With another upswell of guilt she brought her meandering concentration back in line and focussed once more on Siren… for she no longer bore any resemblance to the Chelsi she had known and loved. Redirecting her emotions as her eyes took in the sight before her, and the cigar that was no longer alright

88

but was still sticking out from Siren's backside, she felt sick with horror. To see her talented, beautiful sister brought to the terrible hell-hole that The Ramparts had become sent a shiver of something cold and unpleasant travelling the length of her backbone.

Yet Charlotte knew it was not from cold that she shivered but from an eerie feeling that the ghostly spectres of all the dissolute Morrison-Grenfell ancestors were gathering round to guide the latest in their line to greater cruelty. How they must be laughing and cheering him on, she thought. She tried to shake off the feeling as ridiculous, but what else could account for the misery surging up from her depths? She could not remember ever feeling so downcast.

As she dwelt on her own misery, she hardly noticed when Tyler carelessly flicked a narrow-thonged whip across Siren's backside and expertly removed the cigar from its star-shaped holder. Nor did she care when he struck again, this time with a spiteful strike that caught the newest Pleasuregirl across the tender, frilled petals of her inner lips which poked, quite ridiculously Charlotte smirked, externally. And as Siren responded with an anguished, muffled bleat of pain that even to Charlotte's ears was almost tuneful, she wondered if it were at all possible that her own emotions actually created the feeling of heavy malevolence hanging over the place, rather than ghosts.

Insidiously, the thought crept into her mind that everything had changed, and it was all due to her sister! It was with a jolt she realised that she felt no genuine feelings of sympathy, or even anger on Chelsi's behalf… the horror she felt at her sister's degradation was not entirely born out of love at all, but out of something far more feral and selfish than that! She bit into her bottom lip so as not to give vent to her feelings and screwed up her eyes as if that would in some way seal the terrible truth inside herself…

wipe the evil from her mind. But it was not to be. Some previously unknown devil whispered so harshly in Charlotte's subconscious that at first she thought it must be a malicious spirit!

"What do you care?" the voice said. "She deserves it!"

Charlotte was saved from further haunting by the sound of Tyler's voice as he continued.

"Soon, anyone who can stump up the membership fee'll have the chance to fuck, flog and abuse the latest addition to my stock. She's no superstar, she's just whipping-meat like all the other whores!" He paused only fractionally. "If I ever hear her old name pass your lips, Charlotte, I won't just flog you, I'll unload you on the Jamaican. I'd get a good price, too… he makes a frigging brilliant living selling white slaves in Africa. I've told you before, bitch, they go a bundle for blondes! And, while your so-sensitively-pale skin crisps under a hot, African sky, you can wonder if your devious little sister ever managed to escape. More to the point, Charlotte, would she ever come and rescue you? I doubt it," at this he rocked Siren back and forth beneath his feet. "She's always been too full of herself to give a monkey's about the rest of her family! And she's the bitch who's responsible for the very worst time of my life!" And so it had been, despite only lasting a matter of hours!

Without moving his eyes from the slave at his feet nor moving his body even a fraction, he diverted his skill from one trembling sister to the other and cracked the whip at Charlotte's bare feet in order to press his words home.

Although that was only the start of a painfully-sweet discipline session that stretched long into the night, the thoughts Charlotte took with her to her underground cell had nothing to do with her physical pain. With nothing else to occupy her mind, once again she wondered why it was that she was the only one still called by her real name. All the others… Sparkle… Kismet… Saxon… the list went on and on… there was not one other amongst them who had kept her own name!

***

It was on Wednesday afternoon that Tyler prepared to interview Snick for one of the few remaining, vacant posts. In order to give Snick a clear idea of what The Ramparts Club was about while giving Tyler the opportunity to observe his reactions and gauge if he would be too distracted to work when sexy, available girls were exhibited like artworks all around him, Tyler gave the order that some of the girls should be displayed around the room. He was currently waiting for the Escorts to deliver them.

He had chosen to hold the interview in the recently completed Members' Bar on the first floor. What had once been the Music Room was now transformed into a sizeable, traditional English pub, complete with flock wallpaper and a collection of Toby jugs on shelves above the bar. Except these were not the ordinary type of the antique mugs of that name that were used for ale, and fashioned in the shape of seated men - often caricatures of prominent men of their time, usually dressed in breeches, waistcoats, jackets and tricorn hats. The ones on display in the Members' Bar were far more in keeping with the ideals of the club! As a reluctant newcomer to the World Wide Web, it had taken Tyler months to find the Toby Jugs that were all were depictions of women, some seated while others were tied to a pillar of some sort that doubled as the handle. A few were naked but others were women of bygone days in various stages of undress, with their ripped bodices spilling creamy tits, and skirts pulled up to reveal their drawers. One or two had no drawers at all and daringly revealed hairy cunts, something of a rarity at The Ramparts since it was a rule that all the girls were clean shaven and smooth. All in all, Tyler thought, his collection of Toby jugs were a

91

more amusing distraction than the Egyptian idols and other artefacts so valued by Whitby that used to grace almost every available space.

Leather tub chairs were arranged in conversational groupings around small, round tables and as in most other rooms, devices were set up so that the members could display and torment the Pleasuregirls in whichever room they chose. In time there would be drinks waitresses to move between the tables with orders, as well as uniformed barmen behind the bar. But as Tyler sat waiting, there was only Charlotte.

Seating himself in one of the chairs near the centre of the room, he sent her to fetch him a Scotch on the rocks, and one of the cigars that time had taught him to appreciate. Next, he had her place a couple of disciplinary items around the room to test Snick's initiative. That done and with his cigar lighted, he settled back and, for something to pass the time, he ordered Charlotte to stand in front of him with her back toward him.

"Bend over and grab your ankles."

She obeyed instantly, curling her pearly-varnished, short-nailed fingers around her ankles.

"Move forward."

It was not just the wobbling of her arse that amused him, nor her awkward, stiff-legged gait as she clung onto her ankles, but the way she had to take care to avoid stepping on her own long curls and tripping herself up as her hair hung down over her head. He doubted she could see through its silky abundance that blocked her view, but it acted as a very nice backdrop indeed to the star attraction she thought; a honey-coloured curtain against which her dewy, coral-tinted pussy lips were exquisitely exhibited through her legs.

"Stop!"

She stopped.

He knew she would not right herself without permission and so sat back to enjoy a few moment's contemplation of the delights framed by her splendidly pale and shapely legs, then spent a few more moments checking the qualities of her generous backside as the Scotch warmed his throat; each whip-striped buttock was perfectly rounded, smooth and warm to the touch just like the skin of a peach, with the crack between her cheeks further reminiscent of the fruit. In fact it was her peachy arse that had first attracted him to her, and now it beckoned him with the seductiveness of Eve.

Placing the cigar on one of the cunt-shaped ashtrays dotted around, he shook out his favoured whip.

Charlotte rocked on her feet under the impact of the strikes as each time the terrible lashes fell as one, cutting deep into the crevice of her delectable arse. Yet she did not cry out, even though his skill ensured that the nine, nasty tips burrowed into the tight, puckered opening that was concealed from view.

Slowly he stood up, placed the tumbler of Scotch on the table and put the whip aside. Without speaking to her, he took the few steps that brought him up behind her, his fingers already freeing his phallus which stood out proud and rigid. Drawing back the foreskin, he spat in his hand and wiped them over the shiny head to moisten it. Then he wiped his hand quickly over her cunt, gathering the female sap dribbling like honey from a spoon, then smeared the outpouring into her bottom crack. Still without addressing her, he gripped her hips tightly, dipped at the knee and then in one swift movement drove his impressive cock unerringly into her dainty bottom hole.

"Aarghh!"

"Yes, my sweet bitch, that made you scream, didn't it!" There was no thought for her pain other than as an end to his own enjoyment. Besides, he knew her well enough by then to know that her gasps and moans were not entirely engendered by distress.

**

Charlotte could hardly believe the blessed, cleansing agony that washed her fears of ending up in Africa, as well as jealousy of her sister from her mind. Thanks to her Master's harsh use of the whip, nothing mattered except pure sensation, and her love of him.

The sensitive area around her anus was on fire, burning rawly when his shiny helm made contact with her puckered skin, which only served to fuel her arousal. While her clitoris throbbed and her pussy pulsed with wild excitement and aching need, she merely accepted that this time her cunt was not to be the recipient of his favour. And as the image of her defilement scorched its way across the back of her eyelids, his penis pushed its way inside her. Her sphincters protested vehemently as his terrible, adorable cock forced its way past them. Acid tears pricked at her eyes for she had no choice but to endure the physical pain of his deep, brutal entry inside her secret, shameful tunnel, and the mental anguish of being sodomised. On top of that was the painful emptiness of a scorned cunt. She heard the heartrending cry that filled the room, and belatedly realised it was torn from her own inverted throat. Her fingers gripped her ankles even tighter in response.

As he thrust in and out, yieldingly and without complaint she accepted his misuse of her body as his right, her penance... and the feral eroticism of a mating pair that none could set asunder. It was shiveringly exciting and her heart pumped wildly, sending blood blazing through her veins as he ravished her rectum in the most brutal fashion... in the way she was accustomed to. Yet such was her devotion to him and craving for his attention that she savoured each inflexible, inward lunge and each agonising, partial withdrawal in the same way other girls savour a lover's warm embrace.

Her skin tingled beneath his touch and she was acutely aware of every point of contact between them; her fleshy buttocks welcomed the hard fingertips of the hand pressing into the soft, welted cushions before he shifted it back to her hips to hang on for a better, firmer grip that enabled him to thrust even more forcefully. She felt the tickling heat of his hairy thighs as they pressed against her generous behind, and his heavy ball sac which slapped against her as he continued to persecute her rectum with wonderful, animal lust. She pushed back against him in her joyful eagerness to please him.

She heard his voice, rasping and cruel as he derided her considerable charms as if she were a back-street whore. In response she merely focused her attention on the patch of deep pile carpet between her feet as if it were the most interesting thing in the world in order to bear his scorn. His fingers gripped so tightly that she knew they would cause yet more bruises, and as the ferocity of his fucking increased she felt the first chill of dread that she always did, fearing that he would inadvertently rip her insides beyond reasonable use. Of course, she knew very well that he would never cause permanent damage to her or any of his girls… for one thing they cost too much to replace!

She embraced his callous ravaging of her behind and prepared to accept the yield of his climax as if it were a valuable gift he bestowed. Her cunt may have been spurned in favour of the tightest of her holes, but she consoled herself with the thought that while her cunt had indeed lost out, her deserving back passage was about to reap a just reward.

***

"You filthy slut!" Tyler drove madly into Charlotte's tight

bottom hole as if it were a well-lubricated and overly-frequented cunt. Hanging on to her as his fervour increased, hoarsely he told her, "You'd let anyone shag you up your behind!" He did not add that that was exactly what she would be required to do after the club opened on Saturday. She already knew that. Instead he rained insults upon her. "You'd better shape up, bitch. Call yourself a Pleasuregirl? Displeasure more like! You don't have a fucking clue how to please a man. You have to turn a man on, not make him think his prick was docked at birth! It's no good you gagging for it if you can't satisfy the customers!"

All the while he dug his fingers deeper into her softly yielding flesh, and his iron shaft brutishly hard and deep into the orifice he knew she found extremely painful. He was well aware how much the most accommodating of all his girls hated it! Except that was at the root of his own enjoyment. After all, what was the point of a man having girls at his disposal if he did not use them as he pleased? His need to satisfy his primitive and insatiable urge was all that mattered.

Approaching his climax he was caught in the grip of passion and flung his head sideways. Quickly he withdrew his cock and folded his fist around it as the pressure mounted. Slackening his hold he ejected his precious seed in a scalding, arcing fountain.

"Bet you thought you'd get an arse full!" he laughed as he emptied himself, making a very impressive puddle indeed in the middle of her back. "Well, fuck that for a game of soldiers! It's too valuable to waste up a whore's bum!"

He wiped his phallus across her buttocks a couple of times before extracting a tissue from one of the thoughtfully provided boxes placed around the Members' Bar and cleaned himself more satisfactorily. Making no move to clean up the thick, creamy fluid he balled the tissue, walked around in front of her and stuffed it in her mouth. With a terse command of, "Stay there!" he made a detour to the table and collected his Scotch on his round trip across to the French windows that led out onto a balcony overlooking the front of the house. He raised the tumbler to his lips - a man needed a drink after an arse-fucking as good as that! he mused as he put all thoughts of Charlotte from his head and focussed his attention on the girls outside instead.

Ruby-haired Saxon had been mounted on a wooden cross on one side of the drive and Crikette, similarly displayed on the other side, facing her… a welcoming sight for any visitor, he thought. For a moment he considered the practicalities of making it a permanent feature. He would have to change the girls at regular intervals, he reasoned, not for their sake… they could stay there for as long as they remained interesting as far as he was concerned. But that was the point; the punters would get bored by seeing the same girls every time. For several more moments he stood in quiet contemplation, with the sound of Charlotte's breathing relaxing him and slowing his raging heart.

He did not turn when the door opened, but merely listened as the footsteps approached. He knew who it was standing beside him before he heard the plum-in-the-mouth tones.

"The sluts, Milord,"

"Thanks, Alfred. That will be all." Quite frankly, Tyler thought the man huffed his displeasure on his way back to the door, he wished that it was really all from the disagreeable old git! He could not wait to be rid of him. But somehow it seemed disloyal to his grandfather to replace him.

Leaving Charlotte bent over with the jism-infused tissue soaking up her saliva and drying out her mouth, still clasping her ankles and with spunk drying on her back, reluctantly Tyler turned his attention away from Saxon and Crikette to the three Pleasuregirls who were currently being led into the room by Escorts.

He retook his seat while the Escorts lined the girls up in front of him. Just the sight of them was enough to give a man a hard on and, even though Tyler was used to seeing naked girls, it was with remarkable willpower that he managed to display his usual air of detachment. As charming and varied a collection as one could wish for: golden-skinned Stephanie from the kitchen, standing beside the nymphet he had named Rawnie, and Siren at the end had all been issued with black stiletto sandals that brought them all to roughly the same height, as per his instructions. Siren's were so high it was a wonder she could balance! He smirked. In accordance with house rules their cunts were completely hairless and smooth. All three wore collars… Stephanie's brown kitchen one had been replaced with a Pleasuregirl's black one… and wrist and ankle restraints. They quivered in a most enchanting manner as they stood obediently with their legs apart and hands clipped together behind them, thrusting out their tits.

To begin with, Tyler pointed to Stephanie, and told the stocky escort, "let's keep her anonymous, Tul. Stick a hood over her head, one of the black silk ones with clips that'll fix to her collar."

Stephanie's brown eyes glittered with venom and opened wide in horror. "I'm not fucking anonymous! You've got no right to treat me like this! My boyfriend'll come…"

"Actually, I do," he told her with a sardonic twist of his lips. "You belong to me. And who's this boyfriend you keep prattling on about? You mean your Dominant? Kirk? That part of your life's over! I've dissolved the partnership between me and… " he gave a little laugh, "your man. Oh, don't look so shocked, you must've known it was on the cards. Don't worry about him, he's done very well out of it."

"Kirk'll come lookin' for you! He won't let me rot in

this place. And when he finds you, you'd better watch out. If you knew what Kirk's capable of…"

"I don't care what he's capable of! Forget him, he's old news. As for you… well, you've been promoted!" His hungry gaze zoomed in on breasts that were in sorry need of a good leathering. Well, if a Dominant can't keep his sub's tits reasonably marked… especially such delightfully malleable ones as these… then he deserves to lose her! he told himself as he noted the wide, knobbly, dark brown areolae that were tipped with exquisitely long, fleshy nubs. To Tully he said, "Gather her hair up inside the thing," using his tumbler to indicate the warm brown hair that kissed the bare skin of her shoulders, "then take her over there and have her stand one side of the French Windows. Use a chain fixed to her collar to keep her hooked-up to the wall. Open her legs as wide as they'll go without splitting her cunt open, then keep them that way with a spreader bar. And get those fucking tits marked up a bit! There's a cane behind the bar. Give them a quick dozen then leave the cane over there on that table."

As her tanned skin took on a reddening flush, he gave one final command concerning the former kitchen slave.

"Get a marker pen from somewhere, Tul, and use it to write PAGAN across her lower belly."

Tully collected the cane from behind the bar where he found a black marker and led her toward the designated spot where he fitted the bar between her legs and placed the hood over her head. Then he had her kneel on the floor and with rough, tattooed hands, the loutish gypsy arranged her delightfully pliable breasts over a table for a thrashing.

Within moments the room was filled with her shrill cries as Tully set about his allotted task. And against the backdrop of each whack and accompanying cry, Tyler appraised the remaining two girls as he knocked back the last of his Scotch. He used the empty tumbler to indicate Rawnie, and the escort with her obligingly pushed her forward.

She had open, youthful features, and short, glossy hair that Tyler thought was the same colour as a golden retriever's coat. Once again using his tumbler as a pointer, he told the escort, "nipple clamps and gag."

"Ok Boss. Where do you want her put?" the escort asked.

"Over there," he gestured dismissively away from him to where a chain hung down in readiness from the high ceiling. "Suspend her by her wrists with her feet about a foot or so from the floor. Put a bar between them"

***

On first entering the room with Elvis gripping her arm, Siren had spotted her elder sister doubled over, clutching her ankles. She felt a moment's intense hatred for her master as she sensed Charlotte's humiliation. Forced to endure the intolerable wait while her Master dealt with the other two girls, she knew she had to get out of the place before it was too late, and she became as weak and senseless as her sister! She had seen such terrible, shocking things, Siren told herself, and if she had any chance of survival, then either she must escape to freedom or... she could hardly bear to even think it... or somehow get rid of all the other girls so she could give herself up to him completely! God help her, she wanted him to herself!

"Ah, Siren." Tyler rose from his seat and covered the short distance needed to bring him within inches of her. Using a long, tapering finger he lifted her chin to tilt her face upward toward his, at the same time the fingers of his other hand slipped between the intricate petals of her labia minora.

Her kohl-lined, mascara-fringed doe eyes met his blue ones. Behind her Elvis drawled, "What shall I do with her?"

Tyler raised his hand to stay him a moment. Then, as her Rosy Mauve glossed lips moved to utter insults which came out soundlessly, he dipped his head and placed his mouth over hers, stifling her with his tongue. As his fingers continued their agitation of her sap-filled cunt and his tongue entwined with hers, he felt her resistance melting beneath him. He drew her closer and, using the thumb and forefinger of his free hand he took hold of her engorged nipple and pinched it mercilessly.

"I'll get this pierced," he breathed into the warm cavity of her mouth.

Siren knew she was lost. Her cunt was a bubbling cauldron of lust, and there was nothing she could do to stop the aching need inside her. Damn the man! Luxuriating helplessly in the despicable, nerve-tingling sensuality of his enforced embrace, with her hands joined behind her back, she had no choice but to let him take any liberty he liked with her body. And the liberties he was taking were driving her over the edge. She tried to cry out against the pain in her nipple as he continued pinching it with pincer-like fingers but the warmth of his lips pressing over hers and his tongue exploring every secret place of her mouth silenced her most effectively. He would be sorry! she told herself helplessly as her blood galloped through her veins like a runaway stallion.

He released her nipple but the ghost of the pain remained and throbbed terribly. She felt his hand, powerful and hot, as it slid down her back from her shoulders, as if he were feeling for the evidence of his own savagery. He found it, of course, and she could not help but flinch as his assiduous fingertips traced the latticework of welts he had laid down the night before, not as punishment but simply because, as he had told her and Charlotte at the time, she was there.

His nails raked the welts sharply and in an effort to stand it she scoured her brain for some kind of definition, for some … Ooooohhh… for some meaning. Surely this was not the life she was supposed to lead? Hers had been all mapped out... she was a singer... she was famous... she was drowning! His body was so close to hers that her throbbing nipples were pushing against the firmness of his chest through the coarse fabric of his shirt... making them even harder and... throb, throb, throbbing... no, that was her heart! she argued as his devilry made her more... more what? She struggled to make sense of the maelstrom of emotions, fought against swooning as... just as it had before... her treacherous body reacted to his brutally thrilling sensuality in a most inappropriate way... if she did not hold on she would come... really come... squirt everywhere like she always did! She must hang on!

She was Chelsi Laird, she reminded herself, refusing to admit that that part of her life had been over the moment she had willingly... yes, willingly... surrendered to him on his bloody boat! But then, perhaps that had all been mapped out too, for she remembered how she had once, so long ago it seemed, wanted to run away with the skinny gypsy. It was a curious destiny that brought them together like this. If only Charlotte were far, far away... and it struck her then that it had been Charlie, all those years ago, who had warned her to stay away from the dangerous didakoi. And the ill-judgement that had plagued her throughout her life flared in her brain once more as she realised that what she had always taken for sisterly concern was something else entirely! And she found herself thinking how Charlie must have hated it when it was she, Chelsi, and not Charlie who had so enraptured him all those years ago!

The fires in her back raged anew as his nails continued to score her welts and the heat in her mouth was unabated as his masterly tongue took her breath away. The flames licked up inside her belly and her vagina became an inferno that needed an orgasm to extinguish. But she knew he would not allow that! His fingers continued to thrust hard and brutal into her as she trembled with fear... jealousy...

joy… and the need to come!

The sound came to her of jingling chains and she remembered that one of the girls was to be suspended, and she found herself praying that he would not do the same thing to her. She heard a guttural grunting and realised that one of the Escorts was probably shafting the girl by the window. But what about Charlotte? Poor, snubbed and neglected Charlie! Now she thought about it she could just make out the faintest, muffled bleating.

Overriding everything was the alarmingly loud squelchy, gurgly sound emanating from her own pussy as Tyler's fiendish fingers continued to work their evil spell. She had to fight him, or lose herself forever. One day, she told herself vehemently as he tongued her deep, she would free herself from his delicious cruelty and return to her real life… her career that, if she was honest… she needed to be honest… maybe was not as glittering as it had once been. But today… Ooooohhh… today was possibly not that day… she needed air, she needed… Oh! Oh! Oh! She needed to come! When would he let her come?

She staggered backward as Tyler suddenly broke all contact with her body, disengaging his tongue from hers at exactly the same moment as he yanked his fingers roughly from her cunt and snatched his hand away from her welts, leaving her breathless and humiliated. Her shoulders shook with the effort of keeping her tears in check.

"Don't cry, you'll ruin your make-up!" he laughed while inwardly applauding the effect she had achieved with only the cheapest of cosmetics - there was no way he was going to supply all the expensive stuff that she had demanded. All the other girls were grateful to be supplied with any cosmetics and toiletries at all, but not this ungrateful bitch! he thought churlishly. All she had done since he had first taken possession of her was whine, complain and demand.

Unlike Charlotte, who was more than happy to abide by

his decision. For although he permitted Siren and the others to wear a wide range of cosmetics, Charlotte was allowed only mascara and a clear lip gloss. It was the same with nail polish. While the other sluts painted fingernails and toenails in vibrant colours ... currently Siren's toenails and her long fingernails were a pinky-mauve colour... he allowed Charlotte only the barest colour, a sort of pearly, apricot varnish applied to fingernails only because... well, Charlotte was Charlotte and he had always thought that all she needed do in order to be sexy was merely exist.

Siren was still trembling. Not caring that her ravenous body craved relief or that her heart was shattered into tiny fragments, he waved his hand in the direction of the pillory at the end of the bar. "Gag her, then stick her in that."

When Elvis had secured her in the pillory with a blue ball gag between her mauvy-pink lips, Tyler dismissed the Escorts. Then, with them gone and Alfred mysteriously but thankfully absent, Tyler wandered slowly around the room and examined at close quarters the hooded Pleasuregirl chained at the side of the open French windows. After a perfunctory groping of her assets, he chose to disregard the others and returned to his table.

He took a few moments to adjust the positions of the little group of tub chairs in the centre of the room, casting three aside and placing them together in a grouping of their own eventually settling himself in one of the two remaining ones, with his back to the windows and the vacant chair facing him with the small round table between them. Next, he had the biddable Charlotte, still gripping her ankles, back up slightly and position herself within easy reach with her backside toward the door. Still bent double with the foul tissue still in her mouth, the glistening centre of her femininity was blatantly on view and the first thing Snick saw when, moments later, Alfred announced him.

CHAPTER SEVEN

As he stood in the doorway awaiting entry, Snick stole several moments taking in the sight of the luscious girls.

He was well acquainted with whores though he had never seen anything quite like the sights that greeted him in the Members' Bar. His momentary frown was replaced by a widening of his eyes as he appraised the dangling body of the young girl suspended by her wrists, with her sinews clearly stretched to the limit as her own weight pulled her down. The nipples of her gorgeous, firm young titties were cruelly clamped, her mouth stuffed with a bright red ball and her legs held open, about two feet, by a metal bar. In addition, her body carried the marks of what Snick assumed was a recent flogging, and he wondered whether the man in the chair noticed the tenting at the front of Snick's trousers and, given the current circumstances, wondered if it was a good sign or a black mark against him. He swerved his attention back to the girl whose amazing arse was facing him as she gripped her ankles. It too had been marked, and Snick knew at once that the cutting strikes had been delivered by an exceptionally cruel hand.

"Thank you. That will be all, Alfred."

Snick was surprised by the terseness of the servant's dismissal, and it was with some effort that he tore his eyes from the girl's striped arse and the dewy cleft between her legs, and instead he fixed them on his host as he entered the room and looked the lord over. He was not sure what he had expected a lord to look like, but whatever it was, the man loafing in the chair was not it! Mid thirties and looking like the devil himself with heavy eyebrows which sloped down toward the bridge of his nose, he wore a western-style shirt and faded jeans. Then his eyes returned to the girls and he decided that his lordship was a very unconventional lord of the manor indeed.

***

Dragging a tapering finger through his long, reddish-gold hair, Tyler indicated the vacant chair with his other hand.

"Take a seat," Tyler said with a civility only one step removed from hostility. It was a characteristic due entirely to a lifetime of distrust and antipathy directed toward himself and his fellow travellers, and one that Stapleton was keen he abandon.

With a smirk, Tyler knew that as he sat down, Snick was probably reminding himself of the reason for his visit and forcing himself to concentrate on Tyler himself rather than his whores. But Tyler had not made that easy for him and had deliberately had the hooded girl placed by the window behind him so that she would be visible to the man throughout his interview. Moreover, if his gaze deviated even slightly either side, he would be tested further, either by the suspended girl that he had already noticed on the left, or the delightful… and surely familiar-looking… beauty in the stocks on his right.

While Snick eyeballed the girls, Tyler appraised the grey-suited, ex-army man whose receding hairline was reminiscent of a much older man,

"Drink?" he made the offer sound like an accusation, and Snick's acceptance was equally terse and laden with derision as he kept his eyes on Tyler's blue ones.

"Scotch and soda, my lord."

"Call me Tyler," the lord said with what Snick thought was rather forced generosity, then added pointedly, "Here at The Ramparts we keep our contempt for the sluts!"

Whack!

To Tyler's surprise, Snick barely started at the sound as Tyler delivered a hefty slap to Charlotte's adorable behind, something he put down to the man being used to the sudden noises of gunfire and bombs.

"Fetch the drinks, whore!" Tyler commanded. "And take that fucking tissue out of your mouth!"

As Charlotte straightened up and removed the tissue, Tyler's gaze latched onto Snick, who seemed to be mesmerised by the waves of long, honey-blonde hair that tumbled down Charlotte's welted back.

"That's Charlotte, one of the Pleasuregirls," Tyler told him as she hurried to obey her master.

In an unconscious gesture Snick raised his hand and wiped it over his pink-marble baldness that was emphasised rather than diminished by the remaining grey wisps of hair. As Snick moved his head to focus on a charmingly naked Rawnie, suspended by her wrists just feet away, Tyler saw that it had been pulled back into a two inch ponytail and secured with a rubber band. He suppressed a smile. He called that a ponytail? His grandfather's had been a magnificent white one that reached half way down his back!

"The one by the window's Pagan," he gave a brittle laugh, "at least, that's what it says on her belly! That's where the tattoo's going to be. The bitch that's suspended is Rawnie, and…" now for the test, he thought as he continued casually, "the filthy slut in the stocks is Siren."

***

The tissue had soaked up every drop of moisture and Charlotte's mouth was arid. Yet she did not ask for any refreshment as she fixed drinks for her Master and Snick, since Tyler would not have allowed her one until he was good and ready. Naturally, she resisted the temptation to help herself, though she had no doubt that if her sister were not restrained she would head straight for the vodka. Ah, poor Chel… Siren, she thought, as she deliberately knocked against her sister's backside before carrying the George II silver salver back toward the men.

Once she had set the little hoof feet of the salver with the

Grenfell coat of arms in the centre on the table, she stationed herself beside Tyler as the two men simultaneously reached for their drinks. With no order to the contrary, she took up her usual position with head bowed, legs splayed and hands crossed behind her back. She stood silently throughout the interview, although her master frigged her mercilessly. Tyler asked a few basic questions. Although he made a real effort to appear businesslike as he conducted the interview, just as Stapleton had advised, the air was thick with animosity. And lust, of course.

The concise answers to his questions yielded nothing beyond the facts that Snick, the tall and brawny, ex-service man had left the army some two years earlier, having signed-up for the minimum term. Since then he had been working as a night-club bouncer. He had a flat in Kings Langley, but had no family or regular girlfriends.

"The sluts here have one purpose only, Snick… to be the source of pleasure. Ultimately, they all belong to me. To put it bluntly, I'm their master and they're my slaves. It's their duty to do as I please, suffer for me and do it all with a willing heart and obedient nature. The Ramparts SM club opens on Saturday, and then their duties will be extended to take in the needs of the paid-up members. For one of the Pleasuregirls… whores to you and me… to either offend or disobey anyone who's paid good money to thrash them or fuck them to kingdom come bloody well offends me too! That's where the real punishment comes in as opposed to Pleasure discipline."

He went on to give Snick a rough outline of what the job of Escort involved, ending with, "Naturally, the Escorts get to take their pleasure with any of the bitches that are not in use. So, what do you think of my sluts?"

Snick looked him directly in the eye and Tyler tensed as he sensed trouble. He did not, however, stop his sharp agitation of Charlotte's squelchy pussy.

"What about the sluts themselves?"

Tyler was nonplussed. "What about them?"

"Do they get any pleasure out of it? I mean, look at that poor cow over there… what pleasure does she get from dangling from the ceiling? Or that one with the hood over her head and the welted tits? Or…"

Tyler's bark of a laugh cut him off. "You're asking if they enjoy it?" He extracted his glistening fingers from Charlotte's quim and held them up to Snick. His scepticism reminded Tyler of himself, when he had first come to the house and had asked similar questions. "What do you think? But don't take my word for it. Go and feel them up for yourself!"

Standing up, it took Snick several seconds to decide which girl to start with. At last he made his choice and strode to the end of the bar.

"Amazing! I could swear I've seen her somewhere before. But I guess that's impossible."

"No, not impossible," Tyler told him, swivelling round in his chair to watch. "She's one of my latest acquisitions. Though strictly speaking, the hooded whore's the latest to submit."

Snick looked down at Siren. She stood at an angle, her back sloping and her bottom sticking out. He reached out to touch her head which stuck out through a hole in the centre of the beam, with her hands on either side. Then, changing his mind, he snatched his hand away. With a nasty smirk, he raised his hand again. This time he put his palm over her eyes and, using a slow and grinding motion, he wiped it backward and forward. Satisfied, he removed his hand and then laughed at the sight of her kohl, smeared beyond repair.

Tyler laughed also, then lifted his tumbler to his lips as Snick glanced down at his black-smeared palm. With an oath and exaggerated grimace Snick wiped it roughly in her chaotically tumbling raven hair. Then he reached for her globes which hung downward, and squeezed them harder than he had ever squeezed mammaries before.

And as Tyler watched, he could only assume that it was knowing that it must hurt her that brought a smile to Snick's face, a smile that broadened at Siren's muffled protest. Her legs were held open at an uncomfortably wide gait, and he saw her feet were held in place by metal straps, one across the toes of each foot to stop her from lifting her feet, and others across the back of her heels which stopped her from sliding them out.

There was no way any woman would enjoy being so humiliated, Snick thought and, telling himself it was merely to prove his lordship wrong, he felt between Siren's legs for her opening, naturally concealed between dangly lips that sent bolts of fire through his balls as he manipulated them clumsily. He could not help his salacious smile as he finally located her slit and slipped his finger inside, at once beginning thrusting it in and out of the surprisingly wet channel. He had no way of knowing, of course, that rather than the stocks it was Tyler's earlier ministrations and her own expectations of the indignities to come which excited her.

"You might as well fuck her, seeing as she's ready," Tyler told him matter-of-factly as he took his whip from his belt and used the handle to fuck Charlotte.

Snick needed no further encouragement. Bending at the knee, he replaced his finger with his cock without further and obviously unnecessary foreplay.

"She fucking loves it!" Snick grunted as he gripped her hips and rammed frenziedly into her.

Though her head and hands, were held fast between the beams, they shifted with the force of it as he rammed hard.

"Of course she does! And that's okay…" Tyler hesitated only slightly before adding with a vicious smile, "providing it's you and not her who controls her pleasure! You can't just let the bitches enjoy themselves any old time they want to."

Suddenly the door burst open and Tully flung a naked girl into the room with a cry of, "Sorry, boss, she's a wild one! I can't do a thing with the bitch!"

The girl landed in a heap and the Escort backed away.

"Okay, Snick," Tyler told him, see what you can do with her to bring her back under some kind of control!"

Reluctantly, Snick pulled out of the madly juicing Siren, his cock still pumping out the last of his spunk, and tucking himself away, swaggered across the room to where the girl was sprawled beside the little table at which her Master was seated.

***

With the first part of the interview concluded, Tyler sat back as Snick demonstrated how he would deal with a non-compliant girl. Seeing as Tyler did not own any non-compliant girls… even Pagan, as he now called Stephanie, and Siren were willing despite their little acts of defiance, and in any case, Siren was still in the pillory with a belly full of spunk that was slowly dribbling out and pudding on the floor… he had arranged for Fionola to role play. She was a willowy girl with pale breasts and elfin features topped by short white-blonde hair. He had a soft spot for the slender blonde because she had been the first slave he had actually purchased, some eighteen months or so ago, from the Jamaican who paid occasional visits to his clan, on the lookout for wayward daughters and unruly wives, to snap up. As Tyler looked at her now, he recalled how he had made an appointment to view the man's stock and, with a "loan" from the old lord tucked in his pocket, on first catching sight of the girl he had promptly named her after a gypsy horse he had owned as a child and handed over the exorbitant fee. After that she had travelled around with him, locked in a cage in the beat-up caravan in which he had lived and towed around with his old truck.

Whether it was just that Snick was overwhelmed by the other girls, or the surroundings in which he found himself, or perhaps even the stunning Fionola herself and the effectiveness of her endeavour Tyler could not say. Whatever the cause, Snick seemed oblivious to the deception, as Tully slowly left the room

Apart from delicate little cries that were as genuine as a crocodile's tears, Fionola made no sound as Snick sprang helpfully into action and caught hold of her. He dragged her to her feet.

"Let me go!" she squealed prettily. "Take your filthy hands off me!"

Twisting this way and that in a most erotic manner in an effort to tear herself from the man's grasp, her willowy body almost mesmerised the two men as it moved with a fluidity barely witnessed among the non-submissive variety of womanhood. Except perhaps at the ballet, Tyler thought, and almost laughed aloud as he considered adding it to his ever-growing list of "things to do now I'm rich enough."

Tyler could only assume Snick was prolonging his own enjoyment as he held Fionola around her slender waist and let her wriggle her lovely drum-of-an-arse against his crotch. The indications were that he would make a fine Escort.

Her delightful, sexily breathless squeals continued. "Let me go!"

But it was not long before Fionola began to tire of her part. As Snick held her wrist tightly in his unyielding grasp, she decided to spice things up and kicked out at his ankle and used her free hand to thump his chest. Tyler had instructed her to put as much effort into her performance as possible to make her struggle seem authentic. It was with this in mind that she rolled her fingers into a tight fist and foolishly brought it up under his chin.

"Aghhouchhh!" She gave a cry of distress as for a moment she thought her own bones had shattered as the pain shot through her. She shook her hand wildly as if that would somehow ease the pain.

Snick hardly felt the blow on his iron jaw. Yet it was in that moment that he seemed to feel, quite wrongly, that the job was slipping away from him. It was the job he knew he was born for and he gave a quick glance toward Tyler who was behind the bar refreshing their drinks. He knew he had to find some way to redeem himself! After all, he reasoned, he was a fighting man, not some puny punk gypo who had nothing to occupy himself all day but count his fucking money! There was no way a trollop - lovely as she was - was going to get one over on him!

All at once he remembered the cane that someone… probably his lordship, he realised… had left lying on one of the tables. Tightening his grip with his left arm around the struggling bitch's waist, he lifted her right off the floor. As her long, slender legs flailed madly, Snick edged toward the table where he had seen the cane, then snatched it up with his right hand.

Tyler nodded his approval as with commendable forethought Snick aimed his first strike so that it took in her upper thighs and cunt while he held her fast.

Her resulting shriek was both genuine and high-pitched. Bending double over her assailant's arm with her tight bottom pressed even harder against his burgeoning cock, she flung her hands protectively across her vulva.

With impressive dexterity Snick flung his left arm to the side while still curled firmly around her middle, exposing her backside, and let the cane fly delivering six very fine strikes indeed across her bottom that brought the tramlines flaring instantly and tore a long wail from Fionola's throat.

Tyler laughed and watched Snick's mouth slowly break into an appreciative grin, though whether it was his own appreciative laughter that amused Snick or Fionola's wailing as limply she hung over the man's arm, Tyler could not tell.

Even as Snick glowed with pride he knew his task was not yet completed. Still holding the limp girl over his arm, it was instinct alone that prompted him to look around for something to tie her with. Spotting a length of cord draped over a chair back... again he suspected it had been planted there for him to find as if the lord thought the soldier unable to ferret out the materials... Snick dragged her toward the chair where he deposited the cane and snatched up the cord. With impressive speed he placed her feet on the floor, took his supporting arm away, grabbed her arms with both huge hands and yanked them behind her back, winding the cord tightly around her wrists to join them together. Job done, Snick flung her aside and she fell in a surprisingly graceful and erotic heap of femininity to the floor.

"Well done," Tyler congratulated as he came and placed their drinks on the table. He took out his mobile, flipped it open and called one of the Escorts to fetch Fionola. Returning it to his pocket he smiled, offered his hand in sudden and genuine friendship and said, "welcome to the firm, Snick!"

***

Thursday morning

A maelstrom of emotion shook her to the core as, painfully subjected to her Master's whim, Charlotte resisted the temptation to cry out in agony, even though her hands and knees felt the excruciatingly numbing effects of the solid wooden board beneath her. Besides, it would not have done her much good since there was no one to hear her for she was alone in the sumptuous, red, Members' Lounge. Instead, she merely whimpered at the crick in her neck, and the painful pulling of her long hair at the roots.

She raised her bowed head the fraction that her bondage allowed in order to ease the horrendous strain on her neck. But with her forehead only marginally clearing the board the strain on her roots was inevitably increased, because her honey-blonde tresses had been plaited with hemp and fixed to the underside of the board. It was an unnecessary cruelty since a chain or rope passed through the ring in her collar would have prevented her from raising her head equally as effectively. Naked and on all fours, she was prevented from moving further by archaic-looking rusty bolts to which black leather wrist and ankle restraints were attached, locking her in position. The friction the restraints engendered as they rubbed against her skin chafed her terribly. Not only that, but due to the inverted position of her head, her leather collar rubbed her sore as it dug into the skin beneath her chin. As if that was not enough, the blood pounded in her head.

Of course, she was used to such discomfort by now. But what she was not used to was waiting this long! She had been brought to the room early that morning and displayed to Tyler's specifications, so where was he?

***

Out in the stable yard, Tyler was seeing to Siren's training himself. Standing in the centre of the yard surrounded by out buildings that included garages with the ponygirl stables on one side and the equine stables other on the other, he had a whip in one hand and the end of a blue, training rope in the other. At the end of the rope, a naked, stiletto-heeled Siren was high stepping in a circle while Tyler turned.

"Fucking useless! We've only got two days, do you hear me, you stupid bitch? Two days before the Grand Opening.

What I want from you is the performance of your life. But you're more like a lumbering old carthorse than a beautiful, high-stepping pony!"

All Siren wanted as she put every ounce of energy into trying to please him, was to get the session over and done with so she could be relieved of the discomfort of the butt plug which held the long, black pony tail in place. It filled her to capacity and the ingenious way it was kept inside without a harness was unimaginably painful. This, coupled with the burning sensation in her thighs from having been trotting and high-stepping for so long brought her dilemma sharply into focus. Should she give in entirely to her most base desires and allow herself to become totally subjugated? Or should she fight the bastard and keep her dignity? And then there was the question of escape... surely they could not keep her here? The other girls maybe, but not her... she was famous! Someone was bound to come looking for her sooner or later.

A thread of sadism coloured his tone as he told her, "If you were a carthorse you'd have gone to the knacker's yard long ago. As it is, you're a worthless lump of slutty humanity masquerading as a ponygirl, fucking badly I might add, and I've got no choice but to beat the crap out of you. When we're through here, I'll punish you till you can't stand let alone trot. And then I'll punish you some more, till you understand I expect nothing less than excellence from my star attraction. Did I say star?" He gave a derisive laugh. "You're no star, you're just another pathetic collection of whoring-holes. We've been through it all before, but you don't seem to get it yet... I'm the one with the power now, I'm the one with the money. You, on the other hand, are nothing and have nothing, except what I give you."

The bastard had given her nothing, as far as she could see! she thought peevishly as she raised her knees as high as she could - didn't he realise she would do much better if he untied her hands so she could balance better? He had taken more than he had given, including her rings. And not just the ones she had worn on each her fingers, she thought as she stomped angrily, but even her toe rings. Knowing Tyler, he had probably had one of his cronies go through her flat and rifle through her jewel box as well... the bastard had probably taken all of it! Still, it was a comfort of sorts that he would never get his hands on the really good stuff, the jewels she had bought as investments for when her career came to a natural end... that was safe in the bank vault.

He yanked her to a stop. "Take five."

God, what she would give for a vodka! she sighed longingly as she fought to get her breath back. Up until a short while ago, she had always had a bottle close at hand, through all the ups and downs of her life as a celebrity. It struck her as a strange irony that it had been Tully who had first introduced her to the drink that she had considered her friend... not life support as the tabloids claimed... and, all these years later, it was Tyler who had deprived her of it.

Tyler's attention was momentarily caught elsewhere, and she turned her head to see Mistress Lilith, a haughty, well dressed, dark haired woman, entering the ponygirl stables. Her face was like thunder, and Siren had to stifle a giggle... looked like Mistress Adria was about to get another of the elder woman's "lectures." With a mental shrug of her shoulders, Siren returned to the safety of her memories.

She had had her very first vodka just a short distance away from where she presently found herself. Stupidly, and fatally as it had turned out, as a teenager she had accompanied Tully... the man who was always on hand to do Tyler's bidding... to The Griffin, the sole pub in the village where she had grown up. It had been on the night when Tully had sought her out to meet Tyler though she had stupidly mistaken his motives. She could not staunch the flow of the unwanted memories and all at once in her mind's eye, she saw again the näive girl she had been then, as well as the shocked expression on Tyler's face when she had informed him that she had school the next morning! And all around her the pub regulars had speculated on what eighteen year old Chelsi was up to. In those days her only fear had been that one of them would betray her to the Aunt with whom she lived.

She was brought out of her reverie by the realisation that she was hungry, and she could lay the fault entirely at Tyler's feet. After all, she had only refused to eat anything because Tyler, whose attention was still focussed on the pony stables where female voices were raised in anger, was prepared to deprive her of her most basic requirements. She would never have rejected the food laid before her if he had not refused, point black, to have her own toiletries and make-up brought from her flat. He had explained that an ample supply of both would be provided for her, though her usual, more exclusive brands were out of the question. Instead she would have to make do with the same cheaper brands, in her mind poor imitations, that he provided for all the other Pleasuregirls. But there had been no reasoning with the man! Didn't he realise that her skin was used to the best and would probably break out in unsightly blotches if she were to so much as dab a finger-tip's-worth of the stuff on her face? What was wrong with the bloody man? It was not as if he could not afford it. Hell! She would pay for it out of her money if he would just allow her access to her credit cards! How the hell did he expect her to be in prime condition, athletically fit for all the high stepping and stuff if she was not eating?

As her memories congealed with the present, Mistress Lilith came storming out of stables again and headed for the main archway that led to the car park. A breeze set Siren's tail flapping against the back of her legs as Tyler watched the departing woman, then his attention reverted back to Siren. He carried on where he had left off.

"Remember, Siren, you belong to me and I can do whatever I like to you. I can make your life real miserable, if you let me down, so fucking miserable you'll wish you'd never been born. And I'll go on making your life a misery until you get it right. Get my drift?" For good measure he cracked the whip at her heels once more. "You'll bloody well get it right, Siren, or God help me, I'll turn your back into ribbons of flesh! I'm going to put on a good show for the punters and you can either be part of it or not. If you're not up to scratch you can stay locked in your cell all day and someone with more class can take your place. Now, once more."

***

Indecently exposed, Charlotte was acutely aware that the first things anyone would see on entering the room were the rawly-striped buttocks of her peachy backside and the arousal-flushed split between her pale thighs.

The rudimentary structure on which she was so shamelessly mounted was one of Tyler's own design, it was about three feet high with the board fixed on top.

The platform itself, fashioned from time-worn, ink-stained floorboards that Tyler had had ripped up from the old, disused nursery, had been fitted with special bolts to lock a captive securely. In addition, it was centrally pivoted on a column base so that it could be tilted at virtually any angle, though on that particular day Tyler had decreed it be kept level. The sturdy column was made from two old railway sleepers joined together and stood on end.

Despite her naturally submissive nature, with the arrival of Siren, Charlotte had experienced all kinds of new emotions and was particularly troubled that morning. Unaccustomed resentment bubbled at the forefront of her mind… she had already been waiting for two hours in humiliating, muscle-cramping bondage. Her Master, having commanded one of the more thuggish of the Escorts to prepare her in the manner she was now beginning to endure rather than enjoy, had still not deigned to look in on her! She had, however, been mauled by Tully, groped by Alfred, with whose bony fingers she was only too well acquainted, and had sucked the cock of the newly-employed handyman.

Her pale flesh had reddened with the most delicious shame when he had entered the room a short while ago. He had let out a low whistle at the sight of her. For what had seemed an age he had stood admiring the salacious view before coming round to stand in front of her, while her clitoris had taken to thrumming madly.

"Well, well, look who we have here. It's Charlotte!"

Up until a few weeks ago the man had been the village's only odd job man, a man the sensuous blonde had known her entire life. Then recently, perhaps in a bid to win over the villagers, Tyler had offered him employment. It was a . job the man had taken to with relish!

He had briefly released her hair from its bondage so she could raise her face, and , unable to escape as he had pushed the bulbous head of his penis between her soft lips, Charlotte had been acutely aware that she had gone to school with his daughter. Nevertheless, she had flicked her tongue over its underside and drew him in. After all, she had reminded herself, her beloved Master had given permission to all and sundry who worked on the estate to make use of his slaves when they were not otherwise engaged… "perks of the job" Tyler called it. Besides, she had hardly been in a position to refuse, and anyway, she was horny as hell!

When he had finished and tidied himself, the handyman

had crossed the room with his metal toolbox in hand. He had proceeded to fix a row of shiny brass hooks on the wall, set between two large oil paintings, Cleopatra's Boudoir and The Pharaoh's Slavegirls. Shortly afterwards, one of the Escorts had hung a collection of whips and other implements upon them.

Alone once more with the taste of his semen still on her tongue, an empty, dewy cunt and still no sign of her Master, she momentarily gave way to tears of crushing humiliation engendered by the very subjugation she usually enjoyed so much. She rested her forehead on the platform once more. And as the shame took hold, it sizzled as hotly as the arousal that coiled in her belly, and gave rise to the hope that Tyler's fascination with her suffering would in time transmute into affection… and from there into the love that would give her life even greater meaning. But the very notion was ridiculous, she knew that, because he always treated her worse than a gypsy's cur.

Chiding herself for giving in to her distress, her over-tired and befuddled brain sought to apportion blame. Everything had been OK before Siren's arrival, she told herself once more, then realised she was smiling at the memory of the cigar jutting from her sister's behind. If only he would get rid of her, then things could return to normal. It was odd, but she had never resented any of the other girls the way she resented her sister.

If only Tyler would come to her now, everything would be alright.

Alone and ravaged with despair, it was the longest period Charlotte had ever been kept in bondage. Over the hours her thoughts skittered between the reassuring idea that her Master was a busy man who simply hadn't the time during the morning to look in on her, to the more troubling notion that he had tired of her and had sought amusement elsewhere. Her bonds had ceased to be uncomfortable and were edging fast toward agonising, and it took all her willpower to stay conscious. For the most part it was the bonds themselves which kept her from crumpling in a heap.

Eventually, somewhere around early afternoon, she reached the point where she simply had to accept that he had forgotten her. And when the mantel clock struck two o'clock, she was not just in agony but had reached her lowest point ever; she really believed that she was doomed to stay alone in the Members' Lounge forever... or at least until the club finally opened and someone came across her! It had all been for nothing, she told herself... her obedience, her willing subjugation, her suffering, her devotion, all of it! Yet crushed as she was, it was still more than she dared do to risk Tyler's wrath by crying out for someone to release her.

Just as the clock struck the quarter hour, the heavy oak door creaked open and Tyler arrived at last. She could not see him, of course, but familiarity had seasoned her to the sound of his footsteps. At once, the unusual petulance and totally uncharacteristic resentment she had felt during the long hours of waiting, began to melt away. How could she, his most faithful and devoted slave, have doubted him? she chided herself. If he wanted to keep her waiting for so many hours, that was his prerogative, he probably had his reasons. She would forgive him, of course.

At first, as was often his way, he ignored her and poured himself a drink. She heard Alfred's polite "hem!" from the door and knew her Master had made a *faux pas*, in his manservant's eyes at least - probably just used the wrong glass! With anticipation gnawing at her, she listened as the ice clinked in the glass. Heartened by his presence, she tried to shrug off the pain. It was not that the tension drained away from her, not exactly... it was more a case of her clitoris waking up again and resuming its maddening throb that diminished everything else.

As Tyler sauntered toward her, she knew he had just showered for she could she smell the citrus woody fragrance of the expensive toiletries he had taken to using. She tried to imagine which piece of furniture it was that he kicked across the room in front of him. She could picture him perfectly, oversized chunky green goblet in one hand, decanter in the other, and scratch marks across the polished floor. She winced at the couple of worrying thuds as he plonked the glass and crystal decanter down on a little table, then relaxed when she realised nothing was broken. He drew the table closer and positioned both pieces of furniture beside the structure on which she was mounted. It was only then that she caught a glimpse of the walnut stool, and she wondered if Tyler appreciated its importance; it was a lovely piece and still had its original needlework upholstery intact. Its cabriole legs and ball-and-claw feet gave it an elegance that was totally in keeping with the rest of the room, with the exception of the crude display and stand on which her abused body was exhibited so lewdly.

Tyler settled himself comfortably, facing her side-on with his long, jean-clad legs straddling the stool. He did not speak to her, but merely admired the view while he drank. Then he downed the last of the brandy and, for the sheer hell of it, called to Alfred to replenish his ugly goblet, despite the decanter being mere inches from his own fingers.

With a fractious sigh, Alfred stepped smartly across to the table, a deep scowl adding even more lines to his already age-worn face.

Having replenished Tyler's goblet, Alfred returned to his station at the door.

Tyler took another swig.

There was a tentative knock at the door. Alfred opened it and then stood aside to allow one of the new, correctional-facility-supplied and scantily-uniformed maids entry. Click-clacking across the polished floor on impractical heels, unsteadily she carried a silver salver upon which was Tyler's especially chosen "lunch," which consisted of an overflowing bowl of luscious, juicy strawberries and a jug of cream. Colouring up as she tried to keep her eyes averted from the horrendously displayed blonde, with a perfect curtsey the maid placed the salver on the little table, next to the decanter.

With his gaze fixed on Charlotte's enticing and generously dangling breasts, Tyler reached out his hand and, without speaking to the maid, gestured that she move closer around the table. When she was in position, standing with her legs apart as all the maids were taught to stand, he slipped his fingers beneath her short skirt and sidled them inside the white frilly knickers that were part of her uniform. Without preamble or courtesy and with his gaze still riveted on Charlotte's breasts, which quivered alluringly as she breathed, he delved straight into the maid's moist vagina. Watched by Alfred at the door, he agitated her insides.

"That sister of yours…" he said suddenly, burrowing. ever deeper into the maid's squelching quim.

"My sister?" the maid asked with an expression that was a mix of indignant humiliation and puzzlement. "I haven't got a sister."

"Shut up!" he roared and jabbed his fingers sharply, eliciting a rather pleasing little squeal in the process, "I was talking to the whore, not the fucking cleaner!" he said unkindly. Casting a glance from the corner of his eye, he was gratified to see the exceptionally pretty little maid's lip quivering and eyes filling with water.

"That sister of yours," he continued as if there had been no interruption, "she's a right fucked-up little slut, but she's got a throat to die for! Swallows spunk like its going out of fashion. The punters are going to love her, especially if they have her the way I did… in the straw of one of the pony stalls with her legs held up by ropes over the rafters, and her shoulders held down in by Mistress Adria."

He felt an upswell of pure pleasure as this time it was Charlotte's eyes that glistened with tears! The way her lips quivered and her face contorted as she tried to control both the agony of the bondage and the tears was a joy that he knew would only be surpassed when he took the whip to her. He must be the luckiest man alive, he thought, to have two such stunning sisters to abuse. The memory of flogging and fucking Siren in the stall and then emptying the boiling contents of his balls down her throat just moments earlier was so burningly fresh in his mind that it was all he could do to keep from doing the same thing to Charlotte. But it was too soon - she had not suffered enough yet, he told himself as with a plop! he extracted his long fingers from the maid's deliciously-tight cunt. He slapped her knicker-encased bottom, she curtsied a second time, then click-clacked back across to the door and passed through into the house beyond.

Tyler retrieved his brandy and took a warming slug.

Charlotte wiggled her fingers as best she could to try and ease the cramps. Unable to endure it any longer, she finally gave in and whined the protests she had kept bottled up for so many hours. Once the crack had opened, there was no stopping the deluge and, broken hearted, she wept uncontrollably. Tears streaked her face and sobs racked her cruelly restrained body.

For a full minute Tyler merely watched her. Then he placed the goblet on the table. Slowly and deliberately, he got to his feet and walked around behind her. Next, he pulled the walnut stool into position and settled himself wide-legged. Finally, he selected a strawberry and popped it into her cunt.

Charlotte's line of vision was filled by her own ripe, hard-nippled breasts but, if she relaxed the tautness of her hair and rested her head on the board, as well as gaining some minor relief through the tears she could see her Master's dark striped shirt as he rested his palms on her peachy buttocks.

He lowered his mouth to her vagina and his hot breath came in waves that flooded her insides as he sucked the strawberry from her cunt. Her tears stopped flowing instantly. Her heart sang with joy and she could not help but moan with pleasure as he replaced the strawberry with another, pushing it deep into her channel, followed by another and another. And so he continued until her cunt was full to the brim with ripe, succulent Spanish strawberries that he then proceeded to suck out again.

Erotic tingles of bliss scorched her insides as his lips brushed against her nether regions, momentarily transporting her away from jealousy and heartache to the realm where fantasy and salacious reality melded into the same thing. Nothing mattered any more except his fingernails that were digging deep into her flesh and his lips fastened over her pussy as his teeth and tongue dislodged the strawberries. That moment was her entire world, her whole existence, and nothing else was of any consequence.

He withdrew another strawberry, sat back to eat it and then dipped his head toward her cunt for another one. Once again his lips fluttered over her most sensitive regions, fanning her skin before finally covering her quim.

Her thoughts were becoming harder to harness as his sensual manipulations continued. Yet concentrate she must, for the indescribable pain of her prolonged bondage was hovering over her consciousness and her realm of joy was too quickly splintered. She needed to focus on something more potent than the pain. And that something was, as it always had been, concern for her Master.

The way he was going, splashing out several of Whitby's millions on turning the place into a haven for SM practitioners, she feared that he would very soon find the kitty empty and end up living in his old caravan again!

An uneasiness settled over her, and there was such a feeling of foreboding that she almost felt she should warn him. Except what could she say? It would come out sounding ridiculous, and he would not listen in any case. He would punish her for speaking out of turn and point out, quite rightly, that it was none of her business what he spent his money on. Yet the foreboding remained… what if he were to lose it all? He would be lost to her forever! She had to do something, but what? Given his background, she thought he would have been more cautious with his new-found wealth. But perhaps he was… maybe that was the reason he insisted on keeping Stapleton, the ex-banker around the place, to keep an eye on his finances. She only hoped he and that wife of his could be trusted!

His abrasive tongue licked her hot, swollen labia so slowly… so sensually that she thought she would die of pleasure! For the next glorious minutes, her pain was magically diluted and her worries abated as his tongue became more insistent on reclaiming the fruits. For the first time she became aware that her eyes were so tightly closed that her eyelids ached! In addition, she was panting. As her lips curved into a smile, she felt as if she were drowning in the ecstasy of her Master's attention and arousal zinged its way to her very core as his tongue searched for its deepest prize. He pulled back, laughed softly, and returned to his stool, leaving the strawberry in place. As he poured himself another brandy, it struck her that the last strawberry could be lost inside her forever.

Once again her thoughts trailed away and were swallowed up by the comforting mists of sensual wellbeing. Despite her hours of humiliation and agony, the eroticism of his ministrations was all too much and she was helpless to control the sheer pleasure… forbidden pleasure… that ratcheted up the scale toward climax.

"Master!" she breathed.

But he had not yet given permission for her orgasm and so, once again, she was denied release. She wanted to come… she needed to come! And then she wondered… had he let her bitch-of-a-sister come?

Tyler stood up and casually strode around to the front of the structure. For a few seconds he merely stared down at her, and she could feel his malevolently lustful gaze burning holes in her skull. After the erotic tenderness of the past twenty minutes, his willingness to once again demonstrate his cruelty came as a shock, surprisingly more so since that cruelty stretched beyond the physical. So very gently he stroked the back of her head with one hand while slipping his clenched fist between her pinioned hands. There were clinking sounds that thudded softly against the wood and then he withdrew his hand. Imagining he had placed some kind of devilish device before her, Charlotte opened her eyes.

She gasped and he laughed. For lying between her pinioned hands on the wooden board, so near and yet so far out of her reach… as with the letters from her sister that he had taunted her with months previously but never allowed her to read… was a cluster of glittering, beautiful and obviously very expensive, rings.

"I forgot to mention that I relieved your sister of them when I took delivery of her the other day," he told her in his uncultured tones that had become even rougher with the hoarseness of his lust. "Oh, don't worry, she knows I've got them. It's not as though I'm stealing them!" Again he laughed, then said on a more serious note, "I thought they'd make nice presents for my Ma. You see, by rights she should be living in this place, and would have, too, if the turd who fathered me had married her instead of treating her with contempt and just using her as his bit of rough." It did not seem in the least bit incongruous to him that he had no intention of marrying any of the women he treated with contempt, and far more cruelly than his father had into the bargain! "I guess the rings'll look pretty good with the dresses she wears these days… your dresses, Charlotte, the ones you so kindly donated!

"You'll be pleased to know Siren's coming along a treat. As I said before, her throat clutches a cock and milks it dry. She's going to be the best Pleasuregirl of the lot! Mind you, she played up a bit out in the stable yard, so I had to give her a fucking good thrashing afterward. Still, it'll do her good."

He retook his place behind her and settled himself on the stool once more. He had a few swigs of brandy, then set the glass down again and returned to the remaining strawberry. With his mouth pressed over the entrance to her cavern his tongue snaked around inside, trying to locate the wayward strawberry. He had forced rather too many into her lovely, juicing quim in the first place and the remaining one refused to budge.

Momentarily accepting defeat and with his gaze focussed intently on her peachily-flushed nether lips, he straightened up and reached out distractedly to the table, groping for the half-empty, lead crystal decanter. As his fingers closed around its neck he leaned forward and with dark and calculated delicacy poured brandy down the deep crack between Charlotte's purple-welted buttocks.

"Ooooowww!" Charlotte flinched as the alcohol seeped stingingly inside her anus and instinctively she drew in her stomach muscles.

Placing the decanter back on the table, he turned back to Charlotte and looked along her body, mentally marking every vertebra from the base of her spine to her bowed head. He raised the green goblet in a toast.

"Cheers, Whitby, you lusty old sod! Thanks for teaching me about suffering!" Then he lifted it to his thin lips. With his hazy gaze fixed on the most tractable, most delightful, most charmingly docile girl in his entire stock, he drank in the joy of her suffering. To see a beautiful girl radiant with joy was one pleasure in life, but to watch her writhe in blissful agony or suffer the withering shame of humiliation were pleasures beyond compare, pleasures he no longer had cause to deny himself. He was the master here and could do as he pleased.

The welcome liquid warmed Tyler's throat as he watched Charlotte squirming ineffectually in her bonds. He remembered that her cunt still contained one last strawberry as he ran his hand appreciatively over her welted, bare arse before delivering a thunderous wallop. His brandy-induced smile as her skin reddened served to bite back the joyous laugh that threatened to erupt from his throat as he watched her backside wiggling and her back arching.

"P... please, Master... please..."

He loved the way that, after all this time, the silly bitch still thought her pleas would move him to pity!

"Please!"

"What?" he demanded.

"Please... Master..." she knew she had no right to ask anything of him, that it was his right to punish her for speaking without permission... except she wanted him to punish her! She deserved it! He had punished Siren. And so, just for the sake of it, she blurted, "the strawberry might get stuck!"

"What if it does? Stop your bloody wriggling, bitch! Keep fucking still!"

Nevertheless, he told himself as he considered Charlotte again and plonked the goblet down heavily on the table once more, it would be rewarding to find the bloody strawberry, even though there was no risk of it staying inside and posing a threat to her long-term wellbeing; it would dissolve soon enough, or be expelled by the strength of her muscles. He leaned toward her once more and she felt his warm, intoxicated breath fanning her labia as he told her, "Keep still or I'll never get hold of it!" He clamped his mouth over her lovely quim and inserted his probing tongue. Where was the bloody thing? he wondered idly, then answered his own question… it had probably already dissolved.

He congratulated himself for having chosen to keep the board level, ensuring that Charlotte's cunt was at just the right height as he sat behind her on the stool.

Once again his lips broke contact with her cunt and he withdrew his tongue. Sitting back on the stool, he noticed that between his denim clad legs, a splattered strawberry stained the fine, age-faded needlework seat of the stool. Oh well, he would just have to get one of the domestic staff to clean it.

Outside, the light was beginning to fade as storm clouds gathered. Drizzling rain was now dampening the entire village of Squire's Langley and the "Big House" itself was suddenly doused in heavier rain as the clouds burst. Tyler turned his head to gaze out of the window as the darkness and inclement weather closed in to conceal the entire estate. With one hand resting on Charlotte's rump, he admitted reluctantly that the British weather could indeed be something of a drawback for the club, just as Stapleton had insisted, at least where the outdoor activities were concerned. But whatever the pros and cons, he refused to believe that his plans for The Ramparts would prove to be anything but successful. He would not be defeated! In his mind's eye as he inserted a long, tapering finger inside Charlotte's unbelievably wet cunt, he saw high-stepping ponygirls pulling traps around the estate; not like the other pony carts he had seen, the ones he had ordered were like the traps the gypsies race at places like the Applegate Fair. Luscious girls pulling traps in which they transported paying customers from the Topiary Garden to the tranquillity of the Chinese Garden and beyond what more could a man want? As his thoughts ran on he paid no attention to Charlotte's continuing whines of discomfort but merely rummaged around inside her until he finally located the offending fruit. Finally he hooked the strawberry with his crooked finger.

"Aaargh!"

The enterprise had taken more force than he had anticipated but at last he held the squishy morsel between his fingers. He popped it into his mouth and swirled it around, savouring its girl-sap flavour which mingled quite pleasantly with the brandy.

"How's your cunt now, bitch?" he demanded, his tone betraying none of the light-headedness he was feeling. He rarely allowed himself to get too drunk these days for he found it interfered with his more brutal pastimes, and lessened the enjoyment.

"Empty, Master," she said sweetly. Then mistakenly believing her Master was drunker than he actually was and therefore incapable of as much control as he thought he was, she spoke to him in a way she had not spoken to him for years and added boldly, "it wants your cock, Master, it's waiting for your seed. Fuck me, Master, fuck me now." Warming to her theme and copying her sister's technique she injected a seductive purr into her voice. "We go back a long way, don't we, Master? We know each other well. You know I'll do anything for you. I'll willingly submit to anything. Yet I've never sat beside you at your dinner table or snuggled up beside you while you sleep. Please, Master, I can be so much more to you than a slave, I can be…"

The demonic frown as he drew his heavy, sloping eyebrows together made it perfectly clear that she had made a terrible error of judgement and was enough to check her.

"You're getting above yourself, Charlotte. How dare you speak to me!"

"Forgive me, Master!"

"Too late! Your stupidity's just earned fifty lashes, and that's more than your sister got!" He did not jump to his feet but instead remained seated, groping around for a butt plug he knew he had somewhere. "I was asking after your cunt's condition, not inviting your suggestions." At last his hand brushed against it and his fingers closed around the inflexible object. Straightening up, he dipped the end into his brandy and then, without preamble he shoved it hard into her anus.

"Aaaarghh! Aaaarghh!" Once again tears streamed down her face as the alcohol burned the delicate membranes of her rectum as he rammed the object home.

"Alfred!"

"Yes, Milord?"

"To make sure it's a mistake she'll never repeat, remove the plug every half hour, dip it in brandy and then return it to her arsehole. She's to keep it in until this time tomorrow."

"Yes, Milord."

Not daring to speak again, she knew the best she could hope for was that he would at least release her from her terrible bondage.

"Brace yourself, bitch!"

She knew several terrible, wonderful moments of anticipation as he stationed himself to the best advantage. Her heart took up a frantic beating in her ribcage. There was always pain with a lashing, of course, but there was pleasure too, joy like no other, especially when dealt by the Whipmaster himself! Sometimes it took the form of warmth that spread outward across her body and set her insides quivering with a hunger that only her climax would sate. Yet at other times a slave's pleasure was overshadowed completely by the pain itself as each strike scalded her flesh and imprinted its fire not only on her flesh but deep into her psyche as well. Those were the times when a slave's pleasure... when her pleasure, came entirely from the knowledge that she was the reason for his pleasure and wellbeing. Yet somehow a slave's body reacted totally differently when it was a punishment beating rather than one delivered purely for a master's entertainment; none of the girls derived even the faintest hint of anything akin to happiness, for then there was no comfort in knowing that one was the cause of a master's displeasure.

Swish!

Thwack!

The leather cracked down across her shoulders and she wrenched painfully at the roots of her hair as she instinctively sought to throw her head back in acknowledgement of the sudden pain. And she hadn't . finished her scream when the second lash smacked down and again made her wrench at her hair.

Such was his fury that by the twentieth, savage strike she was screaming her throat raw.

He paused for a few seconds, not to give her any respite but to rest his arm. After all, he had not long ago laid into Siren. When he started again, it was with a new vigour that inscribed horrendously raw lines across her shoulders, down her back and across her backside. Then he started on her thighs. Such was his anger that instead of extracting any enjoyment from her screams he blocked them out. By the fortieth stroke she had screamed herself hoarse. As her fettered body jerked and quivered uncontrollably, she merely snivelled in a most unattractive way.

Without being able to see herself she knew she looked a frightful mess. She only wished she had a hand free to wipe the snot from her nose. How much more must she endure... surely he was done by now!

But still he thrashed her.

She only hoped he was counting.

It was not until he spoke that she realised it was over.

"Tell me again the condition of your cunt!"

"It's... em... empty and w... wet, Master."

"You want a cock, slave?"

"Y... y..." she feared a trap but knew she must answer... "Yes, please, Master."

"Too bad!" He reached across to the remaining strawberries in the crystal bowl and set about filling her empty cunt with a few more luscious fruits. Cramming the last of them inside her so that the last one poked out invitingly from her nether lips, he dipped his head toward her strawberry-filled honey pot once more and, taking the protruding fruit between his lips, used great delicacy to extract it. Even as he savoured its sweetness he regretted that it had not been in far enough to take on her female essence. But if the truth be known, he was beginning to tire of strawberries.

He swept his hair from his eyes with one hand. "Alfred!"

"Yes, Milord?"

"Stand by her head, Alfred."

Alfred took up his post by her bowed head without a word, and Tyler returned his attention to his slave's fruit-stuffed channel. He clamped his mouth over her hole once more and sucked hard enough to extract the fruit. Then he removed it from his mouth and handed it to Alfred.

"Feed the slut." He watched as Alfred positioned the fruit in the centre of his palm before placing it directly by her mouth. "That's been inside your whoring cunt, bitch! Eat it, taste your own juice. Swallow it!"

135

She took it daintily between her lips. It was true, she could taste herself.

"I said fucking eat it!"

When she had complied with his wishes, the process was repeated with another strawberry, and another, until her pussy was empty once more and she had eaten every one from Alfred's gnarled hand.

Tyler eased himself off the stool. He poured yet another brandy before coming to stand beside his manservant. He patted her head.

"Good girl. And for that, you may have a reward. What was it you wanted?"

"Cock, Master."

If she could have raised her head she would have seen the twist to his thin lips.

"Alfred, shaft the bitch while I go and fuck a whore."

"With pleasure, Milord."

He offered the brandy decanter. "Don't forget, every half hour! Return her to her cell and get the Escorts to see to it."

CHAPTER EIGHT

Friday

They had all given their consent in one form or another, and they all knew why they were at The Ramparts. And it was not to play billiards!

Nevertheless, side by side Sparkle and Siren leaned their elbows on the cushioned edge of the billiards table. Naked apart from their collars, with their legs slightly apart their delightful backsides, one olive toned and the other the colour of flaked almonds, stuck out invitingly, at an angle that masked an otherwise marked difference in height.

At the end of the table, a third girl held the cue loosely in her hands. Willowy and pale skinned, Fionola positioned herself to take the shot. It was not exactly a serious game, in the sense that two of the three Pleasuregirls were not entirely sure of the rules. Only Sparkle seemed to know what she was doing, but it was serious fun nonetheless. In any case, it was unauthorised fun for which they could all find themselves in very deep shit indeed!

Fionola relinquished her hold on the cue with one hand and used her middle finger to hook a wayward strand of short, white-blonde hair behind her ear as she furrowed her brow in deep in concentration. All she had to do was pot the black ball to win the game between herself and Sparkle. Letting her hand fall, she held the cue with both hands as before and leaned along the table. With the ease and grace of a cat she climbed up and rested her left knee upon it while her pale right leg dangled, her big toe struggling to retain contact with the carpet. She inhaled deeply and held her breath in concentration, taking the shot mentally.

They were not sure why, but for some reason they had been left unattended after morning ablutions and, following

Siren's lead, the three lovely Pleasuregirls had taken the opportunity to wander around the big house. Still unguarded by mid morning, they had not been able to resist the temptation of slipping into the Members' Games Room to enjoy a rare opportunity to relax together. Besides, Sparkle thought, there was so much ill feeling between them, bubbling away beneath the surface, that perhaps they had all picked up the vibes and felt a girlie bonding session was called for, though perhaps not by licking each other out as their Master would probably demand if he got wind of their growing ill will toward each other. Ever since Siren had arrived, it seemed that the world had been turned upside down. It was all Siren this and Siren that.

Sparkle watched the end of Fionola's cue come within an inch of the ball and then hesitate. What was wrong now, Sparkle thought as she rolled her eyes heavenward, why didn't the silly cow just hit the thing since she obviously had no idea what she doing? She ignored the shouts from outside the open window as Tully decided to mete out a little discipline of his own, to some poor girl.

***

Siren took a sip of the prohibited vodka she had helped herself to, then hissed friendly encouragement. "Come on, Fi, you can do it!" But her dark eyes were not on Fionola's rapt features, the cue in the girl's elegant-fingered hands or the ball, but instead Siren eyed the girl's long legs enviously. At a smidgen over five feet herself, it would take her a damn sight more effort to scramble up on the table… if she ever got the chance to play! Siren told herself as the vodka added fuel to her capricious nature. Not that it really mattered, she thought as she took another swig, except that they would not get many opportunities to unwind without someone watching over them once the bloody club opened!

Outside, screams from the unseen Pleasuregirl spiralled upward and finally filtered through to Siren's fuzzy brain. Someone was being punished, severely by the sound of it.

Shrugging her shoulders, she turned her attention back to the events inside. As things stood, Siren was to play the winner. She hoped it would be Fionola, because even she could see the dozy bitch had got this far through luck and not skill... she was by far the worst player of the three, which at least gave her some hope. But time was marching on... Siren flicked her gaze up toward the wall clock with a mahogany surround - bloody hell! Had they really been playing that long? They could be discovered at any moment! She gave an inward laugh... if she were back in her own surroundings she would probably still be in bed, having spent a long, enjoyable night at one of London's fashionable clubs, in the company of some celebrity or other. And there would be no one to punish her for bad behaviour!

Oh well, if she was going to be punished again... she ran her small hand over her welted bottom and winced as her fingers made contact with a particularly keen bruise... it may as well be for something worthwhile, she reasoned as she knocked back the remains of the neat vodka. She tossed the glass aside carelessly - someone else would pick it up! That's what this place had maids for. She stifled a giggle as she tried to imagine how it must feel for Charlie, as she had always called Charlotte, to have a decent job with a decent wage for all those years and walk freely around the place, only to have it all snatched away from her. Okay, she told herself, Charlie had not lost as much as she had herself, but it must still rankle. Serve the stupid bitch right, she thought unkindly as she remembered all the letters, and gifts too, that she had sent and that had never even been acknowledged. She had no idea, of course, that at Tyler's suggestion Whitby had forbidden her to write letters, a practice that Tyler had vigorously upheld and improved upon when he had taken over. For Tyler had buttonholed anything addressed to Charlotte.

***

At 5' 10" Sparkle was the tallest of the Pleasuregirls and knew she would have no trouble, either climbing on the table or taking the shot. Her former Master had taught her to play billiards years earlier and often bid her play with him when there was no one else around to oblige. That being the case and despite being on the verge of defeat, she was confident of her own ability and knew she had played well, while the blonde haired tart had just been lucky! And the way Fionola was hanging it out… she was bound to miss anyway… they would be discovered long before anyone got the chance to play the bloody crinkle-haired gnome, as she mentally called Siren. She sighed with self-reproach. She had noticed quite a lot of name-calling and spite between them all lately. She was not sure why, all the girls had been happy enough until a few days ago… it had to be Siren's fault! Siren… what was the point of changing her name when they all knew very well who the bitch was? Why was she here, anyway? Sparkle knew she was not the only one who suspected it was all some kind of weird celebrity pastime, something to do when one got bored of the all the glitter and champagne… "I know, I think I'll be a sex slave for a while - I can always go home when I've had enough!" she thought with an inner sneer as she imagined the girl by her side actually speaking the words. After all, it would be so like her, if the tabloids were to be believed. The bitch had tried everything else!

Nevertheless, there was a part of Sparkle that argued as the unknown girl outside screamed in a higher in pitch, that they should all stick together. It really was time to put all the distrust and dislike to bed. Otherwise Tyler might get wind of it and fan the flames to turn it into something more, like those girls… gladiators or something… that her former Master used to like to watch, along with all the other weirdoes who actually paid to see girls physically fighting each other. Not that any of the Pleasuregirls had gone that far… yet… if one discounted the hair-pulling and stuff in the showers.

Sparkle watched as, still holding her breath, Fionola eased the cue right back…

Tyler's angry roar from the doorway shattered the moment.

"What the fuck do you think you're doing?"

Siren and Sparkle spun round instantly. They straightened their backs and took up the accepted pose with their legs apart and hands crossed behind their backs. Siren opened her glossed mouth to speak.

"No, don't answer!" he snapped angrily.

He rubbed his long, thin finger up the side of his nose as he watched Fionola lay down the cue and make to get off the table, then stayed her with another heart-stopping roar.

"Stay where you are!"

Fionola froze and lowered her eyes to the green baize.

Tyler glanced from one to the other of the charming Pleasuregirls, and could not help but give a tight-lipped smile at the sight of the two standing slaves who, despite their sizzling bodies, looked faintly ridiculous when standing upright, side by side.

"Talk about the long and the short of it!" Swallowing the laughter that threatened to dissipate his anger and authority, instead he let rip. "You stupid bitches! You know you shouldn't be in here alone! I'll beat the crap out of you and knock some fucking sense in! I'll whip your sorry arses with nettles …"

In her accustomed position at his side Charlotte, on all fours with her honey-blonde hair trailing on the floor, could not help feeling smug as her beloved Master ranted, threatening all kinds of dire punishments, while she pressed against his leg like some faithful Labrador and hung on his every word.

"You want to play billiards? Okay then! Siren and Sparkle… get up on the table. I want the three of you lined up. Fionola, you get in the middle."

As predicted, Sparkle hoisted herself up with no trouble, but Tyler sighed in exasperation as Siren struggled pathetically.

"Help her!" he ordered, still watching from the doorway as the other two offered their assistance.

Scrambling to obey him, they settled themselves as comfortably as they were able, given the dimensions of the table, in a line along the centre.

"Look at you! See no evil, hear no evil and speak no fucking evil! Anyone'd think you were chaste little virgins." He took out his mobile, flipped it open and took a photograph before slipping it back in his pocket. "There! I'll get someone to put that on the club's website when we've got it up and running. And I'll get it enlarged and printed too. It'll look really good hanging up in here," he said.

He took a few steps toward them, with Charlotte keeping pace at his side. But the sound of crunching glass brought him to a sudden halt. At once the temperature seemed to drop as the atmosphere turned decidedly chilly. Without a word being spoken he lifted his boot and sidestepped. He did not move his head as he lowered his gaze nor speak as Charlotte examined the fragmented glass in horror.

Stupidly, given the extent of her physical suffering, she felt the loss like a wound in the side as she recognised the remains of the finely engraved 16th Century wine glass with which she was so familiar, having handled the delicate, valuable item with loving care many times. And she knew instinctively which one of the girls was responsible for its present condition!

"Okay, which of you sluts was it?" Tyler did not wait for an answer. "No, don't tell me, let me guess. Siren."

Sitting on the billiard table, hugging her knees, Siren fluttered her eyelids prettily and flashed him her sexiest, ball-hardening smile. When that failed to bring about the desired effect, she returned his accusatory look with a defiant stare. Her tone was equally hostile as she answered.

"Yes, Master!"

"Your brain made of shit or something? I'd have thought even you could've grasped that 'no alcohol' means 'no fucking alcohol!' You've earned yourself forty lashes… you'll have them later, when Stapleton's finished with you. Don't look so shocked. He has the right, but just hasn't had time to try out your charms yet! This will be his only opportunity before the Eve of Opening Party tonight. And Siren…?"

"Yes, Master?"

"They're on top of the twenty all three of you sluts have got coming to you! I hope the vodka - it was vodka I assume - was worth it!"

How well he knows her! Charlotte thought miserably as he started walking again, and she crawled beside him, carefully avoiding the razor sharp fragments as he finally approached the table. Sixty lashes? Charlotte only hoped her sister understood why he was so angry. It was not so much the shattering of the valuable antique, Charlotte knew that even if her sister did not, nor that Siren had broken the rule, but that she had pilfered from him. Theft of his property, no matter how trivial, was something Tyler would not tolerate, even though he was not above taking whatever he wanted, no matter who it belonged to!

"On your backs, all of you! Legs in the air, hands behind heads." He waited until they scooted backward and were

143

in the required position, their hands behind heads that rested on the cushioned edge. "That's better." Retrieving the pocketed balls Tyler placed them strategically on the table, then snatched up Fionola's discarded cue. Telling Charlotte, "Stay!" he backed up a few steps while he decided whether to merely hit the stupid sluts with it! He considered the merits of getting them to hold their honey-glazed vaginal lips open and laughed aloud as he imagined the red billiard balls stuffing their cunts the way ball gags so often stuffed their mouths.

He took a few moments to simply drink in the picture before him as wordlessly he focused his attention on the three hairless furrows presented to him

First, his appreciative gaze considered Siren's duplicitous cunt, as deceitful as the rest of her, he sneered. His eyes feasted on her frilly-edged inner lips, which shamelessly protruded from between her engorged outer lips. It was odd how they seemed to interlock and close fast as if repelling boarders, almost daring one to enter. Given her high degree of wantonness, it was not much of a dare since they curled back easily enough with the right incentive -. usually just a pinch of her nipples did it - and revealed the welcoming, voracious hole at last. In any case, he was pleased to be able to offer the club's members something different, to give them the extra interest of her glorious labia minora. Then his gaze travelled up along her raised, olive-toned legs which she helpfully bowed at the knees. Framed between them were a fair portion of her lavish breasts, her extraordinarily beautiful features with dark doe eyes, and at least some of the abundance of her raven-black, corkscrew curls.

There was no doubt in his mind that the stunning girl was his prized possession. Just like on their first meeting when she had been a knock-them-dead eighteen year old, every time he looked at her he felt the need, like a painful burning deep inside… "like indigestion," he mumbled as his straining cock was thwarted in its efforts to escape the tightness of his jeans… to thrash the daylights out of her before screwing her into oblivion.

That had been his intention when he had first met her, all those years ago. But

they both knew he had not raped her… in the event he had not had the opportunity! Instead the youngster had proved to be one hell of a liar and things had turned ugly. Due entirely to her womanly wiles and eyelash-fluttering popularity which had served to validate her mendacity, Tyler had spent a night in police custody, under the watchful eye of PC Liam Durkin.

It was odd how things had turned out - all these years later, not only had Durkin become a close friend but he was most eager to sign up as one of the club's first members.

And now, for better or worse, he had the bitch! He lined up the shot, hit the ball…

"Aaaarghh!" It thumped against Siren's cunt with the force of a ten ton lorry. "You bastard!"

"It's sluts like you…" he watched the gradual darkening of her features as shame and anger mingled, "give whores a bad name. You'd better learn some obedience, Siren, and soon! And show at least some sign of sensuality or I'll have to rethink my whole strategy. God knows how you came to be idolised by millions," he said unkindly while he fought the urge to fuck her senseless. With a smirk he quoted the headlines from memory. " 'Sex Goddess flies to Hollywood,' 'Sizzling-hot and available - sexy vamp dumped by bad boy lover,' 'Stunning star's sex-romp in limo.'"

Laughing, he moved on to Fionola, whose own long, pale, slender legs brushed against Siren's olive ones on one side and Sparkle's equally pale ones on the other. Fionola's cunt lips were sweetly engorged and glistening enticingly. No deceit there, her cunt advertised exactly what it wanted! Directing his gaze between her elegantly bowed legs he took in her the delight of her firmer breasts that cried out for mistreatment.

Once again he took aim.

Fionola cried out as the ball thudded home.

Lastly there was Sparkle, whose long slit - flanked by warmly-beige cunt lips with a hard-to-miss clitoris at their apex - was always inviting. She was an exceptional piece. It was almost possible to believe that her naked breasts with their proud upper swell and large nipples were supported by some invisible underwiring, such was their firmness and high angle of carriage. Tall, elegant and athletic, she was a specimen he was particularly proud of. It was her photograph that graced the pages of the glossy brochure he had had printed months ago to publicise the club's opening. When he had acquired her from her previous owner she had already been trained as a ponygirl so he had had photos taken of her pulling a borrowed cart around the grounds.

Between her up-to-her-neck legs he caught a glimpse of her remarkable tits and her glittering, frosty-blue eyes which had earned the girl her name. Her loose hair was waist long and its glossy shade of red always put him in mind of horse chestnuts, highly polished for the schoolboy game of conkers. In his case soaked in vodka that Tully had stolen.

For the final time he prepared to take the shot.

"Aaaarghh!"

"Very pretty," he hissed as he took in the sight of the red ball expertly lodged against Sparkle's cunt.

One of the girls was whimpering. He was not sure which, some days they all sounded the same, but all three were visibly trembling. And so they should be! he smiled coldly as he set down the cue.

His fingers located the thirteen inch handle of the whip at his side, it was only right and proper that they should be afraid of him. Yet even though they feared him, even though he told them they were nothing more than lumps of slave meat in his eyes, they also trusted him. For each and every one of the Pleasuregirls knew they were safe in his hands and no real harm would ever come to them, for he adored women! It was just that he adored hurting them even more.

Remembering why he had come looking for them in the first place, he flipped open his mobile once more and gave the appropriate instructions to the Escort at the other end.

"Have someone set up a cross in the new Luxor suite. Stapleton's going to try it out for comfort and wants Siren set up ready and waiting, upside down, for his arrival at three this afternoon. And have someone deliver Sparkle to the stables for three thirty. I don't need Fionola until later so have her returned to her cell. But I want her chained and hooded. Give me half an hour, then collect them all from the Members' Games Room." Ending the call, he slipped the mobile back in his pocket.

He was a lucky man, he thought as Charlotte pressed against his denim-clad leg in an attempt to get his attention. Using his boot and more force than necessary since the most compliant of all his slaves would be overjoyed to oblige him, and probably have an orgasm while doing so he thought mockingly, he nudged her aside and told her tersely, "give me room, bitch!" He gripped the tan, kangaroo-hide covered handle of the whip and shook out all nine of its tails, each one a mega-stinging sixteen inches long. Then suddenly changing his mind, he furled it again then crossed the room and made a selection from the whips that were offered for the members' use. Settling on a nasty implement with a long, plaited single lash, he moved to a more pertinent spot for a shot across all three delicious cunts, and braced himself.

"This is going to hurt," he laughed, "and I'm going to enjoy it so much!"

Swish!

Crack!

"Aaaarghh!"

With the sound of leather cracking savagely against flesh and a matched set of three, simultaneous accompanying screams resounding in her ears, Charlotte smiled.

"Thirty-nine to go!" Tyler said as he drew back his arm.

CHAPTER NINE

The dungeon was redolent with the mixed aromas of spunk, sweat, sulphur and female fear as for hours the four men - and the estate manager who had just left the gathering in favour of a quiet pint and his own slave - had drunk, feasted, flogged and fucked their way through a disciplinary session which was a celebration of The Ramparts finally opening its doors the following afternoon. They could have used the opulence of the Members' Lounge or one of the other recently refurbished public rooms. But instead Tyler had elected to hold the party deep underground, in the well equipped dungeon.

Having shunned the electric light with which the dungeon was now fitted in favour of traditional torches, they stood in the flickering light that threw weird and wonderful shadows across the walls and drank in the malevolent atmosphere.

Rhinestones sparkled as they caught the light and the flamboyantly dressed Elvis lowered his empty glass from his Presleyesque curled lips. "Just help myself to a top up," he drawled in a Presley fashion that masked his true, Liverpudlian accent as he made his way over to the trestle table. It had been set up along one wall, beneath the assorted sets of shackles which hung from a number of hooks, and loaded with party food and a fine assortment of alcoholic drinks. Arranged in the centre was a Pleasuregirl crouched low on her knees and elbows, bound hand and foot with her head tucked in, with a flashy arrangement of deep foliage and flowers set up along her back.

The focus of the Eve of Opening party, now that the other three Pleasuregirls who had been such amusing entertainment had been returned to their cells and put to bed, was the attractively and intensely-welted, olive skinned Siren. Her stunning features were hidden under an abundance of long, raven curls that hung down on either side and was plastered to her face. She was close to exhaustion as she lay along the metal-studded sawhorse with her welted, stinging buttocks uppermost and her limbs anchored to the horse's legs, her lavish breasts with their attractively dark areolae hung down on either side. She screamed in pain as Stapleton withdrew his glistening cock from her back passage, overflowing with his semen.

"I could do with a drink!" he laughed as he wiped his prick across her back before turning to yield his place to another.

"Wait!" Tully tossed him a penis-shaped butt plug that was as thick as his wrist and longer than Stapleton's own lengthy cock. Then referring to her as he always had, he said, "Stuff that up the Princess' tight little arse to keep the hole open for later!"

"My! What a beauty!" Stapleton laughed joyously as he examined the plug, then used the spunk seeping from between her buttocks as lubrication. "This'll make her eyes water!" He pushed the bulbous head of the plug against the crinkly skin that had closed tightly over her hole then forced an entry, closed the fingers of one hand around the shaft as if he were holding a tent peg, then using his other fist as a mallet he hammered it home.

The ear-splitting scream that rent the air was the shrillest, loudest of the evening as the poor girl's anal passage was forced to accommodate the inflexible object which was far too large. Her head jerked up and with her eyes screwed up in agony, her open mouth emitted cries and groans which could have been engendered from consuming pleasure or pain.

Whatever the cause, they all agreed she made a very pretty picture indeed as they gathered round for a closer look.

Craning her head round to see her tormentors, Siren tried to raise her upper body from the wicked studs that, thanks to the force of Stapleton's brutal ravishment of her rectum, had dug even harder into her soft, yielding flesh. Her eyes brimmed with water as she fluttered her eyelids prettily.

"Eyes front!" Tyler barked. "And keep them closed or I'll blindfold you!"

Immediately she did as she was bid. Yet still she struggled to raise herself. It was impossible, of course, for the restraints held her fast. Not only that but she felt heavy, restraining hands on her shoulders, forcing her back down as another of the men stepped into Stapleton's place behind her. Even as the diabolical butt plug stretched her wider than she had ever been stretched before, she felt a hot, stiff shaft sink into her unbelievably sore yet still ravenous vagina. How many more times would they fuck her tonight? How many more times would she be forced to swallow their semen? Was it not enough that they had already used Kismet, Crikette and Brandy? Why had she been singled out for such an ordeal? she asked herself as the cock pounded into her and balls battered against her.

"It's going to be a new beginning… " Tyler kept his palm flat on her shoulders and turned his attention from Siren's tear-soaked face toward Elvis and Tully. As Tully continued to thrust wildly into the snivelling Pleasuregirl, his naked chest dripping with sweat, Tyler treated them to an ear to ear grin that was as rare as it was evil-looking, "for all of us!"

"Don't know 'bout 'new start' Ty," Tully panted raggedly. "It's more like old times gone posh. After all, it's still you, me an' some mates sharin' a fucking tart."

The other three men laughed.

"This ain't the first time me an' Elvis have shared one of Ty's birds, is it, Ty?" Tully directed his words at Stapleton, taking no notice of the girl's yelps as his fingers dug deep into her velvety flesh, making little white marks. As if to prove to Stapleton that it was he who was the outsider here and not the gypsies, Tully was keen to reminisce as he drove frenziedly in and out. "Sometimes, Ty'd invite me and some of the lads along on one of his 'dates.' You should've seen us!" His words came out in gasps as he momentarily concentrated his efforts on the girl, his lustful recollections fuelling his ardour. "We'd all… go out… watch Ty do the… business with some local babe… then…" his grunts became more animalistic and his thrusts more brutal as he watched Tyler side-step.

Giving no thought to the aching of her limbs, Tyler continued to hold her down while his friend, who along with Tully had abducted her a few days ago, took his place. While Tully brutally battered her insides, Elvis grabbed her chin with one hand and fed his cock half way down her throat with the other. As one man rammed his penis up her petal-fringed vagina and the other rammed his down her windpipe, she could almost believe their two helms would meet somewhere in her chest. And all the while, master Tully kept panting his way through his story.

"An' then Ty'd say 'here, you have a go!' and pass… the bitch across… to me. An' after I'd done with her… I'd pass her on to one of the others…"

Pain lit up her rectum anew as someone began plunging the plug in and out. She gagged as she tried to scream against the iron rod in her throat. The hands were removed from her shoulders as instead a leather strap cracked across her lower back once… twice… three times before it was laid against her trim waist before being pulled down either side, forcing her belly down onto the spiteful studs, and buckled beneath the saw horse. Then hands seized her breasts from below and she felt something cold, like steel, slip over each one, and then the steel seemed to tighten, squeezing her already redly-raw, whip-scored breasts tighter, tighter, tighter… and then pain shot through her nipples as they were clamped. The chain which joined the clamps together was unclipped from one clamp, pulled tautly beneath the crossbar of the studded saw horse on which she was restrained and then re-fastened, making it impossible to raise her upper torso even a fraction, just as the strap across her middle held her down against the studs.

Tully was still talking. "And we'd keep doin' that… until we'd had… our… fill. Ah man, they were good days!"

"Back then," standing upright once more Tyler took up the story, "once I'd got a girl all tied up and helpless, I just thought the bitch was ripe for a fuck or a blow-job. There's no doubt I got off on her vulnerability. In the end it was just a case of fuck 'em and forget 'em. It never occurred to me to flog them! I have Whitby to thank for that."

Tully finally reached his climax and shot his spend deep into her tight, cock-crushing, clutching channel. He pulled out of the thoroughly used and quite helpless girl and wiped himself clean, just as Stapleton had done, on her backside, then stepped back and retrieved his drink from where he had left it on the rack that took up the area of the floor behind him.

"I'd set her free afterwards, tell her, 'keep your fucking mouth shut, bitch, or I'll come looking for you!' and that was that." Tyler finished as he took a swig of brandy.

"Then what?" Stapleton wanted to know as he walked across to the trestle table and refilled his glass, then leaned across to the flower arrangement and idly mauled the girl's breasts as he took a slug.

"Then I'd make for the nearest watering hole or share a few cans back at the encampment." Tyler wiped the back of his hand across his mouth.

"An' that's all that's changed!" Tully said. "He used to drink lager, now it's all brandy, whiskey and champagne!"

"Sometimes together!" Elvis drawled.

Laughter echoed around the dungeon as Elvis continued to fuck Siren's lovely mouth.

Although Stapleton would never fully approve of Tyler's gypsy cohorts, he thought as he made his way back over to the group, and would never come to terms with their rough manners and way of speaking, he rather admired their camaraderie. Of course, he had little in common with any of them, he told himself. For one thing he was older - could give them all twenty-five years or so, he imagined. Heavy-jowled with a multi-lined forehead, Stapleton had an abundance of sandy hair despite his middle-age. Always a conservative dresser, he was rarely seen without a collar and tie, a look that owed as much to his former banking career as his upbringing. But the upbringing of these men had been a million miles from his own, and both Tyler and Tully seemed to live in jeans. He was pleased to note that Tyler had at least swapped the grimy, fake-designer labels for the more acceptable authentic Armani jeans of late.

Of the three friends Stapleton found Tully the least likeable. In fact, he was one of the most unsavoury men it had ever been his misfortune to meet. It was his U tattooed. finger that Tully was currently using to poke around in his ringed ear.

Elvis, on the other hand was nothing if not extraordinary, though Stapleton found the 24/7 impersonation rather taxing. It was an odd experience, Stapleton thought, watching the King extract his cock and spurt a pint and a half of thick, white jism over the girl's stunningly-beautiful but make-up smeared face.

Much to Stapleton's surprise, he had himself become Tyler's confidant rather than either of his friends. It was a role that he had initially taken on with some reservation having been slow to admit, even to himself, that there were qualities about Tyler that he found quite acceptable. It had helped that Tyler had recognised his, Stapleton's, talents!

Over the years he had cultivated many businessmen, councillors and the like, and was fortunate in having many contacts which Tyler found useful. And so, as Tyler's reluctant supporter in this business venture, he had been engaged in a senior position regarding finances and the general running of the club. In that capacity he had accompanied Tyler on a four day trip on Tyler's narrowboat, ostensibly to meet with a boat builder but in actual fact a slave-buying exercise which had left him shocked at the squalid conditions in which the girls were kept in a warehouse, though his wife, Lilith, would have been more than satisfied, he mused. He had been even more surprised to find that once the girls had been cleaned up and delivered to The Ramparts, they were actually some of the horniest of all the Pleasuregirls.

Since the trip, which he realised now had actually been to give Tyler the opportunity to spend time alone on his boat with the little tramp before him, his views toward Tyler had taken on a new slant. For one thing, he was a most generous employer! He had given Stapleton his own sizeable office, as well as a free hand regarding furnishings, and had found him a most agreeable young secretary with submissive experience.

He had actually grown to like the man with the clear, deep blue eyes and thin lips, and was proud to be considered a friend. For with that friendship, he realised, came a loyalty such as he had never known before, and he only hoped he could keep up his side of the bargain on that score! But while Tyler treated his friends almost kindly and certainly generously, Stapleton was also aware that he was not a man to cross. It would not just be Tyler that one took on as an enemy but his whole gypsy clan!

As a frequent visitor to the house over many years, Stapleton probably knew the house and its history better than Tyler himself. He was not completely convinced that all the renovations had been necessary but on the whole he considered Tyler had done a good job. At one time, an altogether more sinister building had stood on the same spot and now at last the lingering stench of evil, evil that had nothing to do with debauchery, had been eradicated. However, the air of lust-engendered malice remained. Thankfully, Tyler had not destroyed the house's character and one could still tell on entering the building that it was well acquainted with the pleasures of the flesh. That part of its history went back further than anyone could remember.

The dungeon in which they were gathered for the night's entertainment, maybe even the cells, had long ago been used for the sexual entertainment of the wealthy and was part of local legend. It was believed that long before evil had taken hold and made use of its underground chambers, a castle had stood on the site and some said its ruins still existed if only one knew where to look.

Tully suddenly ripped out the oversized butt plug and produced a scream shrill enough to shatter the chandeliers upstairs. Laughing, he replaced it with a brutal finger which he plunged it in and out.

Standing in front of her, Tyler pulled back his foreskin and stopped her mouth with his cock, filling it to capacity as the long, thick column slid down the throat that his friend had just vacated.

As one, the men turned their heads toward the sound as the heavy door creaked open.

"Yo!" Tully yelled as he watched the new arrival enter and worked his finger in and out even more vigorously.

"Lordy, Lordy!" Elvis drawled. "Better late than never."

Stapleton swallowed his mouthful of Scotch and smiled. "So, you decided to come after all!"

Tyler's expression turned positively stony as Stapleton's thin, hard-faced and black haired wife took a couple of paces inside. An Escort outside in the passageway closed the door soundlessly as Lilith click-clicked her way across the flags to the trestle table before joining the men, with the sound of Siren's pathetic whimpering as a backdrop.

Lilith plucked up a glass and filled it with champagne. With a cursory look at the flower arrangement, she slapped the girl's rump. Then, with all eyes on her, she took up a position beside her husband as they paid little attention to Siren who they abused in their midst.

"Glad you could join us, Lilith," Tyler lied as he continued to make use of the former singer's throat. Just because he had employed Lilith as the sluts' training Mistress didn't mean he had to like the woman, he thought testily. He had only issued the invitation because he had invited Stapleton. He wondered at the wisdom of employing the husband and wife team, but it was too late now. Besides, he needed Stapleton's expertise. And he knew from years of watching the woman with her whip in full swing that she was, no matter how much he would like to believe otherwise, just the kind of person he needed to break in new girls and keep the others in line. After all, he had done his homework and visited a few SM establishments around the country before setting the wheels in motion to open his own club, and had discovered that the finest among them seemed to have a dominatrix on hand.

At the heart of the group, Siren groaned in pain and humiliation... and the need to be noticed. She was used to being the star attraction and, whatever she did, was determined to put on a good show. But nobody paid her any attention as, still fucking her face, Tyler addressed the company.

"Now that we're all here..."

"Except for that ponygirl trainer," Lilith observed,

"Here y'are, Lilith old girl!" Tully withdrew his finger and offered his place to the woman.

157

Declining, she merely stood beside the girl and, reaching out her hand, she spitefully plucked at her heated and painfully striped buttock-flesh. Then, holding Siren's soft flesh between her finger and thumb, Lilith mercilessly continued to pinch and twist it. When Siren cried out in response Lilith gave it a couple of resounding slaps that set the girl snivelling for the umpteenth time that night.

"Adria wanted t'spend the night with one of her charges," Tully supplied.

"I bet she did!" Lilith said nastily.

"Wouldn't mind meself!" Tully laughed. "She said somethin' 'bout one of 'em bein' jumpy again and not settlin' down. Wants a bit of soothin', she said. She reckoned she was goin' to let her sleep in one of the stalls so she gets good an' used to it."

"Okay!" Tyler snapped suddenly. "She knows best! I want them all fit for use tomorrow and Adria's paid to see to it! If she thinks the bitch will sleep better in a stall than a cell then so be it." With his cock still buried up to the hilt inside the luscious Pleasuregirl's mouth, he paid no attention to her gagging as he leaned back, swigged his brandy and raked the fingers of his other hand impatiently through his hair. He sighed heavily then continued with his little speech.

"The Grand Opening tomorrow will mark this place out as one of the best ... the best... SM clubs around." Still ignoring the delightful girl's distress, he reached across her and raised his almost empty glass over her defiled, young body. "And it's all thanks to Whitby! Cheers, you old lecher!"

The assembled group raised their glasses also. "To Whitby!"

They drank and then Tyler finally allowed himself to spend and the company enjoyed the sight of abused celebrity in their midst choking and spluttering on the repeated spurts of thick spunk. Then, finished with Siren for the time being, the group made its way across to the table and turned their attention to the veritable banquet that the kitchen slaves had provided.

While the girl beneath the flower arrangement groaned under the sheer weight of the ostentatious affair, Siren whimpered pitifully in discomfort. Her back burned, her restraints cut ridges into her flesh and the metal studs gouged craters in her belly. Not only that, but no one was paying her any attention at all!

Lilith and her husband stood apart from the gypsies who stood laughing together, eating and washing everything down with copious amounts of alcohol.

"Remember that time you had a run-in with the gamekeeper, Ty?" Tully said as he crammed his mouth and refilled his glass.

"The way I remember it," Elvis put in, "was that you had a run-in with the guy every time we were in the area! I bet he never thought you'd be eating estate food legitimately."

"Don't mention anything to do with 'legitimacy' when Ty's around!" Tully added.

When their laughter had died down, Tyler said, "You mean Driscoll, that was his name! I gave him a choice - swallow your pride and work for me or get the fuck out of my life! He went!"

There was more laughter. Despite wanting to share in the team spirit, Stapleton stood with his wife a little way apart from the other three men. Even though Lilith seemed to lighten up and chatted to him quite amiably about their own slave, who Lilith had left alone that evening tied down on their four-poster with pegs on her breasts, while she came along to the party, Stapleton could not help thinking that she was putting on one of her little acts. He had known for a couple of days that she was up to something but try as he might he could not put his finger on what it was. Donning his "well, fancy that!" expression as his wife told him about one of her training sessions, he phased out her voice and tuned in instead to Siren's continued whimpering. After a few minutes his wife put down her glass and click-clicked back across the room. He watched her buttocks swaying beneath her long, sleek black gown and smiled… she still had what it took! He turned and joined the other men.

Siren tensed as she heard Lilith's footsteps approaching. Since her arrival a few days ago, she had become well acquainted with the bitch and, having already been the recipient of the deliciously thrilling but equally crushing mistreatment for so many hours, she was in grave discomfort; the thought of being left at Mistress Lilith's mercy filled her with terror. But then she heard other footsteps and realised that one of the men was walking behind the woman.

CHAPTER TEN

Siren's sensational body was racked by conflicting feelings of erotic delight as all manner of tingles and quivers assailed her, and agony as all manner of throbs, twinges and raging heat assaulted her. Her restricted and clamped breasts dangled down on either side of the sawhorse and the studded bar along which she was still restrained dug painfully into her belly as well as bruisingly hard against her pubic and breast bones.

Lilith stopped behind her, as did her male companion.

The girl raised her head again and tried to crane it around enough to see who it was but it was impossible. Then she felt a finger… a man's finger… pressing against the star of her anus and tensed. Please, please, not up there again! she begged silently. Besides, she had already received harsh "punishment" and, for all she knew, she thought dismally as the insistent finger worked its way inside, there were still several hours of "partying" ahead of her! Much more and she knew she would be too exhausted to take part in the Grand Opening itself! But it seemed that that was not a consideration as far as her tormentors were concerned.

As the finger worked past her sphincters and deep into her rectum, she tried to keep from howling, because that was what they wanted, of course! They wanted to cause her pain, to make her scream, to humiliate her. As if she had not been humiliated enough already! But, the worst of it was, she wanted them to! And what she wanted most of all, even as the forceful, thick finger drove in and then pulled out of her, before driving in again and pulling out of her, was to be used again and again… she wanted to be the most exciting Pleasuregirl and best ponygirl in the universe… as long as that would please her bastard of a Master!

But it was with a heavy heart as the hard, cruel finger continued its violation of her back passage that she wondered if what the two dominatrices had said was true. For Mistress Lilith had drummed into her that she was not at all what the punters would want! She may indeed have been famous but here she was just another slut… a slut whose short stature would be an unforgivable hindrance for she could not be arranged elegantly on the equipment that had been designed and constructed made with a normal-sized woman in mind! And she realised now that probably the only reason Tyler had chosen her as the party's main source of entertainment was because he needed all the other… taller… Pleasuregirls to be bright eyed and bushy tailed for the big event!

And not only that, but the ponygirl trainer had been equally emphatic when she had pointed out that Siren would never make the grade as a ponygirl - she was far too short and feeble!

As much as she had looked forward to playing her part, Siren was beginning to believe that she would have no role in the afternoon's attractions. Not only was she a liability as far as height was concerned, but seeing as she was famous to boot, she would never be allowed to be seen in public. So if that was the case, why was she not allowed to join in the merrymaking or partake of the sumptuous party food the kitchen slaves had provided? They had not even let her have a drink even though her throat was parched from having screamed herself hoarse. Only master Elvis had shown her any consideration and had once wiped her lips with water.

She had been flogged with whips, canes, riding crops and paddles. Throughout the night her nipples had been repeatedly clamped and unclamped, and the unclamping was far worse than the clamping itself as the blood flowed back into ravaged nipples. And during their partying, never once had she been gagged for the men enjoyed her cries and whines far too much for that! Naturally, she had given them a little extra on that score! They wanted whines so she had whined for England. Throughout the night her pleasure had not been a consideration, though Master Stapleton had commented that in his opinion, her screams were not entirely from pain.

And it was true, she had orgasmed, squirted too… and more than once! Though her pain was the major feature… that was her purpose in being there after all… she had known delirious happiness at various points throughout the evening. But now she was just too exhausted and needed to sleep… preferably until lunch time at least. She had been thankful for the short respite they had allowed her but it seemed that now, as the finger was withdrawn for the last time and they began to unfasten all her bonds and the blood pounded into her nipples, she was to be moved yet again. Ever since the party began she had found herself shifted around, alternately arranged on the rack, one of two St. Andrew's Crosses, draped across trestles of varying heights, restrained by shackles and spreader bars, suspended by her ankles and chained to the wall by the metal fixings of her slave collar.

"I meant to ask, Morrison," Master Stapleton said as he and her Master sat her upright, paying no heed to her pain as she sat astride the bar and giving no thought to the effect on her tenderised nether regions, "what made you want this one so much?"

As together they scooped her up, Tyler taking her under her arms and Stapleton with his hands gripping her thighs, Tyler quickly ran through the story, as if she were not there to contradict, which she dare not of course. They carried her across to the other side of the dungeon again and he ended with, "So I just thought we should give the punters something special."

As she found herself dumped unceremoniously in a sort of chair, even the joy of knowing she was something special in his eyes gave her no comfort as her welted body made contact with the metal framework and she gave a pained bleat.

Apropos of nothing, Tully said suddenly, "I really hope it all goes well for you, man."

Without any upholstery at all, if the chair had been fitted with a comfortable, black padded seat she could have mistaken it for a Dentist's chair for it was about the same size and as she was about to find out, it possessed the same mechanism which allowed it to be raised or lowered.

"Not just t'day but the whole club thing - but yer know I've still got my doubts, Ty. What with all them other clubs, like that one in Berkshire and especially that other one over at Langley Feldon, what with it being so close an' all…"

"Don't worry, Tul. It's all going to work out just fine."

Through her own misery, Siren saw the smug look that crossed Mistress Lilith's face. And for one dreadful moment, she thought the woman was going to say something nasty and concerned for Tyler, she turned her own big, doe eyes toward him. But Lilith did not. Instead she stalked off across to the table as her Master continued.

"Don't forget, we've got the biggest attraction of all! When word gets out that we've got…"

Tully laugh cut him off. "So it's the 'Royal we' now!"

Tyler started again somewhat impatiently. "When people know that we've got the famous Chelsi Laird for a Pleasuregirl…"

Siren could not help the little smirk of her own. There! she thought as she looked across at Lilith, stick that where the sun don't shine, supercilious old tart!

"We'll be arrested!" Tully pointed out.

Working together, Stapleton and Tyler re-arranged her

so she was almost, but not quite horizontal, with her head back and supported by a couple of the metal struts which made up the contraption and dug terribly into her softly pliant and sweetly abused little body. Then, with a gentleness that was so out of character it was frightening, Tyler re-arranged her chaotic, black hair so that it framed her dirty face and kissed her olive-toned shoulders.

As the others made their way back to the trestle table, Tyler commanded tersely, "Put your feet on the rest." When she had complied, Stapleton drew her legs apart and they used her ankle restraints to fasten her feet in position. Tyler yanked her slender arms back over her head and joined her wrist restraints together, paying no attention to her delicate, small fingers which she fluttered so prettily in a failed attempt to entice him to make exclusive use of her. Meanwhile, Stapleton bent down to reach for the chain attached to the bottom of the chair and drew it up and attaching it to her wrists. Lastly, Tyler raised the chair a couple of feet then locked it in place before giving her another short respite while the two men joined the others at the table.

Neglecting her for the time being, they roughly pulled the flower arrangement apart and brutally, one after the other, ravished the girl among the wreckage.

Siren closed her eyes to try and nab even a few moments precious sleep, having discovered over the years that sleep was the best remedy when there was no vodka.

But it was only a short while before she heard their footsteps echo around her again. Keeping her eyes closed and with the faintest of smiles, she braced herself for another round of life-giving attention and sweet maltreatment.

For the rest of the night, the small company used her in the most shameful ways without compunction. And that night it was Lilith's cane which struck most cruelly, not because her skill was any greater but simply because she was angry, though no one seemed to understand the root of her ire. And although the chair was undoubtedly uncomfortable for the wretched girl secured to it, it was immensely practical for those using her because the lack of padding enabled them to reach any part of her anatomy virtually unhindered from almost any angle, even from underneath.

**

The dungeon was in total darkness for the torches had gone out after everyone had finally retired for a few hours of much needed sleep. Despite the unbelievable pain from her abundant bruises and skin-abrasing welts, for Siren sleep had come at once for although she had felt utterly wretched she had been strangely at peace. The other girl had been returned to her cell, and yet Siren did not miss her company, nor that of Crikette who had the cell next to hers and who had shown her nothing but kindness since her arrival. Kindness was not a thing to be taken lightly, for it was not a plentiful commodity at The Ramparts.

And so, encrusted with dried semen and still lying on the metal framed chair with her restraints in place, she slept through the short, dark hours. She slept soundly until above ground the summer dawn broke.

**

Saturday

It was early morning and already The Ramparts was in uproar. Siren had been collected from the dungeon and the Pleasuregirls unchained early and escorted to the cavernous ablutions chamber.

They shrieked and trilled excitedly as the nervous tension of the past few weeks was allowed an outlet at last. They were watched over by the two burly Escorts who stood guard over them, standing either side of the heavy, iron-studded door of the ablutions chamber with whips hanging from their belts. But for once their strict orders were to let the luscious girls have their fun and get it out of their system so as not to ruin the afternoon. And so they stood silently with arms folded and cocks stiffening, as the Pleasuregirls dived in and out of the showers, ducked each other beneath the bubbly water of the old water storage tank that served as their bath and turned the water hoses upon each other.

"No, bigger than that, Crikette!" Siren cried excitedly as Crikette and Sparkle coiled two long handled whips, taken from the rack hanging on the wall, and made two large circles from them. "Here, use these," she said, handing them clips taken from the shelf above the rack. All the girls gathered round as they fastened the clips over the whips to stop them unwinding.

Secreted in the next chamber, unobserved, Tyler viewed them through a one way glass window. With his feet crossed and resting on Charlotte he sipped the hot coffee from a mug cupped in his hands as, under threat of real punishment if they got out of hand, the naked, sweating sex slaves squabbled and giggled as they skidded on the wet floor, their attention focussed on their impromptu game of netball, with no thought of how any injuries they picked up that morning would adversely affect the afternoon's events. Nor did they consider their Master's pleasure or even his long-held dreams regarding the club as for once they were permitted to let off steam.

Having organised themselves into two teams of seven, they used one of the training balls purloined from Mistress Lilith's locked cupboard. And Tyler could only speculate which of his slaves had a past more dishonest than his own and wondered, would he be taking on more trouble than it was worth with Perry's girls? Someone had rammed the whip handles into air vents, one at each end of the room, so they stuck out far enough from the wall for the coiled lashes to serve as nets.

Tackling each other with the riotous indiscipline of unmannerly schoolgirls they squealed and cursed, tearing at each other's welted skin. Breasts bounced in glistening abandon as the girls jumped for goal and shoved each other aside.

"No, Crikette! You're playing Wing Attack not Goal Attack! To me, Saxon, to me!"

As Siren, the shortest and most luscious of all the girls, yelled out instructions Tyler watched and listened with amusement and feelings of pride. Against all the odds and as he had known she would, she had bounced back more vibrant than ever after the previous night's ordeal.

"To me, Sparkle!"

"Shut the fuck up!"

"Get off me, Pixie!"

"Siren! Siren!"

What a bossy-britches she had turned out to be. It was amazing how well she had settled in, he thought happily, . given that she had been a slave just a matter of days. Before that... ah, before that! he smiled... she had been a spoilt, hard-living, celebrity with a bank balance of star quality. Naturally, he would get her to sign everything over to him. In the meantime he watched the pushing and shoving as the girls grabbed handfuls of hair or tit, fell down, slid across the floor and crashed into the wall. One girl slid right across to the showers where a couple were locked in a sweet and horny embrace, each girl with her hand deep in the other girl's cunt. A "schoolyard battle" broke out between the three and the Escorts had to move in to separate them.

That was when Tyler had the men call a halt to the proceedings and the girls were commanded to get on with

168

bathing and perfuming themselves. And then there was their hair to be washed and dried. Later they would be oiled to give them an attractive sheen for the big event.

But still the squabbling and giggling did not abate and afterwards, when they were returned to their cells where they dried and styled their hair with the cheap hairdryers their Master had provided them with, they shouted from cell to cell while they preened in front of paperback-sized mirrors. Using the cheap range of toiletries and cosmetics that were provided for them, they took extra care with their appearance, for each girl wanted to outdo the other and catch her Master's eye.

***

While inside the house the chaos seemed relatively organised and the domestic slaves worked in a happy though uncommonly noisy atmosphere, outside in the grounds it was another matter. While the temporary structures for the entertainment had been built and put in place over a period of time, the marquees that should have been erected on Thursday had only just turned up. Tyler made his way across the lawns to oversee the operation only to find he was superfluous to requirements, for a furious Stapleton already had the job well in hand.

Deciding it was best to leave his associate to it, Tyler decided to look in on the stables and see how Mistress Adria was getting on with the ponygirls. Although there were only to be three ponies actually pulling the traps that day, to add to the glamour Tyler had decreed that several of the other Pleasuregirls were to wear the regalia. When he arrived at the pony stable it was to find there were already several Pleasuregirls in the stalls in various states of readiness. With only one groom to help - one of Perry's girls who had shown no aptitude as a maid but seemed genuinely interested in the ponygirls - Tyler knew he was

169

asking a lot of the lovely Adria. So far the dark-eyed gypsy had proved to be a popular member of the workforce, with everyone except Stapleton's witch-of-a-wife, Lilith.

As he entered, Adria had just taken delivery of Fionola, and Snick was despatched to fetch the black girl who Tyler had named Dusk. Pixie, one of the three chosen for traps demonstration, he noticed, was already in her stall, and Sparkle was currently being attended to. He smiled inwardly as he recalled how Adria had intended spending the night with one of them, and his darting gaze sought evidence of which one.

"How's it going?" he asked.

"If they settle down, they'll be okay." Adria went into Sparkle's stall and Tyler followed. "But the last few days have been hell, Ty. They've been so skittish it's been a fucking nightmare doing anything with them!"

Lustfully eyeing the tallest of the ponygirls Tyler simply nodded. He watched Adria run her hands over Sparkle's juicy, unusually high-seated breasts which blossomed proudly from an arrangement of black straps that fitted like a cupless bra. She called across to the young groom, who was taking delivery of Saxon.

"Tighten all the tit straps. There's far too much slack!" having censured the girl she set about tightening Sparkle's.

That done, she delivered a sharp, backhanded slap to Sparkle's right breast. As she and Tyler watched the flush of red appear, she told him, "what she really needs is a good caning across them to bring out the best in her. But tough shit! If I thrash them too early she'll need more later… she's such a pain slut that I'll be stuck here caning her all day and we'll never get her outside!" To compensate, she slapped her other breast.

At once Sparkle began to toss her head, disturbing her long, chestnut hair. She pawed the ground with her naked foot and whinnied prettily.

"Enough!" Adria snapped. "Settle down or I'll have you returned to your cell for the whole day and you'll miss all the fun." Again she called across to the groom. "She needs something to keep her going until I cane her, so fit her plug first." With that, Adria and Tyler left the sweet-scented stable to stand outside.

Adria was an attractive woman about medium height with shapely hips, slim waist and with breasts that were a good handful for any man. She was wearing the uniform of her own choosing, as impractical and delightful as those Tyler had issued the maids with. She looked a million dollars in the black bustier beneath the bright red, fitted jacket with a peplum which flared over her hips, and a black belt. The black Lycra "jodhpurs" were open crotch, which had been Tyler's only demand concerning her various uniforms. After all, she might be a Mistress and a paid employee rather than a slave, but she was still a woman and must therefore accept male superiority and offer herself freely when required. They stretched tightly over her swaying bottom when she walked and tucked into her knee high black boots with their high, narrow spiked heels, and Tyler was sure he would not be the only man to have the hots for her that day.

"Give it your best shot, Ria. I want these ponies to be the best to be seen anywhere," he told her, knowing full well that she had everything well in hand. It was clear his presence was not needed there, either!

As he left the stable yard, he waved across to the head groom of the real horses and went back to the house to shower.

CHAPTER ELEVEN

Sparkle tingled all over. She could hardly believe the day was here at last! Resplendent in full ponygirl regalia and bridle, she was made even taller than her 5' 10" by her mile high turquoise stilettos that click clicked across the stable yard as she followed Mistress Adria on an equine, blue nylon lead rope attached to her collar.

She was in high spirits and her insides were aquiver. Naturally she was also a little apprehensive, for she knew the importance of the occasion and did not want to put a step wrong... this was the day that she and all the other girls had been looking forward to for so long, their excitement mounting for weeks.

"Keep up!"

Adria, having changed into white jodhpurs and blouse with black waspie and boots, tugged on the rope and led her past the pony stables block and past the block for the real horses, where the head groom leaned nonchalantly against the outside wall and made lewd comments to the Mistress who returned them with a filthy suggestion of her · own. Sparkle felt the heat of embarrassment at the remark and she was blushing as they headed for the Foot Arch between the end of the stable block and the garages along the other wall. Adria gave another, unnecessary yank on the rope.

"You don't want to keep your public waiting!"

Sparkle's heart leapt. Yes, she realised as they turned right and walked along the back of the great house, the South side and away from the course that had been laid out for the pony events, people really were coming to see her, for it was her photo, she reminded herself, in the brochure! And she knew she looked every bit as sexy today as she had on that freezing day back in February when the photographer had taken the pictures.

On her right as they continued on were some of the marquees and attractions. But there was no time for the ponygirl to take in the sights because Mistress Adria was leading her toward the lawns along the East side where guests were already assembling to line the specially laid out processional route.

Adria turned and led her across the grass. The three girls designated for the pony driving demonstration would first be taken along the same processional route, Sparkle leading with Adria, and the other two accompanied by Escorts. The Escorts had all been issued with smart dark suits. The idea was that they would be followed along by the other ponies, and lastly by those of the naked Pleasuregirls who were not needed for the attractions, and would instead take their places at the sides among the guests so that when their Master walked along it after them, they could be pushed forward for him to whip as he passed. It had been planned and rehearsed over several days, Escorts taking the place of their Master while he had been away on his trip. Later, Sparkle and the other two would be brought back to the area designated for the carting.

It was mid afternoon and the sun beat down upon her pale flesh that Tyler said was the colour of flaked almonds. Already there were more guests than she had imagined. And as she high-stepped along the processional route with her heels catching in the grass, she knew that the presence of the long, thick column of the butt plug buried inside her was betrayed by the three-finger-thick, four inch long black shank, an inflexible object which reared upward from between her fleshy buttocks, making them appear even paler than they actually were. Its upward curve ensured that the long tail, fixed to the top of the shank and made of real horsehair, remained at an aesthetically pleasing angle and looked surprisingly natural, given that it was bright turquoise.

After the initial shock and pain of the plug's brutal intrusion into her insides early that morning, the nauseous and totally unfounded fear of her body rejecting it had taken over. But, of course, there was no risk of the combined weight of the shank and tail pulling it out, or her muscles rejecting it, since she wore a leather-strapped harness to hold it in place. The plug-end of the device was inserted through a metal ring and into her anal passage and the flared end of the shank nestled over her bottom hole. The ring was also the junction for the arrangement of straps which framed her bottom in a most appealing way. Other straps snugly edged her smooth, hairless pussy and fitted in the creases of her thighs, over which others passed. One central strap at the front extended upward to where rings joined it to others that formed the bra arrangement which Adria had tightened that morning. Her lovely breasts blossomed beautifully from their frame but it gave little support, and the shoulder straps biting into her flesh made it uncomfortable to wear though the effect was very fetching. It buckled at the back where a final, central strap joined the upper part of the harness to the top of the tail-ring. Although common sense told her there was no way the plug could fall out in front of the well-heeled men and women, the way the infernal thing moved inside convinced her otherwise and so, as she made her way along the route, where guests gasped and applauded at the sight of her, she brought anal muscles into play, trusting in them rather than relying on mere straps of leather. She almost wished that mistress had activated the alternative method of keeping it in!

Although the harness was not strictly necessary since the plug was also fitted with its own, fiendish devices to keep it in place which could be activated by a switch at the plug's base if so desired, Mistress Adria had explained to them all that the harness was a piece of kit that a lot of people found sexy in its own right. In Sparkle's case it was most effective for the black leather emphasised greatly the paleness of her skin. But those of the ponies who were, for that day at least, what Adria called "eye candy only" and paraded around, the leather harnesses were replaced by delicate, gold-coloured chains. However, they all wore the gauntlets that Sparkle, Saxon and Pixie wore, and which buckled all the way up. Running in straight lines along their entire length were two rows of studs, one on each side of the buckles. A set of two large silver rings, like those on her collar, were located at her elbows and wrists, and a larger set, also at her wrists currently joined her hands behind her back.

At that point none of the ponies wore bridles though Sparkle and the other demonstration ponies would have theirs fitted when they were finally put to work. But given her height and high heels that brought her to over six feet, it was the plumes, genuine ostrich feathers about twenty-five inches long and dyed to match the tail, that gave Sparkle the most staggering, majestic appearance of all the girls. And her close-fitting skull cap which so perfectly matched the striking, tawny-red of her chestnut hair that it was not visible at close range, made it appear as if the waving, ceremonial plumes sprouting from its centre were an integral part of the lovely girl's head.

The look was completed by tinkling bells swaying gently from her enticing, bouncing breasts. Enamelled to match her ceremonial adornments, they were prevented from falling off by special clamps to which they were fixed.

Her hair was fashioned into one long plait hanging between her shoulders and almost to her waist. She possessed fine, chiselled features which were expertly made up. Her lips were painted a deep claret shade and then glossed. Her eyebrows were freshly shaped, and her eyelids dusted with reddish-brown shadow. Her lovely eyes, which some said had given her her name, were grey with a hint of glittering, frosty blue and on that day they were made up with dark mascara.

She was not given time to watch the procession and, unlike the ordinary Pleasuregirls, could not wait in line to be whipped by their Master. Instead, as soon as she reached the end of the route, mistress turned her back the way they had come. On her return journey past the back of the house, Adria led her across the grass toward the pony carting area. It was then she caught sight of her Master coming out of the French Windows of the Members' Bar. He was not wearing jeans, she noticed, but a fashionable, baggy-fit blue suit. And the brilliance of the sun picked out the gold strands of his unfashionably long, reddish hair. Her heart sank when he did not appear to see her but set off in the other direction toward the processional route. She was surprised that Charlotte was nowhere to be seen for he hardly went anywhere without her following him on all fours. All the Pleasuregirls were sick of it - she was like some devoted little puppy dog, Sparkle thought unkindly, and she could not understand why their Master did not see that they were as eager to please him as Charlotte was! And now that Siren had arrived, no-one else had got a look-in! Everyone knew those two bitches were his favourites, Sparkle niggled. As she followed Adria and approached the course that had been especially laid out for the occasion, her thoughts ran on. Poor Fionola was beside herself because, up until Siren came along, Fionola had been his favourite alongside Charlotte. Although legend had it that Charlotte was the first girl their Master had ever disciplined, Fionola was the first slave he actually owned and, unlike all the others, she had been with him in the days before he became a rich Lord!

She risked a glance over her shoulder but he had disappeared around the corner. She guessed, correctly as it turned out, that he was making his way to the processional route after which he would go across to the special platform that had been set up. The magnificent ponygirl had seen it the day before when she had been exercised. There were two seats upon it, one which was like a throne and was obviously her Master's and the other, just a common plastic one like those that stack together which she supposed, again correctly, was for Master Stapleton. It was here that those of the guests who wished to meet the new Lord of the manor personally would be presented to him. She also supposed that Charlotte would be there at his feet, but in that she was not correct, for she was already chained in position beside the throne, with her sun-kissed and shiny, honey-blonde hair tumbling in waves about her pale shoulders. Like Sparkle herself, Charlotte was one of the girls Tyler had decreed was never permitted to get a sun tan and so both made liberal use of the factor 30 sun screen which was provided along with the other toiletries. In addition, for the great event every girl's skin had been oiled to make it glisten.

It was strange to think that after today, Sparkle thought as Mistress Adria drew her to a halt, nothing would ever be the same... she would not just belong to her Master, Lord Tyler, but to The Ramparts itself... to the entire new SM club. Personally, she had long been used to the whims of men - had been a slave for many years and discipline was something she was well used to - but she could only imagine what it would be like to be flogged and fucked by so many men... men that would have a right to abuse her in any way they wished. When she returned to her cell tonight it would be as a real whore! Assuming the day went without a hitch, she cautioned herself, as Saxon and Pixie were brought across by the Escorts and tied beside her, though as far as Sparkle could tell the Grand Opening already had the hallmark of a great success.

During the early part of the afternoon Sparkle had found the sensations arousing as the plug stirred each time she moved, sending jolts of excitement ricocheting through her. And by the time that she and Mistress Adria arrived at the pony carting area she was already ridiculously wet between her legs. And as she stood listening to Adria going over the details with Escorts she wanted nothing more than to feel the Mistress' fingers inside her.

When the festivities were well underway and the guests were milling about enjoying the entertainment on offer, a small group made their way over to where Sparkle and the other two ponies were having their bits and bridles fitted in place. And then, with her hands still joined behind her and the plug still inside, her mouth full of steel and the straps of the bridle and harness biting into her flesh, Mistress Adria finally obliged her.

"Okay, bitches," she said as she stood facing the three stunning ponygirls, "it's time for you to prove your worth." Positioning herself between Saxon and Sparkle, with gentle strokes she explored their labia. She listened for the soft and muted gurgles of pleasure which she knew were not far away. When she heard them, simultaneous and sweet, with an almost imperceptible nod of her head she directed one of the two Escorts to do the same to Pixie, not that he needed much encouragement. Addressing the girls again she told them, "Do a good job for me today," her fingers prised open the two sets of wet, engorged pussy lips and plunged inside, "and I'll see that you're rewarded. But let me down... " she agitated their insides and did not have long to wait before the squelching noises began, "I'll give you a lashing like you've never had before. You'll wish you'd never been born by the time I've finished you. But because you won't only be letting me down but more importantly your Master, when I've finished with you I'll hand you over to him to flog you again. I'll recommend fifty lashes but... well... you know your Master! He's a hard man to please and his punishments can be a bit harsh. I should think he'd double it at least, maybe treble it. In any case," she said as she jabbed them both so hard they gave muffled cries of pain, "you won't be fit for use for a couple of days by the time we've both punished you!" She extracted her fingers and wiped them on their thighs, waited until Snick had done the same with Pixie and then, suddenly and without warning, she snatched at the bells on their nipples and yanked so hard that quite decent cries of pain found their way past their bits as the clamps sent pain-bolts through their nubs and reverberated around their constricted, tender breasts. Pixie's cries came close on their heels.

Adria released them as the first half dozen guests gathered around. Snick did likewise and took up a position whereby he could address them all while Adria fixed reins to Sparkle's bridle and removed the blue rope from her collar.

Sparkle tingled and quivered inside and out! She was so excited by Adria's manipulation, as well as the prospect of being shown off to the visitors again, that she temporarily forgot about the plug!

And then, after Mistress Adria had been introduced to their audience and she had answered a couple of questions about her station at the estate and more general questions about ponygirls, even more thrilling for Sparkle was the moment that the Escort untied her and she was, at last, placed between the shafts of the pony trap. It was an adaptation of the brightly painted, lightweight, metal framed traps raced at the bi-annual gypsy gathering at the Applegate Fair. In this case bright yellow, the traps had two, large diameter but narrow-rimmed wheels. Her hands were freed and her gauntlets attached to the shafts at wrist and elbow, after which a wide strap was attached on the left side, using the third ring on her gauntlet and then passed across her waist and fixed in the same manner on her right.

"Attaching a ponygirl in this dual fashion makes them part of the vehicle and inseparable from it. While it adds to their efficiency by giving them leverage - adding considerably to their 'pulling power' and ability to transport heavier loads - it means, of course, that should they crash, overturn the vehicle or take it into a tree, unlike their passenger they will not be able to free themselves which, I'm sure you'll agree, is a good incentive for not crashing!"

The group of men laughed.

"Under such circumstances, you will, of course, be obliged to free them."

Next, one of the Escorts, in this case one of Tyler's gypsy clan who looked awkward in his charcoal, pinstriped suit that was their new formal wear, climbed into the trap. Lowering himself onto the one padded seat he showed the observers the correct manner of sitting and distributing one's weight to get the best from one's pony.

"As y'can see, there's only really room for one but I guess two could just about fit in with a squeeze. Perhaps y'd want to take a Pleasuregirl along - sort of having y'cake," he pointed to the girl between the shafts, then patted the small space beside him, "an' eating it too!"

More laughter.

Sparkle was impatient to get off and began to paw the ground with her stiletto-shot foot. She tossed her head and the plumes waved dramatically. She snorted down her nose and Adria had to reach up and stroke the small area of her cheek that was framed by the bridle straps to calm her.

The gypsy shifted his position. "Assumin' it's just y'self goin' for a ride, y'need to sit centrally an' if y'just want to trot around leisurely for a bit - 'ave a decko at his Lordship's pile…" he paused for more laughter, "y'need to keep upright, just sit normal-like, an' keep y'feet flat on the rest in front." Although there was usually no such foot rest in authentic gypsy pony traps, in deference to the member's comfort Tyler had ordered the narrow wooden rest be fitted to all the traps he purchased. "But if y'fancy going at full trot, feel the wind in y'hair an' 'ave an excuse to whip the ponygirl… " more laughter, "y'need to lean back like this," he gave a demonstration of how the seat tilted backward and how they should position their legs as the footrest in front swung upward also, "with y'feet pointin' up like this."

Adria lowered her hand and stroked Sparkle's buttock while the gypsy gave a few more hints and tips. Then she stepped away so that he could give a demonstration of how to use the single stranded driving whip that was fitted inside a special holder inside the trap. He unfurled it and then, so fast that the men hardly saw it, it snapped sharply across Sparkle's back. Once again she tossed her head as the strike lit a streak of pain across her pale, glistening flesh.

"She's eager to be off!" he told the group, then went on to show them how they could control her direction by pulling on either the right or left rein. "I'll just take her round the course a couple of times so y'can see how she looks when she's going." He flicked the whip a second time as the signal to go.

Sparkle set off at a slow trot around the temporary course that had been laid out especially, using the shorter part of the course which bypassed a section that extended farther Westward… like a motor racing track with a Grand Prix circuit and a shorter one for the lower categories of the sport.

To Sparkle's dismay it was more difficult than the practice sessions, which had all taken place during the past dry weeks when the ground had been hard underfoot. But recently it had rained heavily and the spikes of her shoes sank quite deeply into the soft grass. Not only that but it was difficult in such high heeled shoes anyway! She was just thankful that on normal working days they would run naked and barefoot, unless a member had some particular preference of his own, of course.

The driver pulled on the right rein to steer her around one of the obstacles that had been dotted around the course, in this case a potted shrub that did not block the view, so that the members would have something to steer the ponies around.

"If we're going to fucking do this," Tyler had told them, "let's make it interesting for them."

A little farther on she approached a hurdle that had been placed in the middle of the track . She would have to go either right or left, but she knew better than to make a guess in case it was the wrong one. At the very last minute the gypsy steered her right. And so it went on all around the course. It had been drummed in to the ponygirls that if their passenger dithered, unable to decide which way to go, it was not up to the ponies... their job was to obey orders and if no orders came then they must run straight . ahead, even if that meant crashing into the obstacle. That way their passengers would learn the difference between being a passive passenger and becoming a driver! It would also prove that, rather than knowing the course by heart and just going the way they always had, Ramparts ponygirls allowed themselves to be steered.

As she came round to complete the course for the first time she saw Mistress Adria placing Pixie between the shafts of the blue trap. The group of men had also doubled in size. Then, as they drew level with their enthralled audience, she felt the sting of the whip once more and increased her speed as the gypsy leaned back and tilted the seat, sitting back as far as he was able. He whipped her now and then for appearances only since he steered her expertly, eventually bringing her to a halt in front of the waiting group. The gypsy stepped down and relinquished his seat to the first member of the public to take a pony trap ride at the new club.

They started off slowly while the man got used to the technique of driving and steering a ponygirl in the required direction. Remembering that she was not to make any decisions for him, at first his handling was erratic and it took him several minutes to find his confidence and gain control. But not before she had veered right off the course and was trotting off in totally the wrong direction.

"Where you going, you stupid bitch?" he yelled nastily as he tugged on the right rein.

It was attached to her bit and pulled painfully on her mouth. As he tried to steer her in the correct direction, he yanked again, slashed the whip across her back and eventually gave a little tug on the left rein to stop her describing a circle. After a while he managed to get her back on the course though steering her around the obstacles seemed something of a chore for him and several times she caught one or other of the wheels as she went too close followed by Pixie who caught them up. He took her around a second time, this time with more confidence and she was able to start enjoying herself.

Her plumes swayed majestically as she trotted around elegantly. With her head held high she imagined how anyone seeing her would surely admire her, and recognised it as an honour to be chosen to give the first ever pony trap ride at The Ramparts. Even if her skill outstripped the man driving, for he was surely incompetent!

And then the whipping started in earnest, a series of spiteful lashes accompanied by a bellow from the far-from-satisfied driver.

"Call yourself a ponygirl? Faster, you stupid bitch! Faster!"

At once she quickened her pace and started to run, hampered by her heels. And the long plait that hung down her back swung with the movement as did her tail. But the driver had clearly not understood the instructions or had forgotten them because he was not leaning backward, which seemed to have the effect of holding her back. By the time she had run the course a second time, the shoes had become less of a problem. Not that that had stopped the whipping! Now all three were on the course.

As the passengers changed, Sparkle was whipped again and again throughout the afternoon as encouragement to go faster, turn this or that way or simply for the sheer hell of it. She was into her stride, like the other two learning to cope and compensate when the balance of the trap was off. Then all at once her overriding emotion was, once again fear of the plug falling out. In her mind's eye she conjured up the picture of herself running around, with the shank's movement dislodging the plug with every step, and then despite the harness, the whole thing coming adrift and finally falling out, along a section of the course toward the back where spectators were gathering.

And so bearing its deep, agitating intrusion and keeping it in place inevitably became a matter of pure endurance until, with her session at last over and her viewing about to begin, the stirring was nothing short of unbelievably unpleasant! But the skin-tingling humiliation that came with it… ah, that was something else entirely and, even though she considered herself surely quite mad, she relished it and her heart was fit to burst with pride. She was a ponygirl, with the very real possibility of being fucked that evening… and to think her father had said she would never amount to anything!

CHAPTER TWELVE

Sparkle's skin glistened with the perspiration of her exertions. Her bit and bridle were removed just as Tully arrived at the course to collect her. The blue rope was fixed to her collar once more and the gauntlet rings at her wrists were once again joined behind her back. As soon as she began following him toward the main festivities, her fear of the plug falling out evaporated as if it had never been and in its place, arousal kicked in with a vengeance.

She felt the eyes of the crowd upon her and shivered with delight, tossing her head proudly and , to the delight of those who watched her pass, whinnying. Yet rather than the inevitable pain and exhaustion of her stint between the shafts, it was the agony and pleasure of her humiliation that consumed her. For she realised that everyone probably knew how obscenely and deeply her rectum was filled, thanks to the shank that speared upward. The tail which hung down to her shapely mid thighs fluttered and swayed in the summer breeze, occasionally brushing against her skin as she pranced elegantly, remembering to raise her knees once more as she was paraded before the well-to-do who made up the guest list and milled around on the lawns... and some obviously not quite so well-heeled who made a bad job of blending in. Obviously gatecrashers, Sparkle decided.

Among the surprisingly vast numbers who had turned up to the event, some were obviously men and women who had come along out of curiosity alone. As expected, the greatest number was made up of lone males who groped at her considerable charms as she passed, unhindered by Tully, and others who just walked quietly past as they took in the sights and atmosphere. There were couples, Sparkle noticed, who were accompanied by their own slaves, though some of the "collars" were golden chokers rather than collars in the accepted sense. She noticed too the age range of the slaves, some were quite young while others were women well into middle age. But whatever their age or social status, aristocrats or paupers, it was not hard to spot which of the women present were slaves, even if they wore no collar at all! For there was something almost tangible in their demeanours that marked them out as submissive even if they walked by their Masters' side with their arms linked. Of course, there were those men who paraded their slaves in the same way as Sparkle herself was being shown off, and like herself they wore leather collars and were led through the crowds, usually on chain leashes, and had their wrists cuffed behind them. Sparkle could not help wondering if any of the slaves imagined themselves in her place. And, if they did, was it their dream or nightmare?

The fires across her back raged as the sun beat down across them, and unknown hands slapped the welts as she passed. Fingernails scored them and once someone slashed their own whip across her shoulders. And all the while the enamel bells danced, tinkling tunefully as they swung mesmerically from her high, whip-scored orbs.

"Ooooh, look at the darling little bells!" cried a young voice excitedly.

The high pitch caught Sparkle's attention at once. Slewing her glance to the side as she passed and daring to raise her eyes just a little, she saw that the owner of the voice could have been no more than nineteen and stood staring at her wide-eyed, homing in on the musical decorations and seemingly ignoring the rest of the regalia of which Sparkle herself was so proud.

"May I have some like that, Master?" the girl said as she tugged at the jacket sleeve of the man she was with. "Please?"

Sparkle risked a smile at the girl and whinnied quietly,

wondering at the boldness of the young slave, for Sparkle herself would never dare to ask anything of her Master! But, of course, the girl was five or six years younger than herself, and Sparkle acknowledged that she of all people understood the rashness of youth, for it had been her own audacity that had brought her to slavery in the first place. And she realised that to the youngster she must seem like something really beautiful to aspire to and could perfectly understand the other girl's desire to decorate her own breasts in the same way, promisingly opulent ones they were too, judging by the amount of cleavage she was showing.

Tully tethered her outside the beer tent and dived inside for a pint. She was grateful for the opportunity to rest. But it was not to be. It seemed to the tall, elegant ponygirl that there was an over-supply of eager fingers exploring her exposed quim as she stood alone and tethered for public scrutiny; almost everyone who was on their way inside the tent took the opportunity to touch her up before entering, and just as many relished the chance to "try her hole for size" and declared her honey-drizzling vagina, "wet and juicy!" as they left it.

Yanking on her rope to pull her head down to their level, other fingers prised open her mouth. Some were content to have her suck on their digits while others insisted on appraising her mouth as if she were a horse going to market, counting her teeth and inspecting her gums! They discussed her as if she were a horse to be traded at some upcoming gypsy horse fair.

Cruel fingers dug into her breasts, each intent on eliciting a cry of pain. And as the hands stroked, squeezed, jabbed and dug into her mammaries, mouth or pussy, her arousal grew to almost intolerable potency. All the while, the damn plug filled her back passage to painfully sweet capacity, so much so that when Tully returned with the smell of beer on his breath, she almost begged him to withdraw the damned plug and let a flesh-and-blood cock take its place. It was true that under normal circumstances she hated to be fucked "up there," as she still demurely - and somewhat ridiculously given her long experience of sexual slavery - referred to anal penetration. For her it had always been a truly painful experience which she still believed to be a filthy, indecent act. Yet after several hours of the fiendish plug's stirring coupled with everything else she had endured, she actually prayed for it. But as she glanced across to the main marquee across the way and watched the comings and goings of the well-heeled, she was not entirely sure that God in his Heaven would grant such an immoral request. Still, it was worth a try, she thought with an inner grin.

"Please, God, grant me a cock to fuck my arse!"

Murmuring softly, it was the slightest tremor of her darkly glossed lips which betrayed her rather than her voice, and earned her a couple of harsh slaps to her breast from the returning Tully.

"What did yer say, bitch?" Whether he was heedless of the small knot of watching men with the one woman amongst them, or conversely because of them, Sparkle could not tell, but in any case Tully did not wait for her reply. Instead, he unhitched the rope from the ring to which she was tethered, stood behind her and wrapped her long, glossy plait around his hand in order to drag her downward, pulling her head sideways as she bent at the knees. When she was nearer to his level he released her hair and instead thumped his hands on her shoulders and with unnecessary roughness pushed her down to her knees.

Having her hands bound behind her meant she had no choice in the matter and she merely shuffled her knees more comfortably in the grass, remembering to keep her powerful thighs apart. He came round to the front and those people who still stood behind smiled at the way her tail settled on the grass and the stiletto heels pointed upward as she arranged her feet to keep from injuring herself.

"If yer can't keep your pretty mouth shut," Tully scoffed, "then I guess I'd

better fill it." With that he opened the flies of his ill-fitting pinstriped suit and withdrew his burgeoning cock. Holding the back of her head with one hand and her finely chiselled chin with the other, he rammed it between her lips with no thought as to whether or not she would enjoy it.

Despite her experience and entirely due to the lack of saliva in her mouth, she gagged hopelessly as he forced the ever expanding shaft of hard flesh as far as possible down her protesting throat. But her inability to accept the centre of his being without discomfort only spurred him on as, oblivious to or actually encouraged by the entranced bystanders poor Sparkle still could not tell, he shoved her face into his groin. With splayed fingers he gripped the back of her head tightly and ground her face against his pelvis, squashing her nose uncomfortably against him.

Forced to breathe in his strange, unsavoury aroma at its probable source, her nose and chin were horribly irritated by the profusion of wiry black hairs, while he leant back slightly as her long plumes tickled his own face and hindered his vision.

Worked up into a frenzy he pumped away at her throat like a man possessed. For a good ten minutes they were the star attraction that performed for the crowd, Tully enjoying his chance to show the world what a man could do with a tool as mighty as his and a totally subjugated, brain-fucked slut.

He gave a yell of, "Take that!" and discharged an impressive amount of hot spunk down her recalcitrant throat.

In the manner she had become used to at The Ramparts, he held her face in place until, not caring that she was retching uncontrollably, he was satisfied and his cock had deflated. Then he withdrew and watched as the white, milky liquid oozed down her chin and seeped from the corners of her claret-toned mouth.

Accepting the crowd's back-slapping approval he told them, "I don't know what's up with the fucking bitch today… she's usually one of the better jism-guzzlers!"

That was greeted with laughter, and he looked on with amusement as the only woman present stepped from the little group and used a lace-edged handkerchief poised elegantly between two aristocratic fingers to dab at Sparkle's spunk-defiled chin. With slow delicacy she patted and cleaned the ponygirl's mouth, paying special attention to the corners as she removed the traces of spunk without destroying the appearance of the deep-toned, glossed lipstick.

And Sparkle, still kneeling demurely, was touched by the woman's kindliness and felt its presence like a warm glow inside. Briefly, the two women made eye contact and somehow it felt so natural.

But all too soon the moment was lost. "That's enough, dear," the woman's husband stayed her arm and his firm benevolence was directed toward his wife rather than the ponygirl. "Leave her to the experts."

The woman turned a beseeching eye to her husband, and her words were all the more shocking to Sparkle since they followed so closely on the heels of such tenderness. "May we have her later? Perhaps we could take a room? I would so enjoy squatting over that pretty mouth while you give her a good rogering!"

"If that's what you want, dear, then I'll make inquiries. Perhaps they have shackles we could borrow… " he raised his brows questioningly toward Tully who answered with a nod of affirmation, "and perhaps something to flog her with?"

Again, Tully nodded.

"Is there someone we should speak to?"

Tully pointed his "F" tattooed finger toward a desk set up on one side of the main marquee, behind which sat Tyler's efficient-looking, newly engaged secretary, a good-looking woman of about twenty-seven with an arse that was surely created for the crop, who was accompanied by Stapleton's secretary, an equally attractive woman with a clipboard, who stood alongside.

Like a not-entirely-successful cross between a company rep and a market trader, Tully informed them enthusiastically, "There are some exceptionally good, unrepeatable deals on offer today! Best thing yer can do, mate, is see one of the secretaries. They'll fix yer up with a membership package to suit yer! If yer want my advice, I'd say yer'd - " he gave the man the once over and continued without a pause, "have no trouble qualifying for full membership! The half-membership is really only for the… " he searched his mind for a word that wasn't too insulting, "less eminent than your good self. But the Full Membership now, Squire, well, that's only open to dominant males, but it will allow yer to bring a dominant lady," he smiled his sincerest smile at the man's wife, "along to participate in the privacy of one of the bedrooms or luxury suites! Unless, of course… " again he smiled but more discreetly than before as he tried to put his point across without alienating the obviously well-to-do couple, especially in front of the other people who were still listening. "Unless I've read it wrong and the Lady happens to be submissive. Yer see, dominant wives, spouses and the like aren't allowed in the public rooms or the grounds, except for on special Ladies' Days and other special events, like t'day for instance, and the ball later in the year. To put it bluntly, Sir, Madam, The Ramparts is more of a Gentleman's club and so Ladies aren't permitted in the dungeons, library, dining rooms etc. unless they're actually slaves. But…" the rest of the little group began to disperse, but sure that he had the man's full attention, Tully continued, "as I was saying earlier, the Full Membership deal that Lord Tyler himself worked out is a good one… it's what I'd go for if I was you… and includes a bedroom… or suite… as required, as well as use of all the club's other facilities. And yer can bring your own slave along anytime…" he smiled mischievously, "if yer've got one, and use her in any of the public rooms and the grounds! And the Pleasuregirls too, of course! Now, Sir," Tully lowered his voice in a conspiratorial sort of way, "pop over to see the secretaries, tell them I sent yer, and we may be able to wangle a special, one-off tour of the cells for yer and your lady wife!"

"Thank you, you've been most helpful." He turned to his wife. "Come along now," he encouraged as he drew her away, "we'll inquire about the registration fee and reserving the girl for later. And there's still a lot more to see yet."

Once they had gone and Sparkle was once more alone with Tully, he gave a sharp jerk on the rope, "Get up, bitch!" and wrapped it around his hand. "It's time to mingle. And for fuck's sake, try to look as though yer're gagging for it when punters show an interest! How are we ever going to sign the bastards up if yer sit there with a face as long as a wet fucking Monday in Squires Langley!"

But she had not been miserable, of course! Far from it. She had just been feeling the tiring effects of the day.

While she had been kneeling, and stationary for so long, Sparkle had almost forgotten the presence of the plug in her anal passage but, as soon as she had risen to her feet and began to follow Tully, the plug had stirred again and she had renewed her efforts to keep it from falling out. And such had been her terrible arousal engendered by her deep humiliation, not to mention her contradictory sense of exhilaration that, if she had been able, she would have ripped it from her rectum, plunged it deep into her vagina instead and to hell with the consequences!

***

She was the beauty who followed the beast, Sparkle told herself while he accepted the lewd observations and complimentary comments on behalf of her owner and assured Sparkle's many admirers that she would indeed be available for use that evening.

"First come, first served," he laughed as he passed through the knots of men,

who were enjoying the "village fête" atmosphere of the occasion. And a more incongruous sight would be hard to imagine as Sparkle trotted along, docile and elegant behind Tully. Unshaven as was his natural state, to the casual observer he was merely a dark haired lout who was jammed uncomfortably into the conformity of his pinstriped suit, giving him the look of a mobster, he wiped the back of his dagger-swathed-in-barbed-wire-tattooed hand across his nose, as he always did pushing the small ring through his left nostril sideways. His other hand held the end of the leash, the F-U-C-K tattoos on his fingers starkly visible as they curled tightly around the blue rope.

He glanced quickly over his shoulder. "Keep up, you stupid bitch! The day's not over for you yet."

Sparkle's heart sank a little. Thankfully, Mistress Adria had explained that on normal working days she would not be hampered by the regalia but would run entirely naked, save for the necessary accoutrements, and barefoot. But while working this afternoon, she had had to run not only adorned as she was now but also wearing the high heels!

The paleness of her skin was further heightened by scarlet welts across her shoulders and back, though it was clear to all that her plait had somewhat hampered the drivers' use of the whip. Naturally, she expected to be carrying a whole lot more lines and abrasions by the end of the day, perhaps crop marks to complement the tramlines that already adorned her breasts, for she fully expected to be one of the main attractions that night. Although she did not consider herself overly conceited she was nevertheless cognisant of the fact that men found her stunning, and that today of all days their lustful appetites had to be catered for.

Like the other Pleasuregirls, Sparkle had not been officially informed of the running order of the day's events, nevertheless, she gathered that if the guests signed up for club membership before the end of the day's festivities, as one of certain privileges that would apply, they would be at liberty to use the girl of their choice for the night. But despite her hopes on behalf of her Master that the event would be a success, she rather hoped that guests would not enrol in their dozens for it was still early days and if, as she feared, there were not sufficient girls to go round, it would prove to be a very long night indeed if the girls were obliged to service more than one new member each!

However, the gaiety of the event was contagious and despite her fatigue Sparkle couldn't worry about the night ahead for long.

The extensive and usually magnificently maintained lawns were temporarily transformed into a host of fête-like attractions, though the events leaned toward lascivious rather than charitable. All around her, the atmosphere seemed to fizz with sexual arousal and lustful… and not necessarily benign… fascination. As the sun beat down on the glorious summer afternoon, the songs of birds and buzzing of insects were replaced by female shrieks and screams, punctuated by the swishing and thwacking of canes and whips, to say nothing of the whirr of the machinery which worked attractions such as the "merry-go-round."

Sparkle had not seen it for herself, but while she pranced along she overheard many lurid accounts of that particular attraction from those who had witnessed the spectacle, and their comments ranged from "most entertaining" to "a rollicking evil contraption - no garden should be without one!" As far as the statuesque ponygirl could gather, the structure consisted of a central pole of around nine feet high with a huge wheel fixed horizontally across the top. One of the Pleasuregirls had been spread-eagled naked across its surface while some of the others… reports had been rather vague as to the exact number… had been suspended by their wrists to the outer rim. Then, when the wheel was set in motion, the naked girls were flung around at speed with their legs flailing. Although she was not sure as to the truth of the matter, someone had commented within her earshot that the whole thing had been speeded up and centrifugal force had come into play so that the girls had been flung around while completely horizontal! Personally, Sparkle could not see the point to it but she had come to learn that there did not need to be a point where sadists were concerned, provided the effects were to cause pain or distress, and preferably both, to the girls concerned.

Bedevilled by the infernal plug shifting uncomfortably with every step she took, she wondered at her own capacity to bear it for so many long hours, for although her previous owner had used her as a ponygirl he had never gone in for all the regalia. He had simply hooked her up to a little, chariot-style cart by means of a wide strap around her waist and attached reins to the outer rings of her collar. But it had been obvious right from the start that Tyler's ideas were very different indeed.

CHAPTER THIRTEEN

While Tyler mingled with his guests, Mr Peregrine Green was taking a private tour of the dungeons with one of the Escorts. As there were no girls currently displayed there since the entire herd was on duty outside, they had taken along one of the "young offenders" who had been brought along to work as a waitress. Having caught Tyler's eye when she arrived, the tall nineteen year old with long legs, slim waist and enticingly bouncy breasts had been taken aside and an altogether different deal was struck between Perry and Tyler concerning her.

Her skin was pleasantly and deeply tanned and looked sensational with her straight, blonde hair which was almost long enough for her to sit on.

"Once she's broken in and trained as a Ramparts Pleasuregirl," Tyler had told him, "she'll be unrecognisable. Obedient, polite and willing… always willing! Like the rest of them, she'll live for nothing more than the whip and her Masters' pleasure. If she's only got a week to go before her release and, as you've already pointed out, she's got nowhere else to go, it seems ridiculous to turn her out into a world that gives her no choice but to offend again! Leave her here and I'll see she's taken care of."

As Tyler, out in the grounds, smiled, shook hands and accepted congratulations on "a perfect show, old man!" Perry was ogling the girl's charms for the very first time as the Escort stripped her bare and then fixed her bound hands to a chain. Within moments, the lovely, gagged and bound young offender was suspended by her wrists, stretched tautly so that every sinew of her lovely body was perfectly visible.

"Okay, I'll leave you to it," the Escort said, handing Perry a very acceptable dog whip. "I bet you've been dying to give her a good thrashing!"

196

"You've no idea," Perry leered, wishing he had the facilities... and the guts... to punish the older girls as they so obviously deserved at the Hempstead End Young Offends Correctional Facility. Up until then, he had only groped the sluts and made them suck him off for some misdemeanour, usually fighting with the other inmates. He could not understand, as he slashed at the girl's delightful buttocks and watched her back arch in the most fascinating way, why it had never occurred to him to cane them. After all, he had a perfectly serviceable desk in his office over which they could be bent...

***

In the absence of Adria, who was currently overseeing the ponygirl and trap demonstration, her young assistant - another of Perry's girls who found herself "on loan" from the facility, took charge of Siren when she was brought back to rest after a gruelling time as part of one of the afternoon's main attractions. Four inches taller than the just-over-five-feet Pleasuregirl and five years her junior, if she recognised Siren as the famous singer, she made no mention of it. She was dressed in a uniform of short red plaid skirt without knickers so that she was easily accessible, and white, short-sleeved cotton blouse with V-neck worn with a loosely tied red tie and a white, push-up bra beneath. White stiletto boots completed the uniform, and the overall effect was of a sexy, rebellious schoolgirl, which was exactly what the eighteen year old had been before her arrest and detention at the correctional facility.

She brushed Siren's long, perspiration-soaked fringe from her large, brown eyes but did not remove any of her shocking pink ponygirl regalia. Unlike Sparkle and the "working" ponies, Siren wore the golden chains rather than a leather harness. Her wrists were still joined together behind her back by the rings in her gauntlets. The girl

197

merely rubbed her down vigorously and smiled at the tinkling of the swaying bells hanging from her hard, erect nipples, then returned her to one of the stalls, where she was secured safely by a rope fixed to her collar.

"You should think yourself lucky," the youngster confided. She placed one of the larger than normal ball gags that Adria had insisted upon when taking up her position, in Siren's mouth and buckled it tighter than was strictly necessary, dismissing as meaningless the pathetic whimpers as strands of hair were caught in the buckle. Her jaws were spread achingly wide and unlike the usual kind of ball bag, there was a small bung at the front which could be removed to allow the wearer to drink through a straw since there was a hole right the way through.

"You're not thirsty," the girl announced and left the bung in place. "Too bad if you are! I haven't got time to mollycoddle you!"

Leaving the tail with its butt plug in place she removed the inflexible dildo that had filled Siren's cunt for a couple of hours, smiling in a faintly evil way as she sighed with relief. "Master's giving you a break but not the others, he's having them paraded round all afternoon - even the ones pulling the traps have to be shown off after they've done their stints. But he said something about you needing to rest because you'd had a 'tiring night.' Ah, diddums! Has the poor Pleasureslut had a hard time of it?" she mocked nastily. "You should try working in the tack room…" the youngster snatched up a stiff bristle brush that Siren had seen the stable boy across at the horse's stables use for cleaning out the real horses' buckets, "grooming the tails and plumes, then polishing the leather 'till bloody midnight, then you'd know what a tiring time's really like!"

She upended the brush and, without warning or lubrication, inserted the handle between the lovely pinkly adorned ponygirl's legs, shoving the handle deep inside her, then withdrawing it. As she rammed it hard, she was not concerned as the stiff bristles scratched Siren's thighs, the brutal ins and outs keeping time with her resentment as it tumbled out.

"And all the while, there was Mistress Adria and her pony-lover grunting and howling away in one of the stalls all night long. Don't mind me, I thought, I'm just the hired hand around here! It's 'do this' and 'do that' all the bloody time! I might just as well be at the bloody facility again. Well, I ain't going back there, that's for sure! So I'll just have to prove to everyone here what an asset I'll be."

Letting go of the brush, she let it fall between her charge's feet, then used a paddle to give Siren's backside half a dozen resounding slaps across the marks and broken skin of the previous night's lustful savagery and laughed as Siren pawed the ground with her stilettos and whinnied complainingly.

The youngster turned suddenly at the sound of footsteps entering the stable. Coming out of the stall, she was surprised to see one of the dark-suited Escorts.

"Where's Siren?"

"In her stall, resting. Master said…"

"Your Master's changed his mind… he wants her paraded with the others! Fetch the bitch, now!"

***

As the glorious summer's afternoon wore on Tyler strolled across his vast estate, following the blonde whose chain leash he held in his hand. There was only one cloud on Tyler's horizon and that was the man who Lilith had presented to him earlier. In some part of his consciousness it was as if the tall, thin man with short, slicked back grey hair was already known to him and yet he was sure they had never met before. He could not remember now how he had been introduced... he certainly had not given his name, just an initial... C, B... something like that, he thought distractedly as he watched the naked backside of the lovely girl who progressed slowly on all fours, mentally he shrugged his shoulders... it went without saying that any friend of Lilith's was surely not a friend of his! Until now he had given the matter little thought. The day so far had been an out-and-out success and he was not about to let a ridiculously insignificant thing like Lilith Stapleton's companion play on his mind. After all, every witch had a familiar! he thought with a smile.

Besides, he had more important things to occupy him such as the new girl in the dungeon to examine, established slaves to punish and prospective club members to cultivate. All around him the distinguished visitors who made up the guest list, many with their wives or slaves in tow, enjoyed his hospitality while his own slaves shrieked and wailed their way through the long hours of their first public exposure, yielding when required to whatever was asked of them.

Except for Charlotte, who he had kept with him throughout the afternoon. Appreciatively he trawled his ravenous, blue gaze over her rawly-scored nakedness as she advanced slowly ahead of him, swaying her generously proportioned, peachily-perfect bottom enticingly as she did so. Even more inviting was the tight hole which nestled between them and the delicious, naked pussy which she managed to flash so charmingly as she crawled. Yet it occurred to him that she was having far too much fun... it had been too long since he had last humiliated her.

"You're an embarrassment!" he told her unkindly. Uncurling his long fingers he released his grip on the leather loop of the chain and flung it to the ground. "Get behind me where I can't see you."

Obediently, the lovely girl halted to allow him to pass.

But without lowering her eyes, he noted as he slewed his gaze sideways as he passed. Assuming she would fall in behind him, he increased his speed.

It was not uncommon for a slave, especially a long-serving slut like Charlotte, to "try it on" merely to receive attention, either in the form of the punishment she craved or in the hopes of a rare moment of tenderness. But to discipline her now would be for him to submit to her will, which was totally out of the question, of course! He strode ahead across the grass, then flicked an oblique glance over his shoulder. His face broke into a smile as he saw her, still on all fours, inching her way along behind him with the chain attached to her collar hanging down between her lovely breasts and trailing between her thighs as she progressed forward. Every time she lifted a hand and then planted it on ground again, she trapped her long, honey-blond hair beneath it, causing her to wince and slow her pace further.

"Keep up!" he commanded.

She was still his most obedient and devoted slaves yet there had been something in Charlotte's pale gaze that alarmed him… if he did not know better he would swear it was jealousy!

Cognisant that her dreams were of sharing his bed every night, he knew also that her nose had been put out of joint by the arrival of her sister. But that was what he had wanted, he reminded himself. He suspected she would have preferred a greater role in the day's proceedings. She may even have wanted to wear the regalia of a ponygirl but quite frankly he much preferred to see her body naked and oiled. Besides, this was his day, not hers!

The stupid tart obviously expected more from him than he was prepared to give, and it was entirely conceivable that she harboured some kind of delusion that she was entitled to a reward of some description, as if she considered herself somehow responsible for his ownership of almost all he surveyed. And it struck him that because of those past events, she had probably deluded herself all these years and now believed there had always been something special between them.

But he was enjoying himself far too much to concern himself with the sensibilities of slavegirls. Where once he was shunned and reviled, everyone was keen to make themselves known; a few overawed villagers, dressed in their "Sunday best," made a bad job of blending in as they took in the cruelty and delights of the attractions, and the notable and elite of the land were eager to shake his hand and call him "friend."

He glanced back at Charlotte. She was falling behind and in danger of slowing him down. Tossing over the possibilities in his mind, he knew it was safe to leave her un-chaperoned… she could hardly escape without clothes. Besides, he knew it was not freedom she wanted. In any case, one of the Escorts or perhaps a guest would soon pick her up to make use of her. Alternatively, he could allow her to get to her feet and walk, but what was the point in that? he thought with cynical smile. She had been in his company for several hours already and, to be quite honest, he was beginning to grow bored with her. There was no need to explain himself to the bitch, and she would not dare regain her feet unless someone gave the express order.

Coming to a decision, he veered off suddenly in the opposite direction, leaving her behind as he was swallowed up by the crowd.

***

Alone and frightened, Charlotte was devastated to be separated from her Master. Pushed around and tripped over as alone she remained on the same spot.

"Get out of the way!"

"Stupid tart!"

But she did not dare to stand up for she had not been given permission. Why didn't they just walk around her? she wondered. She had not been given the green light to move.

Heavy feet stomped all around her.

"Oh look!" The surprised voice belonged to a woman. "Someone's lost their little doggie!"

The woman stroked Charlotte's head. Then, bending down, she offered her palm to Charlotte's nose in the same way Tyler often did. At once, Charlotte sniffed the woman's hand, then licked as if she were an affectionate puppy.

"Oh! What a sweetie! Can we take her home?"

"She is lovely, isn't she?" Charlotte felt the man's heavy hand on her head as she continued to lick the woman's. "She's also his lordship's! I just heard someone say that he's looking for her."

Charlotte would have wagged her tail with joy if she had had one. Master was coming back for her. He had not meant to leave her behind. Her heart began thumping wildly, pumping excitement through her veins.

The man's hand smoothed her hair and continued over her back in an unbroken caress down over her bottom to her vagina, where two fingers gained entry. As people milled around them and Charlotte continued to sniff the woman's hand which smelled, surely, of woman juice, the man vigorously agitated her quim while the woman's other hand disturbed the chain as she reached down beneath the delectable blonde's head and groped her breast, before finally alighting on her cork-like nipples.

"Should we be doing this, dear?" the woman asked belatedly. "Won't his lordship mind?"

"Shouldn't think so. He'll be pleased to think someone's taking care of her in his absence."

In actual fact, Tyler was looking for Siren not Charlotte. Calling one Escort after another he tried to locate her.

When Tully's mobile rang, it seemed to Sparkle that she had been following him around for hours! And by that time the comments of the people rarely registered since she had heard them all before. But what did register was Tully's anxious tone as he took the call while they walked.

"What? Well yeah, I know yer want to parade her but no, man, I ain't seen her! Who'd yer send?"

Sparkle's eyes remained downcast and she tried not to flinch when hands groped at her charms as the cries and screams from the girls on the various attractions continued to waft around. Not far away, she saw Snick leading Pixie who, like Sparkle, was still wearing her regalia. So, the pony rides were over, then?

"Well, yeah, Max is kosher," Tully's hoarse whisper into his mobile was growing more troubled. "So what's he sayin? What? The stupid bitch had let someone else take her?" He stopped walking and Sparkle came to a halt behind him. "Okay! Look, I'll get some of the lads from the clan to scout around… yeah… they dropped in to take a gander. Yeah, right. An' I seen Durkin, he's around somewhere, so I'll get him to keep an eye open."

Sparkle sensed the change in his tone and, raising her eyes, she saw that Tully was frantically gesturing for the tall ex-policeman to come over and join him. He kept up the conversation until the man stood beside him, looking down on the gypsy with an unmistakable dislike. "Perry? Nah! I last saw him over by the coconut shy. Look, gotta go. I'll tell Durkin. Let me know if she turns up."

Returning his mobile to his suit pocket, Tully gave Liam Durkin a quick run through of the facts which Tyler had related to him.

"Earlier, Ty had Siren taken back to the stable to rest. A few minutes ago he decided he wanted to show her off… yer know, the star of his show… this whole event's just for her, really… anyway, he sent Max to collect her but it seems someone else beat him to it. Some Escort - don't know which one - had already taken her. No one knows where the bitch is!"

Sparkle's heart leapt. Siren gone? Then there really is a God! she thought as she suppressed a smile.

"Ty's a bit worried. So can yer see if yer can find out anything? I'll see if some of our own la… " he seemed to think better of it, shrugged and said, "well, yer see what yer can find out."

As soon as the ex-policeman had gone, Tully began ringing around, presumably, Sparkle thought, to enlist the help of their gypsy clan members, telling them, "But keep an eye out for Durkin. If yer've been up to any tricks lately, well… once a copper, always a copper!"

Before long, they were on their way again, Sparkle following as before as they passed among the crowds. And as they walked and people groped the tallest of the Pleasuregirls, Tully informed them that "the use of the Pleasuregirls tonight is restricted to those who sign up for membership today," before inviting them to, "test her tits. Feel her cunt."

**

Still wearing her shocking pink regalia and with her hands still joined behind her back, Siren was led out of the stable yard by the Escort. The horrendous ball gag had been removed, but Siren knew better than to say anything to the rough-looking man who took her away. Besides, her jaws ached so much she doubted she could manipulate them! Instead she bit into her lower lip as she followed on the red rope attached to her collar. But he did not take her by the earlier route but made a detour that took in Tyler's old wreck-of-a-caravan, hidden away in the grounds.

"He says it's to remind him of his humble beginnings," the Escort sneered. "If you ask me, he should've fucking stayed away! Him and all his didakoi friends!"

She gave the caravan a cursory look then returned her gaze to the ground. They were not anywhere near the public yet, so she did not bother with the high-stepping because there would be enough of that later.

As the Escort mumbled into a mobile, she realised there was something vaguely familiar about him, though he was obviously not one of Tyler's clan. But she had met so many people… she must be mistaken, she thought and, pushing all thoughts of her past to the back of her mind she mutely followed where he led.

Except they were heading away from the festivities…

Feeling the stirring of unease in her bowels, she raised her eyes and looked around her. They were heading for the woodland garden. Still she followed, even when they left the path of bark chippings and headed into the woods themselves. What else could she do?

He halted suddenly and spun round. She lifted her head but before she had a chance to react, he used his work-roughened fingers to open her mouth and stuffed a rolled-up wad of cloth between her lips. Next he produced tape which he stuck over her mouth to keep the cloth in place. Returning the tape to the suit pocket, he removed the plumes and tossed them aside, then removed the rest of her regalia. All except the tail, held in place solely by the butt plug. But he was privy to its terrible secret and, flicking the tiny switch at its base and caring nothing for the agony it would engender, he activated the hundreds of nasty little studs that were sprung loaded. It was unimaginably painful as they dug into the tender fabric of her rectal passage! No matter how filled to capacity the plug had made her feel before, she had known that its removal was just a simple matter of removing the harness and withdrawing the thing. But now, no matter how hard her muscles tried to dispel it, the object stayed in place until someone decided that she had suffered enough and flicked the switch to retract them… which one look at the Escort's face told her would not be any time soon. With her eyes filling with tears as her stilettos sank into the loamy ground, she doubted her rectum would ever be the same again.

"So, how does that feel, girlie? Bet your bum hole's on fire! And I know a thing or two about fire!" He threw back his head and gave a loud, open mouthed laugh that curdled her innards. "I wonder if my girlfriend's had that little beauty up her yet? It's no good asking you! You've got a mouthful of my underpants to contend with! Still, at least it'll stop that fucking caterwauling you call singing! I used to hear you, all them years ago, when you used to come back from your singing lessons, or whatever they were! You'd walk up the lane, past our place and you used to be singing your little heart out." He paused for another laugh then said, "He's got her in there, you know, got my girl. Oh, don't look like that, she's not what this is about! I don't give a toss about her, never did, but that stupid arse of a fucking didakoi paid me - yes, actually paid me - to dole out a bit of punishment, like! She thought I hadn't got the heart for it but, do you know what? The more I did it, the more I wanted to get my hands on some of the real classy bints that he's got up here! So I tried to get myself a job up here. But all the vacancies were gone, so I had to rely on my girl, Steph, persuading Alfred to let me in. Then I just made myself useful. Security? Ha! No one even noticed they've got one extra 'Escort.' But as it turned out, it was a good job I was here, 'cos when I heard that his lordship - the real one - was coming back…"

207

Tully noticed as he led his charge through the throng that, while the men seemed perfectly happy that he should be in charge of such a delightful specimen as Sparkle, the women turned up their posh little noses at him. And while a surprising number of the women turned a lustful eye toward the tall ponygirl, others chose to show their disdain. Of course, there was nothing wrong in that! he told himself, wasn't that what slavegirls were for? No, it was not that that bugged him, it was the hypocrisy of women who were dressed up to the nines and treated him as something to be squashed beneath their dainty shoes when all the while their supposedly well-bred manners were no better than his… or Tyler's, for that matter! But due to the importance of the occasion he bit his tongue. He had more to worry about than manners.

One of the Escorts had reported a guy, wearing a suit like theirs, claiming to be a new man, hired just the day before. Someone said he looked like someone from the village. Great! Some idiot trying to wreck the party… that was all they needed!

Up until then, his own worries had been for Sparkle. After her stint with the trap at the carting area, he had been concerned by the exhausted state of her. After all, it was no use running the bitch into the ground, he had thought as he had walked her across to the beer tent where he left her to recover while he went inside, when she was supposed to be bright, ready and waiting for the punters that night. But it had not been his decision to use only three, Sparkle Pixie and Saxon, between the shafts, the others being used to bolster the numbers of the other Pleasuregirls for the other attractions. But he need not have worried; the girl seemed to have remarkable resilience.

From tomorrow, ponygirls pulling the pony traps, usually

without the regalia, would be a common sight around The Ramparts grounds. The members would be able to take the ponies for a drive around a specially laid course. But during today's demonstration and armed with a buggy whip, the men had been encouraged to urge the pony on by whipping her. Naturally, some of the men were experienced at pony carting and so needed little encouragement, while others were complete novices. Of that number, one could separate the men into two groups, those who used the whip wisely for its intended purpose, and those who slashed away, clearly more interested in the exciting brutality of the exercise than getting the most out of the pony. And so it was that Saxon, who in Sparkle's absence had been unfortunate in taking the majority of the latter group, had later been deemed unfit to work further that day and was on her way back to the stable to recover. And that was why now, in the distance, Tully could see Max leading orange-clad Fionola in the direction of the carting area as her replacement.

Having circled back toward the main marquee again in order to show Sparkle off to what he called "the Pimm's and Strawberries brigade," Tully's path took him toward a couple who stood outside together sipping champagne.

The man was tall and distinguished looking and, Tully guessed, in his mid-sixties. His wife, a particularly well-dressed lady who was some ten years or so younger than her husband, had a haughty demeanour. She hissed nastily to her husband as Tully approached.

"Is that him?"

"Who?"

"The new Lord Morrison-Grenfell! Is that him?"

"I presume so." Then smiling affably as Tully drew closer, the man raised his glass in salute. "Lovely show, old boy. Good health to you!"

Deciding not to embarrass the man in front of his wife

by pointing out their mistake, Tully merely nodded toward him and put on a snooty voice of his own. "And to you!" he returned as he led Sparkle past.

The man's wife sneered nastily and, in a voice which she made no attempt to lower, said to her husband, "My God! What is the world coming to when they put gypsies in charge of a virtual palace and fill it with painted, vulgar, sewer sluts!"

Tully halted abruptly, and Sparkle just managed to avoid crashing into him as he stood his ground.

The woman said, "It really doesn't make a scrap of difference whether you dress them in furs or like these Las Vegas-style showgirls, one is still left with a common whore! And no cheap suit will ever turn a gypsy into a lord!"

Tully heard the note of embarrassment in the man's voice. "Keep you voice down! That may not be him."

Tully slowed his pace and, looking over his shoulder, was just quick enough to see that she followed up her snide remarks by making a contemptuous 'tutting' noise at Sparkle. And that was the point when he had had enough. It wasn't her contempt of Sparkle that bothered him... hell, there was nothing wrong with that! It was the whole "upper class snobbery" that annoyed him, the same snobbery he had been faced with all his life. Bringing Sparkle to an abrupt halt and tense with aggression, he faced the woman.

"Yer're no fucking better than I am, darlin,' all done up in yer finery with the manners of a pig. Don't they teach yer nothin' at finishin' school?"

"Oh my! I've never been so insulted!" She put a quivering hand to her mouth and touched her husband's arm with the other hand. "Say something, Archibald. Do something!"

But Archibald said nothing, just looked on with a quizzical expression as Tully continued.

"You're no better than the ponies yourself, darlin'! Yer

210

need a fucking good bollocking, or better still, a belting." He turned to her husband, who was clearly amused by the whole incident. "Shall I have her taken away and taught some manners, Sir?"

"That would be very kind of you, your lordship."

His wife shrieked. "Archibald!"

Tully raised his hand and almost at once, two similarly suited men appeared. Tully gave a sign and at once, one of the men grabbed her arms and tied her hands behind her back.

"Archibald! For God's sake! Do something!"

Archibald smiled at his wife and listened as Tully told the men, "take her away and educate the lady. Return her to… sorry, Sir, I didn't catch your name."

"Lord Bradstock. That is Prunella, Lady Bradstock."

"Oh, pleased to meet yer. When do yer want her back?"

"Well, I shall be having dinner in your restaurant, so perhaps… why don't you hang on to her until I leave… possibly in the morning if I'm able to book a room?" Archibald, Lord Bradstock told him.

"Right you are then, your Lordship. Oh, by the way, I ain't the lord. He's over there," he said, pointing as Tyler entered the marquee. He turned towards the men. "You heard Lord Bradstock. Here," he delved in his pocket and extracted a folded piece of black cloth which he handed to one of the men. While Lady Prunella kept up a barrage of protest, he shook the cloth out and, revealing it to be a hood, he placed it over her head, then fastened the Velcro at the neck. Several heads turned her way to watch as she was led away through the crowds.

CHAPTER FOURTEEN

With all his men and more besides searching for Siren, Tyler told himself as he raised his glass of Champagne that the stupid bitch was merely hiding somewhere in a pathetic bid to escape. He had already dispatched a search party to the house itself. He tried to raise Alfred on the mobile, but it seemed the old fool had buggered off out of it for the day.

He took a few moments to take in the charms of Perry's waitressing girls. He laughed softly and as he often did, mentally gave a silent salute to Whitby. If it had not been for his father refusing to marry his mother, life would have turned out very differently indeed; his mother would have been dressed in finery and attended the most dazzling parties hosted by the country's elite, he thought, as he looked around at the well heeled who currently gorged themselves on his hospitality. Putting down his drink , untouched, he left the stifling marquee for the fresh air, and all the while his thoughts ran on. As a child, he himself would have played with children of the landed gentry. Yet he could not help wondering if his mother would have been happy living in the great house for she was descended from the proud Romanies of Southern Europe. Besides, he had had the most wonderful childhood, free from the constraints of the house dwellers and had been privileged to roam the countryside, play in streams, swim in rivers and have adventures in the woodlands and fields that coloured the land.

Stapleton slapped his back as he walked past with Kismet in tow. "Good show, Morrison," and continued on his way.

Tyler realised that now he had everything he had always dreamed of, and with it had come power, real power, to influence others and do as he pleased. And where the fairer sex were concerned, he exercised his power without mercy or regard, and especially without love. So if it was love Charlotte was after, she was out of luck, along with all the other beauties who populated his world.

As he walked every once in a while he caught sight of one or other of them as they were escorted through the crowds by his men, some in pony regalia, others naked. In the case of those who were naked, the girl had her hands tied behind her back and her breasts thrust out temptingly. But in keeping with the carnival atmosphere, brightly coloured balloons danced above their heads, attached to nipples that were kept erect by their blood-flow being interrupted by the narrow string tied around them and the mauling of their breasts by passers-by. It was an amusing idea that had certainly caught the imagination of the crowd and, he noticed now, several of the female visitors had bared their breasts too, either willingly or on the orders of their male companions and, like the beautiful Pleasuregirls themselves, had balloons tied to their nipples also. This turn of events was entirely due to the resourcefulness of one of the gypsies who, never one to miss a trick, had removed a couple of the youngster waitresses from their posts and had set them up with bunches of balloons which they were selling at an exorbitant price, which the guests seemed only too happy to pay! As far as he was concerned, as long as the money found its way into the Ramparts' coffers, Tyler thoroughly approved of his man's method of making sure the girls did not run off with the takings; each girl, still wearing the catering uniform that she had been issued with, was staked to the ground by a chain attached to her ankle.

**

Tyler strolled across the lush, well-maintained lawns, accepting the hearty praise and best wishes from his notable guests, curious visitors and gatecrashers. This afternoon, he reminded himself, they were merely spectators at the event he was hosting in the stately home's grounds but hopefully, by the end of the entertainment, a good number of them would have signed up as members and some might even stay on for a meal in the new restaurant and use the bitches that evening.

He approached The Wheel of Fortune to discover it was doing a roaring trade, the spectators almost obliterating the event from view. It was a particularly enjoyable pastime Tyler thought, since its variables made the whole thing quite random. With one girl to unwittingly determine the punishment of another, it took a punter to operate the system which randomly selected the procedure. The attraction itself consisted of a large frame upon which was vertically mounted a brightly coloured disc of about six and a half feet in diameter. Around the outside edge in large letters, several punishments were listed, ranging from the innocuous, "Face Fuck," and "Cunt Screw," through "Shoulders 10 lashes," "Tits 20 lashes," "Cunt 30 lashes," "Rump 40 lashes," to "Needle Play," "Candle Wax," and "Tit Crusher." Positioned over the disc was a similarly painted but smaller turntable. Strapped in the centre of it with arms bound to her sides by transparent tape and her ankles similarly bound was Rawnie, naked and blindfolded. There were two long needles crossed through each breast and a big-enough-to-see butterfly-shaped, weighted clamp attached to her clit. On her head was a preposterous large, red arrow head to serve as a pointer. On the left hand side of the contraption, a naked girl called Brandy was bent over a trestle, awaiting her fate. Her hands were tied behind her and she was arranged as necessary by an Escort, who was on hand to dole out the punishment which the "arrow" would determine by the spinning of the wheel by a punter, using the special mechanism on the right hand side of the construction.

While everyone enjoyed the carnival atmosphere and especially the attractions, as the heat of the afternoon wore on many of the guests were heading for the main marquee that he had just left, where, at great expense and fit to rival anything available at Henley Regatta, "afternoon tea" had been laid on. Flower arrangements made showy centrepieces on the tables, around which chairs had been placed, and were a tasteful contrast to the pale cream colour of the starched linen tablecloths. Elaborate bows of cream ribbon hung as decorations.. Apart from the champagne, Pimm's and liqueurs which had been flowing all afternoon, coffee and tea were also provided, in delicate pots with cups and saucers. Such was the success of the event that a couple of the Escorts had been dispatched to the nearby villages of Abbots Langley, Squire's Langley and Langley Forge to obtain more strawberries and cream.

Everything was served by waitresses, their hastily provided uniforms surprisingly formal, the only concessions made to the nature of the event being the shortness of their black skirts and the transparency of their white blouses, beneath which their breasts were naked. The girls themselves were everything Tyler could have wished for. Despite his worries that Perry Green would let him down the girls who were on loan from the local facility, only the prettiest having been selected, were causing quite a stir among the guests. Despite their initial belligerent behaviour on arrival and slovenly appearance, they had all scrubbed up nicely and, once made-up and dressed in their uniforms, they had proved most acceptable. They went about their business in an able, efficient and, to everyone's relief, a polite manner. Of course, that could be attributed directly to the host of the event himself, for Tyler had promised each and every one of the youngsters that if they behaved themselves and carried out their duties with humility he would personally intervene with the authorities, in this case an influential representative of the Youth Justice Board that Perry Green had invited to the event, on the girls' behalf.

Ahead of him while he walked were Sir Maynard Pickering and his dark-haired, female companion. Her short hair was topped by a pink hat worn at a jaunty angle. It was one of those neat little jobs with a net veil at the front, Tyler had noted earlier, that had done little to hide her haughty eyes. She was also wearing a matching pink, short sleeved, lightweight summer dress with a flared skirt, the back of which was currently hooked up to her waist to reveal her tanned nakedness beneath. Tyler kept one eye on her voluptuously wobbling, rawly striped backside as he followed. Whether or not she was Sir Maynard Pickering's wife or slave Tyler had not yet established since, as was right and proper if she were a slave, she had not been introduced when he had met Sir Maynard a couple of hours earlier. But as they walked side by side ahead of him, Tyler was of the opinion that she was accustomed to both roles for her natural, aristocratic bearing as well as her obviously expensive outfit was gloriously undermined by the trappings of her subjugation. Her cuffed wrists were fastened to the back of her collar so that her elbows stuck out, and Tyler noticed that at some point since their arrival, Sir Maynard had also fitted a chain between her lovely ankles which was clipped to the actual ankle straps of her expensive pink sandals, the heels of which were so high that they emphasised greatly the wobble to which Tyler was so drawn. If he could have seen her front view again, he would also have approved of the way Sir Maynard had unfastened the tiny pearl buttons to the waist to reveal her nipple-clamped, ample breasts.

Sir Maynard drew to a halt in order to exchange a few words to a friend. Beside him, the woman also came to a halt. Regretfully, Tyler walked on past.

One of the most popular attractions was the coconut shy, where for hours a handful of the most delectable Pleasuregirls, their jaws held wide by ball gags, were still being used as a variation of a coconut shy, and there seemed to be no lack of contestants. Each competitor was given five special balls with which to try and knock the "coconuts" from their perches which, of course, was as likely as a Pleasuregirl becoming a leading light in the Women's' Rights movement! Instead, the balls exploded on impact and splattered the helpless, darling girls with bright body paint. To ensure the girls were held in place and were unable to free themselves, having first been hammered into the ground special poles impaled their cunts. There were small platforms positioned near the tops, and it was on these that the girls appeared to sit. With their feet tied to footrests and their hands bound behind their backs, they were wonderfully vulnerable and tempting. And, as one of Tyler's men had laughingly pointed out, "They can't frig themselves! You know how some of these sluts are exhibitionists, and being on show for so long will probably give them a buzz fit to send them sky-bleeding-high!"

Tyler had found that idea unbelievably erotic and, during the latter part of the afternoon, he had had modifications made; the girls were blindfolded and then balloons, like those tied to the other girls, had been tied to their nipples. Every once in a while, Tyler had one of his men walk behind them and at random prick a balloon with a pin, which set all the girls screaming into their gags and made the victim herself jump delightfully and come down heavily on her pole. The crowd loved it and the coconut shy became one of the most popular attractions of the afternoon. One of Tyler's men been allocated the task of hosing the girls down every now and then, and the appreciative crowd would "ooh" and "ah" in delight as the wealth of bruising was revealed beneath the paint.

In the distance Tyler could see Sparkle as she was led by Tully through an assemblage of men. She was proving to be a great crowd-pleaser. Not that he had ever doubted Sparkle's sex appeal. When he had first set eyes on her, the colour of her lovely hair was so strikingly, deeply red that it had reminded him of the polished horse chestnuts with which he and his childhood friends had played the traditional game of conkers.

In those far-off days of his "other life," when they had gathered the fallen nuts still encased in their spiky green coverings, Tyler had selected his allowance from the yield with an almost uncanny knack of picking a potential winner, the same skill he now put to use when choosing Pleasuregirls… only the hottest and sexiest girls would do! It did not matter too much whether or not they were naturally submissive, for subjugation was a thing that was easily taught. For apart from his qualified eye, another skill that served him well back in his conker-playing years was his quick, sharp and accurate shots, a skill which was especially useful when using the whip on naked girl-flesh.

The crowd assembled around the specially constructed "T" shaped structure. Around eight feet from the ground, the crossbar was some ten feet in length.

Pagan the former kitchen slave, and Dusk, the pretty black girl, were made ready for another of the attractions, a new take on the old schoolboy game of conkers, the idea for which had been planted by the attractive colour of Sparkle's hair. As he watched the preparations, Tyler recalled that he had almost always won the traditional game. And winning was something he determined to enjoy in all his adult activities. In a contest between himself with a whip and a girl who refused to scream for his pleasure or submit to his authority, there was never any doubt about the outcome. And hardening his "toys", as once he had hardened conkers, had become a way of life, and he put his slaves through many hardships, sure that his methods of hardening their hides were extremely effective.

And Pagan was proving a delightful subject on which to practice his skills, he laughed as he noted her sullen expression. The two girls were stark naked apart from their collars and their hands were tied behind their backs. Then they were rendered appealingly anonymous as they had protective head gear fitted. Another function of the padded hoods was to keep them quiet by means of an integral gag, like a rubber penis which blocked their throats. Pagan gagged terribly as it was inserted, but Tyler's prime concern was that any cries of pain from either girl were stifled so as not to impair the spectators' enjoyment.

Once hooded and with their whip-scored assets wobbling enticingly they were led over to the "T" shaped construction by the Escorts. The eagerly awaiting audience seemed mesmerised by the two beauties as the Escorts used canes to prod them into position, making them lie face down on the grass. Then both Escorts placed a foot in the small of each girls' back and, like a couple of magicians at the beginning of a trick they held up the leather straps they intended to use to show the crowd. With an "O" ring at the centre of the arrangement, there were four short leather straps in an "X" formation, with one longer strap between the two upper arms of the "X". When ordered, the girls drew their legs up, bending them at the knees. The straps were placed on their backs and the ends strapped around their ankles and wrists, and within moments Dusk and Pagan found themselves hog-tied as the last strap was fitted to their collars, rending the girls very effectively helpless.

Hog-tied and vulnerable, they were then lifted into position beneath the arms of the "T" structure, where at each end an oversized hook hung from a rope. Using a simple pulley system, the hooks were lowered and attached to the girls' limbs. Then they were raised again and the ropes locked into position, leaving the girls suspended like fruits from a tree. Applauded by the crowd, the men stood aside and waited while those who felt inclined laid bets. Once all bets were taken, one of the Escorts grabbed hold of Dusk while his companion did the same with Pagan. Holding the naked, hooded Pleasuregirls tightly they walked backward, pulling the girls with them and raising them. When their progress was checked by the rope, on a given signal, they let the bundles of girl-flesh go. The momentum of the girls as they swung toward each other sent them crashing into each other.

The cheers that went up were deafening and at once, the two Escorts repeated the process. Again and again the girls crashed together until, to cheers from the crowd who, greatly approving of this new take on the old game of conkers, laughed and applauded all the way through. The winner was deemed to be the one with the least bruises after ten collisions, as decided by the estate manager, Cotterel, who seemed only too pleased to play a part in the . festivities.

Pagan and Dusk would be replaced with fresh girls once they had been spun and battered and the winner had been declared.

CHAPTER FIFTEEN

It was late afternoon when Tyler spotted Stapleton leaving the throng with Kismet still in tow. Seizing the arm of one Perry's girls who had clearly had enough of waitressing and was trying to make her escape, Tyler followed. Snagging a piece of cream coloured ribbon that had come adrift from the main marquee, he used it to tie the girl's hands behind her as he walked.

"Don't ever try and run out on me!" he told her. "You'll be returned to the facility soon enough, so for now just do as you're told, relax and let me control your pleasure. I promise you, it'll be worth it."

"Not on your fucking life, my lord!"

He placed his fingers round the back of her neck. "While you're here, you'll call me Master!" He squeezed. "Do I have to tie a lead around this pretty little neck of yours or will you behave?"

"You wouldn't dare!"

Keeping Stapleton in sight as he moved among the attractions and crowds, Tyler delved in his pockets. "Shit!" he mumbled, remembering too late that he was wearing his suit and had very little in his pockets. He gestured to one of the Escorts who produced a blue length of rope for one of the ponygirls. Thanking him, Tyler tied it loosely around her neck and gave it a tug. "Behave, or spend the rest of your time here in the dungeon. It's up to you."

At last Tyler caught up with Stapleton and fell into step beside him. They congratulated each other on the success of the event.

"The thing that bothers me," Stapleton began, nodding and smiling to the guests as they passed, "is that we still won't have enough Pleasuregirls to meet demand. I mean, even if only half the guests sign up…"

"We'll manage for tonight, and after that… well, at least we've got that consignment coming from China," Tyler said as he watched Lilith laughing girlishly with the black-suited man whose side she had not left since his arrival. He remembered now that the rather gaunt-looking, grey haired man, whose severe appearance was heightened by the black T shirt and black suit, had actually cut Lilith's introduction short and insisted he be known as… Tyler still could not remember! As he watched the two together, just as before Tyler felt stirrings of unease… … it was hard to trust a man who was clearly on such good terms with Lilith, and for the umpteenth time he regretted giving the fucking woman an official position. After all, he had hated her since that very first meeting, years ago, when Whitby had invited the young gypsy who had still been unaware of his own identity, to join him and the Stapletons in disciplining one of his sex slaves.

"Stapleton," he said at last, "do you know that guy talking to your wife? I didn't quite catch his name."

Stapleton looked uneasy. He ran his finger round the inside of his collar. In his habitual way he cleared his throat before answering. "That, my dear chap, is Digby Morrison-Grenfell, the unfrocked Reverend… your Father!"

Tyler stopped dead in his tracks.

Stapleton walked on a few steps before he realised Tyler was not beside him, turned and rejoined him.

Tyler's heavy brows were drawn together in the darkest of frowns that seemed strangely at odds with the shining, golden flecks in his hair as the sun beat down upon the two men.

"What the fuck's he doing here? You invite him? I thought you said you'd lost touch with him?"

"No, no, of course not! It must have been Lilith. I knew she was up to something, has been for days, but I never…"

To Tyler's surprise, Stapleton took hold of his arm and

steered him away, out of sight behind the beer tent. Once again, he cleared his throat before speaking.

"I hoped I'd never set eyes on him again! I also hoped I'd never have to discuss the subject with you." He paused, had the naked Kismet bend over a beer barrel and freed his cock. He spat in his hands, wiped his cock with his spittle and bending at the knee, drove unerringly into the Pleasuregirl. As he began thrusting in and out, he cleared his throat. "Look here, Morrison, he broke your grandfather's heart. Or, more correctly… " he turned his head to look Tyler in the eye, "it broke his heart to see the young, pregnant, gypsy girl head off with his grandchild in her belly!"

Knowing he always thought clearer when he had a slut to flog, Tyler tore off the waitress' uniform. When she was stark naked he pressed her face down over a stack of colourful plastic crates and told her to stay put. Using a clip attached to the end of the rope, he secured it to a wooden post that earlier had been used to tether some of the ponygirls. Then he withdrew his favoured whip from where it was concealed beneath his jacket, tucked into the waistband of his suit, and without warning let it fly. The fanning lashes fell across her shoulders.

"Aaaarghh!"

He struck again.

"Aaaarghh!"

"Quiet! Make as much as a squeak and I'll put aside the fact that you're new to this and really lay into you!"

He struck again, and this time there was only a muffled noise in reply. Satisfied, he began in earnest, concentrating on building up a rhythm. Only then did he speak to Stapleton.

"If Whitby was so concerned for Ma and me, why the fuck didn't he see her all right, at least give her money or something? And why did he care anyway that his son had fucked a gypsy? Was that it, fucking below his station? The Whitby I knew would have applauded him for it!"

"You don't understand…" Stapleton withdrew, roughly turned Kismet over so that she was lying backward over the barrel, then entered her again. "It was one thing to sexually abuse girls… Whitby did it all the time… but he believed in marriage and never abused his wife… that's what he had sex slaves for! And, for the sake of his lineage, he abhorred the very notion that his grandchild would be a bastard and insisted that Digby…"

"Ah yes," Tyler said suddenly, "his initial… D!"

"That Digby," Stapleton continued as his face grew red with exertion in the heat, "marry your mother. He had her brought to the house to have it out. Ranting like a madman, Whitby ordered Digby to marry her, but he would have none of it and had her thrown out. But Whitby went looking for her the next day, he was too late, the travellers had moved on, taking your mother with them. Your grandfather never forgave Digby… a Morrison-Grenfell… for treating the girl who carried his child so despicably and denying him a grandchild. He threatened your father with cutting him off without a penny, but it was Digby himself who smoothed the path for him to do just that!

"Digby claimed to have found religion and, much to Lilith's annoyance I should add, entered the church, vowing to destroy Whitby and purge the place of depravity." He pulled out of the girl and came over her belly. When he had got his breath back, he brought the story to its conclusion. "But, of course, Digby has always been a hypocrite and it soon got back to your grandfather that not only did he abuse the church he professed to love - stealing funds and amassing great wealth, but he also acted improperly with parishioners and, instead of carrying on the family tradition of taking slaves, he used his wife instead. Although many would find no fault with that and even applaud him for not looking outside the marriage, it was something Whitby could never come to terms with, believing that a wife was not only a necessity for carrying on the family name, but also someone to love, cherish and pamper, as he had done with his own late wife!"

Preferring not to dwell on those particular eccentricities of his grandfather's, instead Tyler channelled his anger toward the waitress, in particular patterning her shoulders with an intricate design that she could later perceive in the mirror and know that she had been disciplined by The Whipmaster. Making the lashes dance, he drew fires across her back that blasted furnace-like into her very being.

Had he bothered to enquire, he would have discovered that, far from feeling as though she were being punished the nineteen year old believed she had been singled out by a cruel but redeeming God who would teach her not only the error of her ways but show her the way to sacred pleasures. For even as each terrible, wonderful strike sent pyrotechnics exploding across the backs of her eyelids and lit up her brain, in a converse reaction it engendered such peace and feelings of wellbeing that she could almost believe she would float up into the air if it were not for the rope that anchored her to the ground.

"Feel her cunt," Tyler directed as Stapleton tucked himself away. Then abruptly he announced, "I won't speak to him, Stapleton. When we're done, just get rid of him."

"Of course. Glad to." Taking care not to hinder Tyler's aim or find himself the recipient of a strike as the bearer of sad tidings, Stapleton bent down behind her. "Perhaps I can persuade him to take Lilith, seeing as he left her behind last time!" Without a word to the girl he plunged his thick finger between her glistening vaginal lips and into her not-as-tight-as-he-hoped pussy. Nevertheless, he was pleased to announce, "wet as a true slut's cunt," and take the opportunity to enjoy its delights. Agitating her roughly while Tyler kept up his unrelenting rhythm, Stapleton summoned Kismet. But it was Tyler who gave the order.

"All fours in front of her." He watched as Kismet hurried to obey. "Back up, stick your arse in her face. No, closer than that or feel the lash across your back! That's better," he said as, with her feet either side of the crates she squirmed delightedly into the required position with her bottom pressed against the girl's face. "You! Yes, you with your face in her arse! Don't panic about being able to breathe, just stick your tongue up her arse and be done with it!"

At once the poor girl was engulfed in shame. She could never do that! Would they know, could they even see that she was too ashamed? Whether they could or not, his lordship... master... must have a sixth sense, she decided, because he knew!

The next strike was more vicious than any that had gone before, and she realised now as each tail was laid down savagely, just how easy he had been going on her before. And the other man was doing the most exciting things to her quim!

"I said stick your tongue up her arse! Do it! Now!"

Despite the crushing humiliation and sick feeling in her stomach, the feeling of wellbeing returned as she obeyed. Curling her tongue, she tried not to think of where she was putting it as she wiggled it into the tight hole, up into... no, no... forget where it was... she told herself, just let the peace, the tranquillity, the pleasure wash over me... forget the shame... just accept...

***

"Your Lordship!

With the naked girl walking beside him, Tyler turned round. Smiling, he retraced his steps to where Sir Maynard-Pickering was beaming happily and beckoning him.

"Call me Tyler," he invited as he joined the little group

that had gathered.

"Have you met Lancelot Boothby?"

Tyler shook the outstretched hand. "Pleased to meet you."

Once the formal introductions were completed, the men struck-up a conversation. Sir Maynard clicked his fingers and at once his female companion, with her hat still in place and the netting doing a bad job of obscuring her eyes, dropped to her knees in front of Tyler.

Needing no further encouragement, he unzipped his trousers and withdrew his penis, already eagerly stiff. Pulling back the foreskin he presented his cock to the woman whose lips accepted it with hungry gratitude as the girl looked on, the woman's saliva lubricated his shaft and without preamble she took it down into her throat. Tyler used the toe of his shoe against each of her knees to encourage her to open them wider, not so much because he wanted access to her pussy for he had that already since her knees were already well parted, but because he knew that it would increase her discomfort.

Cursorily he looked her over. "Wider," he told her as she gagged on his still burgeoning cock, "until you feel the burn."

When he was satisfied that her knees were stretched to the limit of their ability and that her thighs were aching, he reached down to her clamped breasts and, without being invited, tightened the little screws at the sides, turning them until she finally gave a whimper of pain. Having achieved his objective, he relished her ministrations as her head bobbed back and forth.

And all the while, the conversation continued.

"I must congratulate you on a good show," Boothby told him. "The exhibits are wonderful, and the attractions some of the best it's been my privilege to enjoy. And I have been in the field for many years."

"Thanks." Tyler's heart thumped with pride. "Good of

you to say so." Since his transformation from a common gypsy outcast to one of the richest men in the UK, he had become adept at finding new ways of utilising girls for entertainment. And now he looked about him with pride and amusement as his girls were lewdly displayed and put to lascivious use. If only he had word of Siren, to just know her whereabouts, then perhaps his mind would have been at rest.

CHAPTER SIXTEEN

It seemed hours since Siren had known the safety of the stables. As the man continued to pound into her pussy, she prayed for deliverance... for Tyler himself to come and rescue her. But the very notion was absurd... saviour? He was the devil!

"That's enough, Kirk!" The voice belonged to a stranger who strode through the wild vegetarian toward them, another of the Escorts following in his wake. "Get those things out of here! Bury them or something," he said, waving his hand dismissively in the direction of her regalia strewn about the ground.

Kirk Stoner! Of course, the village grave digger! How the hell...

But Siren was not given a chance to continue with that train of thought as the thin-faced stranger came and stood in front of her while Kirk hastily tucked himself away. Sneering down at her, the stranger told the other Escort, "untie the rope, bring the girl and follow me."

When the escort - one of Tyler's own men - had untied the rope, unhooked it from her collar and then used it to bind her upper body, poor Siren found herself plucked from the spot and heaved up over the Escort's shoulders. The last thing she saw as she was carried away was Kirk digging a hole. Unable to move, the once stylish dresser could do nothing but cry at the fate of her lovely ponygirl costume.

After they had gone some distance, the Escort following the stranger in the black suit, as he headed deeper into the ancient woodland, they came to an abrupt halt and she found herself unceremoniously dumped amid the stinging nettles. She wriggled frantically but was too afraid of stinging herself to move and could not make any sound other than a "Mmmmphh" that was nowhere near loud enough to alert anyone.

There was a strange grinding noise, like heavy stone being shifted and scraping across other stone, and then she was raised once more. With her hair tumbling down the Escort's back as her nose was buffeted against the back of his suit while he gripped her legs tightly, she could see nothing as they descended stone steps.

And she knew nothing of her master's anger with the young stable girl who found herself flogged by Tyler himself for not having alerted him that Siren had been collected when he had left express orders that no one was to collect her but himself, Max or Tully!

Having no choice but to breathe in the overpowering aroma of the earth, the only thought in her head as they marched her along the damp, claustrophobic tunnel was to bemoan the fact that her beloved Master had failed to come for her. It occurred to her that it was Tyler himself who had condemned her to this. But if that was the case, what had she done to deserve such a fate? How had she failed him?

And then, as her stilettos caught on a root and caused her to almost topple over she realised the terrible truth… Charlotte was behind this!

***

Far away, the festivities came to a close. But Siren knew nothing of its success or that so many of the guests had taken out membership. She knew nothing of the new restaurant's accomplishments, nor how many of the Pleasuregirls were made use of well into the night. For Siren, it was all a world away.

Although time had ceased to exist for her in the strange, dimly lit chamber in which she found herself, it was in fact the next day when, following Digby's orders, Kirk and the other Escorts sat her upright on the hard floor, propping her up against a huge boulder. Pulling her legs so wide apart that she thought they were using her as a wishbone, they secured her feet to bolts sunk deep into the floor. Untying her hands, they brought them round to the front and attached them to her collar. Next, they fitted steel rings, like the devilish ones Tyler had used in the dungeon, over her breasts and tightened them. The hard metal bit into her flesh, cinching the roots tightly so that the luscious, ripe fullness spilled over in a banquet of mouth-watering flesh that Tyler would have loved.

Then the men stood aside. At once Digby took their place. Standing over her, eyeing her scandalously welted breasts scornfully as they blossomed from the rings.

"My name is Digby Morrison-Grenfell," he told her pompously. "I am the true heir to The Ramparts. You're here at my invitation."

"What do you want with me?" she asked. Only afterwards did she realise how stupid a question that was, seeing as she was alone with three men.

"Me? I don't want you at all! I have no time for whores and I intend to cleanse The Ramparts once and for all from the shame that has tainted its past. You may be familiar with the dungeons and a couple of the other chambers. And the cells, of course! You may even think you know something about the underground passages. But in that you are wrong. Excavations during the nineteen fifties revealed the network to be far more extensive than anyone had previously believed... anyone save myself, of course. Unfortunately, they're all in a pretty bad state of decay these days, but I can assure you they stretch for miles," Digby told her proudly. "You probably know of those that link with the canal and the house. But there are many other, narrower passageways that go off in all directions, under Squires Langley itself... under the church and The Griffin... all the way across to Langley Feldon. Believe me when I say it's a labyrinth. Anyone who gets lost down here stays lost... forever."

Quivering, she looked up at him. He was making it up just to frighten her... she knew he was! She had lived in the village for most of her life and was pretty sure that if it were true, someone somewhere would have mentioned it. Oh, she knew the old legends of the passages, everyone did, but if there were as many as he claimed and under the pub and church - if there really had been excavations - knowing the good people of Squires Langley, they would have held "Save our tunnels" summer fêtes and insisted they be opened to the paying public as part of the Hertfordshire Heritage Trust or something.

"You don't believe me? Shame on you!" His shoulders shook as he sniggered nastily. "Also uncovered around the same time were crumbling manuscripts, which survived only because they were stuffed inside sealed jars, just like the organs stored in the knopic jars that my father brought back Egypt with their contents removed and replaced by pipe tobacco. But I digress. The parchments they uncovered proved most enlightening. Their general contents... mainly to do with the price of grain and sheep, proved that the tunnels were already ancient by the time of the Civil War, when they were used by supporters of the King to escape Cromwell's armies."

"What has all this to do with me?" Chelsi asked bravely.

"I've already told you, I intend to close down the sinful club, cleanse The Ramparts of its shame and take back all that is mine. The house is full of secret rooms where I used to play in as a child. The point is, I came across them accidentally and kept their existence largely to myself, sharing the knowledge only with a friend from Oxford. I doubt even Alfred knew about them and, even if he did, they've not been used for years! My Father was too wrapped up in his silly collection to pay any attention to me, and probably went to his grave without realising that he'd had treasures of his own hidden away in chambers almost as secret as Tutankhamun's tomb! Of course, the treasures have dwindled over the years since I pilfered them on a regular basis, until I left to join the Church and renounce my foolish ways. Today, with the help of some friends, I was able to gain entry and check that they are still there. There are chests of gold, great works of art and other delights, all stashed away by my ancestors to save them from Cromwell's men. And so, my dear girl, I'm probably the only man alive who knows of the existence of both the treasure and the chambers which contain them. I tell you this because I'm planning to keep you in one of those very rooms!"

Ashen faced, she stared up at him, her eyes wide with terror.

Smiling at her distress, Digby continued, "Don't look so worried, my dear, it won't be forever, just until I have gained possession of what is truly mine! In the meantime, I intend to punish you for your sins and cleanse your soul. More importantly, locked away from that common gypsy who wormed his way into my Father's affections!"

"How can you talk like that? He's your son!"

"Do you really think I'd impregnate a gypsy whore with my seed? Come, come, my dear! Just because I fucked the bitch when I was… what, nineteen?… doesn't mean the filthy sprog she dropped was mine! I am the rightful heir to…" he swept his hand in a gesture which was supposed to take in the tunnels, lands, house and its contents, "this, and I shan't give up without a fight. Besides, I have something he wants even more than the estate… more even than the title… and he will be only too pleased to hand it all over in exchange for the one thing he really wants." He tightened her bonds, then made to leave her. "I just thought it would be amusing to give you something to think about while you're out here alone. Oh don't worry, I will come back for you… if only to take you to your new accommodation. You'll like it, you know; it will be so much better than that stark cell you're kept in now. You'll be surrounded by beautiful things."

The two Escorts looked behind them, them together made for the tunnel.

"You'll even have freedom to wander around rather than being chained," he continued to the backdrop of scuffling noises and men's voices. "Of course, you won't have the company of all the other sluts, but instead you'll have wonderful things to keep you company. And when you get bored with frigging yourself, you'll have all those beautiful objects to keep you occupied. Until I sell everything, then you really will be alone. But that will take some time yet… possibly years!"

The noises grew louder.

"You can't do that! Any of it! You can't leave me locked away! And … and Tyler will never let you take it all from him! You were disinherited and Whitby named him as his legal heir! You are his father, whether you care to admit it or not. Though God forgive me for saying it, but he'd be better off like me, without a father! Besides, what could you possibly have that he could wa…" Her words trailed to nothing as the full horror dawned on her. What if Digby were wrong and Tyler didn't want her as much as Digby believed he did? She would be locked up in a secret room forever!

"You won't get away with it. I'm… famous… yes, I am! They'll come looking for me."

"Sorry to disappoint you, my dear, but it may have escaped your notice that you've already been 'missing' several days and no one has come looking yet. Besides, even if they did, one of the new members of the so-called club is a very senior policeman and, incidentally, a personal friend of mine," he laughed. "I told you I had a friend at Oxford - I always knew he would do well for himself!

Now shut your mouth and make the most of the light. It will be the last you see until that... that gypsy leaves and takes you with him!"

He turned to go then, as an afterthought, he looked over his shoulder and said, "whatever am I thinking of? That the gypsy will hand it all over just to get you back? Maybe. But then again he might be more co-operative when he discovers that you're not the one he really wants after all."

At that moment, the two Escorts returned with a third man. And with them was a blindfolded, naked and bound blonde girl who they threw down beside her.

"Charlotte!"

To be continued... ... ...

'He had never held a real cat-o-nine-tails before or any other kind of whip and, as he approached the girl and positioned himself for action, he weighed it as if assessing its force. The handle, around thirteen inches in length, with a loop at the end, was covered in animal hide, though he was not inclined to guess from which animal.'

Tyler Morrison sets out to become a true master of the whip and aided by a fortuitous accident of birth he is able to devote himself to his art.

This spells big trouble for Chelsi; a girl who spurned him in his youth. He is determined that she will pay for his humiliation and he has all the means to accomplish his aim.

This is one of the most erotic books we have been privileged to publish for a long time; Francine is on top form.

A unique event in erotic literature; a collaboration between a submissive authoress and a dominant author. The result is a real treat for the reader! Vivid and knowing descriptions of the delights of SM adorn page after page of erotic action.

Vanessa and Rae have been rivals since school days, but when Rae walks off with Vanessa's boyfriend a series of events is triggered which will irrevocably alter both their lives. A fascinating cast of brilliantly portrayed submissive women and dominant men are set on collision course by the girls' enmity and the climax is one of the most intensely erotic episodes that Silver Moon has been privileged to publish for many years.

The Night Master
Cora Devon

Jessica Millar is secure in her power as a successful businesswoman. However, she doesn't realise that one person she has offended in her dealings is about to take a devastating revenge. Evan has built up a slave-trading empire and uses this as his instrument of retribution when Jessica taunts him.

The results of her imprisonment and the dominance of Evan's most trusted lieutenant surprise everyone. But as Jessica comes to terms with her new life, she is also plagued by the presence of the most dominant master of all. The night master. Who is he?

Cora Devon is another new Silver Moon author who makes an impressive entrance onto the erotic literature scene with this tale of sensual submission and devotion.

When Claire comes to in hospital after a minor traffic accident, she finds that her behaviour seems to have altered dramatically. She also finds that she is the focus of attention of a mysterious stranger who commands her sexually in a way she has never experienced before.

As she recovers he leads her into more and more extreme encounters that she finds herself taking more and more pleasure in. But then she goes on holiday with her husband and he disappears just as the mysterious 'X' makes ever more stern calls on her body.

Stephanie Kenny makes an impressive debut with this tale of lost innocence and pleasure gained through submission.